Charm

Reverse Fairytales

book 1

J.A.Armitage

Contents

The Funeral

The sun shone brightly in a way it had no right to do. Not on a day like this. Today should have been a day for clouds, for rain, for anything but the promise of summer. A summer that Grace would never see. I realized that this was my first time on the royal balcony as I gazed out over the crowd, a sea of people swathed in black and united in grief. I could even hear them all the way up here. Wails of anguish and tears of sorrow over the untimely death of Her Royal Highness, Princess Grace.

I had no such tears. It just wasn't protocol. I had been schooled to stand, wave, present a face of stoic composure, not to show the desperate abyss inside me that the death of my elder sister had left.

To my right, I could hear Elise sobbing quietly. She knew the protocol as well as I, and yet she was breaking it in the most public way possible. My younger sister was a favorite amongst the people as well as with our parents, and I knew that she would get away with it in a way I wouldn't. Not anymore, at least.

Someone somewhere played a somber tune on a brass instrument. It sounded a little like our national anthem, but slower somehow as if the trumpet itself couldn't quite understand how a healthy twenty-one-year-old girl could suddenly drop dead for no apparent reason. When it happened two weeks ago, rumors abounded that it was poisoning. That somehow one of our enemies, someone from a neighboring country with a grudge, had infiltrated the kitchens and slipped something into her food. I'd even heard gossip that it might have been one of the Magi.

When the doctors did the autopsy, they found it was much more mundane than that. An undiagnosed heart problem. She'd probably had it from birth. Not that it was much in the way of consolation. She was still dead. Thriving one minute, cold on the floor the next.

She would have loved it up here, the adoring crowds, seeing how much she was loved. The royal balcony was only used for special occasions when the public would flock to the driveway below just to get a glimpse of us at weddings and coronations and, of course, funerals.

In my whole life, I'd only ever been to one of those, and that was today. The next one was to have been Grace's wedding in six months' time, but, of course, that wasn't going to happen now.

I looked over at the crowd, all of them in black, united in grief. Even the Magi had worn the color of mourning, forgoing their usual purple attire as a mark of respect. Either that or no Magi had shown up. It was hard to tell.

Yes, Grace would have been in her element up here. I just felt uncomfortable and itchy in the long black dress that had been chosen for me to wear.

The noise gave me a headache, and if I didn't get away from the people soon, I was going to burst into tears, protocol or not.

Thankfully, when the sad tune had finished, my father, King Aaron, decided enough was enough, and we were finally allowed to head back through the large doors into the formal sitting room in the palace where we could grieve in peace.

All I wanted to do was head to my room, throw myself on my bed, and cry for a week. And that was exactly what I was planning to do when my mother and father collared me.

I watched as the servants and Elise left, so it was just the three of us in the large ornate sitting room usually reserved for formal meetings of state and times when we let the press into the palace. Today was not one of those days. The press had all been confined to a pen near the front doors and had to be content with filming us on the balcony. They would have to wait another day to let the public get another glimpse of this golden room with its high ceilings and crystal chandelier that threw rainbows around the room when the light was just right.

My mother sat next to my father on one of the golden upholstered sofas. This was their usual position when they were interviewed by someone in the media. The view I had of them now, was the same one the public always saw. I took the chair opposite, the one that the carefully selected reporter usually took, and yet, despite our positioning, I felt that it was me in the spotlight.

While I spoke to my mother frequently, an audience with my father was much rarer, and something told me that whatever it was they wanted, it wouldn't be good. The solemn look on their faces confirmed my suspicions. Although, having buried their first child only today, perhaps I was being too hasty with my assumptions. Didn't they have every right to look solemn?

"We need to talk to you about the ball," my mother began.

She was sitting with a perfectly straight back with her hands in her lap, the way she had been taught and the way Grace would have done. Grace was the epitome of the word princess. I slouched.

The ball my mother was referring to was really Grace's coming out party. Or it had started that way. A way to officially introduce her role as princess of the people. After which, she was to take a more active role in the running of the country. As we were on the verge of war with more than one country, not to mention the problem in our own kingdom of Silverwood with the Magi wanting more power, it had been decided that she would also take a husband. A hundred potential suitors had been invited— men who were dignitaries and lower princes in their own countries, and who would provide not only a political match for stability of the kingdom but also at some point in the future would provide an heir.

"What about it?" I'd assumed it would be canceled. What was the point of having all those people come if there was no princess to choose between them?

"It's in two weeks. The catering has been ordered, and it's too late to cancel."

I sighed. My mother had a way of telling me things without telling me anything at all. Somewhere in the back of my mind, a little voice was telling me that somehow this had something to do with me, but I didn't want to acknowledge it. I squirmed in a very unladylike manner in my chair.

"I don't see the problem. So what if we all have too much food for a while? We can give it out to the local homeless. It will improve our popularity among the people." Our popularity among the people was at an all-time low thanks to problems between the Magi and non-Magi and all the protests that went with it. The Magi wanted a democracy with no royal family and to install one of their own as a president. The non-Magi, like ourselves, wanted things to stay as they were, fearful of having someone with Magical abilities in charge.

My mother shifted in her chair, the first sign she was uncomfortable with the conversation. "The people are expecting a ball. They need to know that the future of Silverwood is in good hands, and your father and I aren't getting any younger."

"The people will get over it."

"That's just it, Charmaine. The people won't just get over it." It was my father's turn to talk to me. For some reason, his words weighed more. I guess because he used them so rarely, only speaking when he absolutely had to. He was not a man to waste words, and used them as though they were worth the same as diamonds. "Our situation is a precarious one. Our nation is relatively young, and we do not have enough troops to withstand much in the way of battle. Our only defense is to form strong ties with one of our neighboring countries. We need a powerful ally to do what we cannot do alone."

I fiddled with the edge of a cushion next to me, a nervous habit of mine, wondering why they had chosen to speak to me about this. That little voice in my head already knew, but I was actively ignoring it, hoping that I'd somehow gotten the wrong end of the stick.

"Why are you telling me this?"

My mother smiled. Her smile had a way of putting people at ease. I'd seen her use it countless times on nervous subjects. That's what made her a good queen. She flicked her eyes towards my father who just nodded, and then she turned back to me. Reaching forward and taking my hand in hers, she spoke softly to me. Another trick of hers to keep me calm. I wondered briefly what exactly she would need to keep me calm about.

You already know

The little voice was persistent.

"We cannot cancel the ball. Too much is at stake, and while it is unfortunate timing, it would be madness to stop it at this late stage. Your father and I have talked extensively about this, and we have decided that you are to take Grace's place."

I opened my mouth in shock. We had only just begun the official mourning for Grace, and here they both were, asking me to take her place at some stupid party.

"You mean to dance with the men?"

"Not just dance with them. We need concrete ties. The country is in a period of great instability, and we need a leader to take our place when we are gone. We need you to choose a husband."

"Why do I need a husband for that? I could lead Silverwood with Elise."

"This isn't a question about your leadership abilities, Charmaine. I have no doubt with a little schooling; you'll grow to be a fine leader, but what then? The line has to continue after you. You will need to pick a husband. The people expect it. If we don't go ahead with the ball, goodness only knows what will happen. By inviting all those men, it gives not only the princes from other countries a chance but also the men within our own kingdom. A wedding will have to go ahead, but it cannot without a bride. It's already planned to go ahead in six months' time. You are heir to the throne now, no matter how much you don't want to be, and now the duty falls to you."

"No!" The tears that had been threatening to fall all day were now prickling at the corners of my eyes. I let them fall. "There must be some other way. What about Elise? Couldn't she do it? She would do a better job than me! I won't know what to do."

It was true. My younger sister had the poise and grace that seemed to have skipped a place when it came to me. With her stunning white blonde hair, two or three shades lighter than my own, and her darling face, she would make an excellent queen. Just like Grace had been, Elise was a natural at this whereas I had spent most of my childhood climbing trees in the palace gardens and actively avoiding any kind of royal engagement like the plague. It wasn't that I didn't like meeting people; it was just that I never quite knew what to say. Grace had always been able to converse on any topic thrown at her and remembered all those little details about people that made them like her so much. Elise was exactly the same.

She could speak to a dignitary she had only met once, years previously, and inquire about his wife and children, remembering all of their names. I'd just stand there and say something inane such as "I like your socks."

It's not that I was stupid. In fact, out of the three of us, I probably knew the most, thanks to hours spent pouring over books in the huge palace library, I just didn't know people.

"Elise is only seventeen. She is too young for this. You are nearly nineteen, and though we would have preferred you to have a few more years out of the limelight, unfortunately, we have to push ahead now."

I stopped playing with the cushion and started working on the hem of my dress instead, picking away at the seam, desperately trying to think of a way out of the mess I was in.

"She will be eighteen in ten months. Why can't we postpone it until then?"

"Everyone is invited, the palace is ready. We cannot wait another ten months. With Grace gone, we need someone more than ever to take her place in the public eye—"

"No one could ever take her place!" I was sobbing really hard now, the tears free falling down my face.

I felt my mother's soothing arm around me. A mother's touch that could cure any ills, all except this one. My heart ached at the thought of taking Grace's place. She had been so looking forward to the ball, in a way I could never do. She was born for it. I couldn't hope to ever be as good as she was.

"You're right. No one will ever replace her in our hearts or in the hearts of the people, but someone must step up to her title, and you are the next in line. It is your duty."

"My duty to marry someone I don't even know and couldn't hope to love?"

My father, who had been pretty silent all the way through, spoke up.

"That's not the case at all. The king of Pearlia has been wanting to marry his second son into our family for the past few years. If we didn't care, we would have set up a match with him for Grace, but we wanted her to be happy and marry for love, just as we do you. That is why we have invited a hundred men to the ball. A hundred chances for you to fall in love. After the ball, you will choose five of them to stay on. They will stay here while you court all of them and get to know them. When you are ready, you will be the one to make up your mind about whom you decide to marry. You will get to choose."

"Not really. What if I don't like any of them?"

It was my mother's turn to talk again. She gently pulled my hem out of my hand and smoothed it down.

"Charmaine, a hundred men is more than you've met in your lifetime. You are bound to like one of them and remember, at the end of the day, the final decision will be all yours."

It was true. I'd been woefully sheltered my whole life and the only men I'd met apart from a few passing dignitaries, were palace staff.

In the end, I agreed to do it. Not that I had any choice in the matter, and took myself off to my bedroom. I needed the solitude, to be allowed to grieve in my own space without hundreds of thousands of eyes staring at me.

My maid, Agatha was waiting by the bed for me, handkerchief in hand. I could see by her red puffy eyes that she had been crying too. Just like the rest of the staff, Agatha was wearing the requisite black, a color she'd be expected to stay in for the next two weeks. I barely recognized her out of her white and purple maid's uniform. You see, just like the majority of the palace staff, she was a Magi—the name given to the magical people. It made sense to hire them because they got the job done much more quickly with only a flick of their wands. As there were so many of them, the palace had adopted the color purple as a trim for the staff uniforms of the Magi, although the uniforms themselves were either white or gold depending on the position. The maids and kitchen staff wore white with purple trim; the butlers and wait staff wore gold and purple. All the non-Magic staff wore the same but without the trim.

She passed me the handkerchief and curtseyed. I could tell that she wanted to say something, but what was there to say? She was my personal maid and wouldn't have had much contact with Grace, but I knew she thought very fondly of her. Everyone did.

"Is there anything I can do Your Highness, or should I just let you be?"

Agatha knew me very well. She knew I'd want to be alone.

"You can take the night off Agatha. I can undress myself tonight." It was against protocol. Her entire job was pretty much dressing and undressing me, but she didn't argue. She curtseyed again and left me to my own misery.

I sat down in front of my mirror and looked at my reflection. A sad girl looked back. She looked nothing like a princess. My sisters and I had all inherited our mother's blonde hair, but where Grace's had fallen in thick, honey-colored layers, and Elise had white-blonde poker straight hair, mine fell somewhere in the middle. A dirty blonde that nothing but the strongest hairspray and lots of pins could tame. I usually left it alone, preferring the wild, untamed look of it, but this morning a bevy of beauticians had teased it into something manageable, so I could look smart for my sister's funeral.

The door opened behind me, and for a second I thought it was Agatha coming back, but when I turned, I saw it wasn't the door to the main corridor, but the door to the adjoining bedroom. The one that belonged to Elise. Opposite was another door, one which would never open again. It led to Grace's room.

Elise ran in and flopped on the bed. She'd changed from her black mourning suit into a pretty summer dress. I wish I'd thought to do the same. The dress I was wearing had so much starch used on it that I itched in places I didn't even know I had.

"What happened?" Elise was the most curious person I knew. She knew the name of every staff member and all the gossip that happened between them. I could tell that she had been dying to come and speak to me ever since our parents had requested to see me alone.

I told her everything. About how Grace's ball was still going ahead except it would be me instead of her that the ball was for. I told her that I'd have to pick a husband at the end of it.

"You are so lucky!" was all she said once I'd finished my story.

"Lucky?" I felt anything but.

"Think about all those handsome men in tuxedos, all there just for you. You can spend the night dancing and drinking champagne, and then you get to marry the best of them all."

"It sounds like hell," I countered.

"Oh, don't be like that. It's romantic," she sighed. I sighed along with her but for different reasons.

I could think of nothing less romantic than a group of men being paraded through the palace like a herd of cattle while I picked out the one I was going to marry. I had one night to pick out five men. How was I supposed to do that? If the ball went on all night, I'd still only get a few minutes with each one. How was I supposed to make such an important decision that would affect my whole future based on just a few minutes?

"And then there will be a huge wedding," she continued, seemingly oblivious to how she was making me feel. "And then there will be another royal baby."

"A what now?" I sat up on the bed

"A baby! Don't tell me that it hasn't crossed your mind? Why do you think Mother and father are doing this? They need to secure an heir to the throne."

As if my week hadn't been hard enough. I'd lost my sister, and now I was getting married to someone I'd never even met and was having his baby.

I fell back on my bed, consumed by my own thoughts. At some point, Elise left, more than likely disappointed by my lack of enthusiasm. As I fell asleep, my thoughts kept going back to Grace, and how I was taking the night she'd been looking forward to for months away from her. Mostly, I wondered how I was ever going to fill her shoes.

The Makeover

As early as the next day, Jenny, my former nanny, came to my room to drag me out of bed.

"Why isn't Agatha waking me up?" I asked, stifling a yawn. The sun was yet to break through my windows. I sat up in bed abruptly. "Is it Elise? Has something happened to her?"

After the events of the past couple of weeks, I could think of no other reason that Jenny would be here to wake me except to tell me more bad news.

"Don't bother yourself, child. Elise is grand. I've been told to escort you down to the dressing room. From now on you are expected to dress in a manner benefiting the royal princess."

The royal dressing room was a room I'd avoided as much as possible my whole life. It was a place where royal women were laced up and squeezed into corsets and dresses and had their hair teased into all manner of shapes. Elise loved it. Grace had too, or, at least, she'd accepted it as part of her life. As the second daughter, I was pretty much allowed to wear whatever I wanted within reason unless there was a special occasion. Even then, I let Agatha pick up whatever the advisors had chosen for me and bring it to my room where she would help dress me. They knew my tastes by now. Plain and comfortable and boring. I liked to blend in with the scenery.

The room itself was much more than a dressing room, with tall gilt mirrors filling one wall and seats for different stations. Each station was for something different: hair, nails, buffing and shining, and makeup. There were three huge gold doors at the end.

"I still don't understand why Agatha couldn't have woken me up," I said as I was manhandled into a seat at the first workstation.

"Because as you and I well know, you'd have just ignored her, and I'd have had to come up to pull you out of bed eventually. This way, I thought I'd cut out the middle man."

Jenny had been my nanny since I was a baby. Each of the princesses had our own, and Jenny was mine. When I was too old for a nanny, she took on an admin-type role within the palace, and whilst she had no official control over me, she still had the ability to rule with an iron fist. I loved her fiercely, and I knew the feeling was mutual. Despite my moaning, I was happy she was by my side. I don't think I could have gotten through this alone.

One of the palace beauticians came in and strode over to the pair of us purposely. Grace would have known her name and said something nice to her. I could only sit there open mouthed, staring at her in the mirror as she picked up my limp hair and sighed.

"This will not do. Not at all." She was talking to herself. It was as though Jenny and I were not in the room, just this woman and my hair. She let go of my hair and wrote something on her clipboard. A beautician with a clipboard? She was wearing a smart black tailored suit, and I had the feeling this was the type of thing she usually wore and had more to do with fashion than mourning. With a severe black bob and blood red nails that matched the slash of scarlet on her lips, she reminded me of a sleek black panther. I expected her to growl like one any second.

I stayed silent as she eyed me up and down, her face contorted into an expression of obvious disapproval.

Jenny pursed her lips. "Will this take long because I'm sure Her Highness doesn't want to sit around here all day?"

Yep, I loved Jenny! She might have been a whole head shorter than this woman, but she took no nonsense from anyone.

"Beauty cannot be rushed, and in this case, we will need longer than usual. I've gathered my elite team to work on her, and they will be up here momentarily. I suggest you go and get yourself a coffee or something."

Jenny looked like she was just about to suggest something of her own in retaliation, but just as she opened her mouth to bite back, a group of about twenty people all walked through the door and stood in a line.

The woman walked down the line, kissing each one on the cheek in turn.

Why did I need twenty people? They looked like an immaculately dressed firing squad. I took hold of Jenny's hand.

"I am Xavi," said the woman, finally turning back to me, "and this is my team. They will turn you from a caterpillar into a butterfly."

"I only thought I'd need a dress," I replied in a small voice.

"Nonsense," Xavi replied. "Chanelle here will be taking you to the marble room with her team first."

I had no idea what the marble room was. I'd walked every corridor in this palace, and even though it housed over a thousand people, I knew every nook and cranny of it. I was yet to find a room made of marble. I was just wondering if she meant the great hall with its marble staircase, when Chanelle pulled me up out of my seat and, along with three others, escorted me to the back of the room. Along the back of the room were three huge sets of double doors painted in gold. I assumed they were full of dresses and royal attire.

The first set of doors opened, and I found myself staring into a room made out of marble. The marble room! How could I not have known it existed before?

"You won't be needed in here," said Chanelle to Jenny and shut the door in her face. I could only imagine the look on Jenny's face. She didn't stand being talked to like that.

Chanelle flicked a switch, and the room came to life. Where there had been only a room with a huge marble table in the center and a channel in the floor around the edge, there now was a waterfall. A huge water fall that covered three of the walls. I wondered if it was caused by Magic or technology. I flicked my eyes to the trim of Chanelle's uniform, but she only wore white. She, like the others, was non-Magic. Water gushed down the channels in the floor and then drained out somewhere. Along each wall were a number of large stone urns. Set against them and to the side of me next to the doors, was a marble bench and some hooks. I noticed a white robe hanging on one of them.

"Strip off and put your clothes here." Chanelle indicated the bench. "I can assure you they will remain perfectly dry."

I gawked at her, wondering what exactly she had in store for me. Because I'd taken so long to move, she clicked her fingers and the other three girls moved forward and began trying to remove my pajamas.

"It's fine! I can do it myself!" I was going to have to be naked in front of these strangers! Had Grace ever had to go through this? It was certain she must have, and yet, she'd never mentioned it. Was this the palace's best-kept secret or just one of many?

Once my clothes had been removed, I was told to hop up onto the marble table. One of the girls fetched three sponges filled with soap from the first urn and passed two of them to the other girls. Under Chanelle's watchful eye, they washed me down, soaping me from head to toe, missing not a single crevice, from behind my ears to between my toes.

When I thought it was all over and I couldn't possibly be any cleaner, they put away their sponges and brought back brushes. Chanelle herself poured a bucket of water over me to wash away the bubbles and then the others got to work, scrubbing my skin until it was red.

My cries of pain went unheeded as they roughly scrubbed off any dead skin.

By the time they had finished with me, my skin felt like it was on fire, and yet, I'd never felt as clean in my whole life. Chanelle handed me the white robe I'd seen earlier and after turning the waterfalls off, instructed me to go through a door I'd not seen earlier.

The next room was bland compared to the marble room. It looked a little like an office, although it too had a table in the center. This one was not made out of marble, however. It was padded leather and looked like it had moveable parts.

Judging by the huge double doors to my right, this room was right off the main room.

I perched on the edge of the table and waited for something to happen. I didn't have to wait long before a young woman walked in. She gestured for me to lie on the table.

Just like the others in the room before, she worked silently. Her job, it seemed, was to cover me in sticky brown stuff that looked a little like treacle. I wondered for a second if it was some kind of moisturizing substance until she added a small strip of fabric to the stuff she'd applied to my leg and yanked it off, pulling the treacle stuff and what felt like half my leg with it.

I yelled and pulled my leg towards myself protectively.

"It's for hair removal," she said in a foreign accent.

I looked down, and sure enough, there was a strip of hair missing from my leg.

"I like the hair on my leg!" I replied defensively. It had never been a problem before. I usually wore trousers, and in the few times I'd been forced to wear a skirt or dress, my legs had been covered with thick tights.

"I have orders," she said, wrestling my leg back into a straight position and applying more of the treacle stuff. "Legs, underarms, upper lip, eyebrows, and bikini line. I make you look like a princess!" She smiled as if she'd just told me something wonderful instead of the horrific torture she was about to put me through. I was just about to argue when she spoke again.

"King tell Xavi, who tell me."

So my father had put them all up to this. Did he know how much it hurt?

"My father would not expect me to go through this...Ouch!"

She pulled another strip from my leg. A stinging sensation hit me for the second time.

"His Majesty gets waxed twice a month."

My father got waxed too? Part of me wanted to know exactly what he got waxed, but a much bigger part didn't want to know. If my father had ordered it, I had to bear it. With each pull of the wax strips, the pain became worse and worse until she finally declared she had finished. I'd been naked in the last room, but now, without any body hair, I had never felt as naked in my life. She wiped me down with a cloth dipped in some strong smelling solution which she told me dissolved any remnants of wax and then rubbed a sweet smelling pink lotion over my whole body. After all the pain I'd endured, the cooling lotion was bliss to my skin. She handed me a simple thin white dress and pushed me through the double doors. As I had assumed, they led back to the large dressing room. As soon as Jenny saw me, she ran over, a look of concern on her face.

Xavi had also seen me.

"Bring her over here," she demanded from across the room.

"Are you ok, child?" asked Jenny under her breath.

I was about to answer how awfully I'd been treated and how painful it had been when I realized my skin had never felt so good. My arms were softer than a newborn's, and I felt amazing. Maybe Xavi and her team knew what they were doing after all.

"I'm good," I replied.

The chair Xavi had indicated was next to a sink. A young man was waiting to wash my hair.

"Jon here will wash and dry your hair. Then Alezis will take over and create a style for you." She indicated another man. This one had long black hair tied in a ponytail and was wearing more makeup than any woman I'd ever met.

Jon carefully put my head back over the basin and began to wash my hair with careful hands, massaging my scalp with practiced strokes. I closed my eyes, enjoying the sensation of his fingertips caressing my hair, shampooing, and conditioning until my hair was spotless. It was so much more pleasurable than anything else I'd had to endure that day that I was almost sad when it came to an end. Jon moved me to another chair and dried my hair until it hung down in shiny waves. It looked so amazing that

I wasn't sure exactly what Alezis would be able to do to improve it.

"Everybody leave!" He shouted as he examined my hair. "I need total silence while I work, and I cannot have anyone disrupting me as I create my masterpiece."

I watched in the mirror as Jenny opened her mouth to argue, but she was swiftly removed by Xavi, who dragged her from the room and slammed the door behind them.

"Jenny isn't going to stand for that!" I mused out loud.

Alezis didn't answer. He was too busy examining my hair, strand by strand as though he might find buried treasure in there somewhere. After half an hour, he was still to pick up a pair of scissors or comb, and I was beginning to get impatient.

"Are you going to cut my hair?" I inquired eventually.

"Hmmm," was his reply. I wasn't sure exactly what he meant, but he finally picked up his scissors and began to chop at my hair. His work was delicate and deliberate. I could see him agonizing over every cut, and when he did snip, he did it slowly.

How could anyone care about hair so much? I'd have happily tied it up at the back with a ribbon and been done with it.

After what felt like hours, he put down his scissors. It looked exactly as it had before except it had a life to it that it had never seen. He'd glossed it and yet it was not heavy. It was difficult to put my finger on what exactly he'd done, and yet, it looked magnificent. I was pleased to see that he'd not changed it drastically. I still looked just like me except somehow better.

"When there is a royal engagement I'll sculpt your hair into something much more magnificent," he said, "but for now, you can wear this."

He picked up a simple golden hair band and slipped it into my hair.

"Thank you," I replied, gazing at myself in the mirror. The next step was the one that scared me the most. Makeup. I hated the stuff, and up until now, I'd gotten away with not having to wear any.

Xavi strolled back in with the rest of her team and gave me an appreciative glance.

"Wonderful job as always Alezis," she kissed him on each cheek. "I'll send the royal tiaras to you next week so you can decide what to do with her for the ball."

"Magnifico!" he replied before leaving.

Jenny ran over to me and clapped her hands. If she was still angry, she didn't show it. Instead, a grin spread across her face.

"You look stunning, child!"

"Not yet, she doesn't," remarked Xavi, "My team of artists will transform her. The first three will create a blank canvas, and then Louis will perform a miracle on her."

Four more people to beautify me. Who knew that being beautiful was such an effort? Unlike Alezis who let me watch what he was doing in the mirror, this time, the chair I was in faced the middle of the room.

The only mirror I had was Jenny's face which was alternating between concern and pride, before breaking into a huge grin which stayed on her face throughout the rest of the session. The three people working on me applied all manner of creams and powders to my face. They took it in turns to use a multitude of brushes, and I heard words being thrown around like "contouring" and "highlighting," none of which I knew what they meant. As they worked, I counted all the people that had worked on me so far. The three in the marble room, the woman with the accent who waxed me, Jon, Alezis and now the three make-up artists. With Louis and Xavi herself that only made eleven. I'd counted twenty when they had all trooped in at the beginning. What were the other nine for?

When the three had finished, they spun my chair around until I could see myself in the mirror. I looked back at me, version 2.0. I looked exactly like I always had, and yet, I was beautiful. How had they done it? Just as Alezis had done with my hair, they had made me something better than I always had been but without seemingly changing me at all. They had put so much on me and yet it looked like I'd just stepped out of the bath, naturally flawless and makeup free.

I'd never known just how beautiful I was. Beauty was not high up on my agenda, and yet, I couldn't help but look at myself in awe.

When Louis came over with a huge case that opened to show a whole rainbow of colors, I almost asked him not to bother. I didn't want to change a thing about my face. And yet, I knew it was fruitless. The people who had gone before had done an amazing job; I had to trust that he would too. He was short and blond, and unlike the exuberantly dressed and made up Alezis, he wore no makeup. Instead, he had a small mustache that sat almost square on his top lip and wore jeans and a t-shirt. He could have been a plumber or mechanic. A small purple elongated star was pinned to his top.

His way of showing he was a Magi without going overboard about it. Nothing about him said make-up artist, and yet, Xavi was fluttering around him in obvious excitement.

"Will you make me up using Magic?" I asked, eyeing up the pin.

"I always perform Magic sweetie." He winked at me, but instead of bringing out a wand, he pulled out a full set of makeup brushes.

Despite his looks, I had the feeling that he knew exactly what he was doing. He was much quicker with his work than Alezis had been, and he even let me watch in the mirror as he applied more powder to me, this time, around the eyes, layering up subtle shades of beige and browns. He made my eyes appear bigger, bringing out the hazel shade of them to perfection. When he'd finished on my eyes, he moved to my cheeks, sweeping the faintest shade of pink before applying gloss to my lips. It had taken him less than a minute, but he'd made me into something stunning. He'd turned me into a princess. I was assured, he'd do something spectacular on the night of the ball, but I wasn't sure how he could improve on the perfection he'd created.

Two more people were ushered in, and it turned out, they were to do my nails. One applied a subtle shade to my fingernails, and the other worked on my toes.

All the while, Jenny danced around, clapping her hands and grinning; the anger at her being ordered around had obviously left her. She was enjoying this.

"Charmaine, you look stunning!" she kept repeating, over and over again, between grinning at everyone around her. When the two nail technicians had finished, she hugged them both before hugging a rather rattled looking Xavi.

The last seven turned out to be my dressers. The last set of double doors opened, and they paraded out, each with a dress in their hands to show us.

They stood in a long line, waiting for inspection. By now, there was only Jenny, Xavi, and I left.

The dresses were extravagant and horrible, each more poufy and fluffy than the next.

"Nope!" I said. I was expecting Xavi to argue with me, but instead, she ushered them all back to the room from where they had come. A minute later, they all trooped back out with seven more over the top gowns.

"Didn't you hear what her highness said last time?" Xavi shouted over at them. "Nope. I agree with her. They are a whole lot of nope. Do better!"

"I think they are beautiful," said Jenny.

"Hmm," I replied noncommittally. They were beautiful, but they weren't me. Not that I could think of any style of dress that would be me.

Finally, after six or seven attempts, Xavi went into the dressing room with them. When they all lined up the next time, the styles of dresses they brought out were much simpler. I had to hand it to her; she knew what she was doing.

"These are much better," she said, taking a place by my side. "I think the white one for your official introduction to the press today. It's understated but regal. The pale yellow for tomorrow. It will go nicely with your hair, and the paparazzi are bound to want lots of pictures of you. After that, I think the pink, then the blue, then the beige. From then on, we'll keep you out of view until the big day. Do you agree?"

The ball! I'd almost forgotten about it in all the excitement.

"I agree," I said. I didn't much like any of the dresses, but at least they were simple. The white one was brought over and the others taken away. It had navy blue piping on it and reminded me of a sailor dress, with pleats along the skirt. A matching jacket was brought out along with a pair of plain gold studded earrings and a simple thin gold chain.

"Now, I know you don't like fuss, but it will be expected that you wear the insignia of the crown."

Grace wore hers as a diamond broach. She wore it at every official occasion and had even been wearing it as she was buried. I waited for Xavi to pin something similar onto the jacket, but instead, she told me that my mother would give it to me later.

The seven women helped me into the dress and Xavi guided me to one of the full-length mirrors. She handed me a pair of white shoes to match, and I slipped my feet into them. They were not as flat as I would have liked, but the heel was small enough for me to feel comfortable in. Before me, stood a princess. For the first time in my life, I looked like the woman I was supposed to be. Despite myself, I smiled. Beside me, Jenny bawled.

The Lessons

My mother's eyes lit up when she saw me in the parlor later that afternoon. Perhaps she'd forgotten for a moment and thought I was Grace. I looked more like her than I cared to admit now that I was dressed up. The light didn't die as I sat down opposite her, so perhaps, I was wrong. Maybe she was just pleased to see me looking so well turned out for a change. One of the servants brought in a tray with platters of tiny sandwiches and cakes. She also placed a couple of teacups down with a pot of Earl Grey – my mother's favorite.

"I must say, you are simply sparkling today. Xavi and her team have done a wonderful job with you. Did you enjoy it?"

"Not at first," I replied truthfully, "but I feel wonderful. I enjoyed the head massage when I was having my hair washed."

My mother laughed. "That's my favorite part too."

I took a sandwich and nibbled on a corner of it, waiting for my mother to continue. The ball was less than two weeks away, and I was woefully unprepared. A nice dress and hairdo was one thing, but knowing how to act was a whole different ballgame.

"I've drawn up a schedule for you. You are to have intensive etiquette lessons, and lessons on deportment and speech. I've asked for the young men to send photos, so you will study them in great detail and try to learn as many of their names and titles as possible."

"I thought there were a hundred men coming?" I asked, feeling overwhelmed at the prospect of remembering so many names.

"And so there are. They may be bringing family members with them, so I've asked that photos be found of those people too. Many young ladies from the finest houses in the district have also been invited to even up the ball somewhat, and some of the ladies of the staff will make up the number. It would be strange to have a hundred men and just one woman to dance. They have all been instructed only to dance with the young men until you cut in on a dancing couple if you so wish; however, your teacher for the next week will show you how to do this delicately."

"Teacher? Who is going to be my teacher?" I asked in horror. I was never going to be able to learn all the things I needed to in less than a fortnight, and the thought of a stranger teaching me all these things filled me with dread. I remembered my horrible teacher that attempted teaching me etiquette throughout my schooling. Needless to say, she failed.

"Jenny has said she'd do it, but I've also hired a dance teacher to show you the basics. Grace has..." she caught herself and then like the queen she was, carried on "had been having lessons for four months. I don't expect you to get to her level, but I do expect you to learn some basic dance steps without falling over anyone's feet. You'll do the dance lessons in the afternoons and the rest in the morning. For now, the press have set up in the sitting room. I've asked that just one person interview you, and I've expressly told them that the interview will be no more than ten minutes. I'll be with you the whole time, and I'll help if you feel overwhelmed."

I felt overwhelmed already. I'd been told hours earlier that this was something I had to do, but with my makeover taking so long, I'd had no time to prepare. This was my first ever interview, and I was terrified.

As I walked through the double doors to the sitting room, hand in hand with my mother, what felt like hundreds of flashes of light from all the cameras blinded me, leaving my mother to guide me to the sofa. It was the same sofa where she had sat and told me about the ball only yesterday except now it was I by her side, and a squat man with a balding head in a smart suit was sitting in the place I had taken.

"Welcome, Your Majesty and Your Highness. Thank you for agreeing to this interview and for inviting us here today to celebrate at what must be a difficult time for you." His voice was even and bland.

"You are more than welcome." I didn't turn to look at my mother, but I knew she was smiling. I tried plastering on a smile and hoped I didn't look too fake.

"So, Princess Charmaine, how are you feeling, knowing that you get to be the belle of the ball?"

Dreadful, scared, annoyed, aggravated... "I'm happy to have this opportunity."

"And are you looking forward to meeting all those eligible bachelors?"

Nope. "Yes, of course, it is always an honor to meet new people and in this case, someone who will change the course of my life. I'm very excited."

"Is there anything you can tell us about the men? Are there any front runners?"

My mother jumped in. "The princess Charmaine has yet to learn the identity of the hundred men who have been invited, but I can assure you, when she does, she will give each and every one of them careful deliberation."

"There has been a bit of controversy over the men who were invited though, hasn't there?"

"In what way?" my mother asked. I could feel her going rigid beside me. What controversy was this?

"Well, it's been noted that no Magi have been invited."

"We put out an expression of interest many months ago, to everyone in the Kingdom of Silverwood as well as to neighboring kingdoms. Everyone had a chance to apply for a position. We had over five thousand applications. The royal advisors, along with myself and the king, handpicked the hundred that we thought would provide a good match, not only for our daughter but for the kingdom as a whole. Then we sent out the invitations."

"But none of the hundred are Magi. Many would say that you are purposely marginalizing them."

"That is not the case at all. We picked the hundred men we thought most fitting for the role."

"Did any Magi apply?"

"I couldn't possibly say," replied my mother. Her usual poise was beginning to crack. It was subtle, but I could hear it in her voice. "We chose the men months ago."

"I happen to know that more than one or two Magi did apply," continued the interviewer.

"Is that so? Well, as I said, there were over five thousand entries. Unfortunately, not everyone could get picked. We hope we've picked out some wonderful young men, and on the day, the final decision will belong to Charmaine. I thank you all for coming, and we hope to see you at the ball in two weeks."

She stood up, signaling the end of the interview. It was the first time I'd ever known her to cut an interview short. It was great for me as I didn't want to answer any questions anyway, but I had to wonder why.

I wasn't given long to ponder it as my first dancing lesson started in less than half an hour. The thought of dance lessons terrified me, but I was pretty nimble on my feet. How bad could I be at dancing anyway?

"Ouch!" cried Stephan as I stepped on his toes for the hundredth time that day. Stephan was a world-renowned dance instructor that my parents had hired. He was also a very short man, at least, a foot shorter than me, and after an hour with me, was professing that he'd never be able to dance again.

Apart from his melodramatic statements, he was a great dance teacher. Unfortunately for him, I was a lousy student. I tried, I really did, but my feet wouldn't go the way either of us wanted them to. After four hours, I'd barely managed a single dance without either stepping on him or knocking him over.

He signaled for one of the servants to turn the music off and called it a day. I had a feeling he'd be spending the evening soaking his feet in a herbal bath.

I felt a complete failure and was ready to give up everything when I bumped into Elise on the way to my room.

As soon as she saw me, her hands flew up to her mouth.

"Mama told me how gorgeous you looked, but she was wrong; you are stunning!" She ran up to me and flung her arms around my neck. "Come to my room and tell me all about it. Did they wax you?"

I laughed at her excitement. "You knew about this?"

I sat on her bed, and she sat right beside me.

"Waxing? Of course. I've been begging Mama for years to let me get my legs waxed, but she always said I was too young."

"But it hurts!"

"Yeah, but you have nice smooth legs. I swear I'm turning into a gorilla."

I punched her playfully on the shoulder. She was anything but a gorilla. She was one of the prettiest girls I knew.

"It's a pretty awful experience, but if you like, I can ask mama if you can have a makeover before the ball. Xavi and her crew have done wonders on me, although I don't know how they are going to be able to improve you."

"Would you? Oh, thank you!" She flung her arms around me again, this time, knocking us both flat on the bed.

"Only you would attempt wrestling after spending all morning being made prim and proper."

I looked up to find Jenny there. There were few people who would just walk into our bedrooms, and Jenny was one.

I sat up and smoothed my hair while giggling.

"Sorry, Jenny," we chorused, although guessing by the way we were both giggling, she could tell we were anything but.

"Her Royal Highness, the Queen, has asked me to give you lessons. I figured there was no time like the present."

"Mama said you'd be teaching me in the morning!" I'd had enough lessons today. My legs were still aching from all the dancing.

"Charmaine, you and I both know that you need to put in the work. Do you want to go into that ball not having a clue how to act, or do you want to study hard and enjoy yourself?"

"Ha!" I replied. She knew I'd rather do pretty much anything than go to the stupid ball, and enjoying myself was not an option. However, I didn't want to let my family down either. It was a huge responsibility.

"Come on, let's go."

I followed Jenny to a part of the palace I'd not been to before. The servant's quarters.

"I thought we'd be having lessons in the classroom?" The classroom hadn't been used since Elise had finished her schooling last year.

"No. There is always someone around to be nosy. I thought you'd be much happier away from prying eyes. A lot of the information I'm going to give you is for your ears only, and you never know who might be listening."

"I thought we were learning about etiquette?"

"Among other things. We'll start on etiquette tonight. I had one of the kitchen staff set a table in my quarters. By the end of the night, you'll know exactly which spoon, knife, and fork to use."

"But I already know that stuff," I whined. Table manners was one of the first things I learned as a child.

"Not like this, you haven't," she replied before opening her door.

It opened into her apartment's living room. Right in the center, filling up almost the whole room was a large round table with a white tablecloth upon it. On top of the table was one place setting with so much silver cutlery, I could barely count it all.

"Why is all the cutlery on one setting?"

"That's how much cutlery there is supposed to be for that one setting. You'll be having a seven-course meal, and that is all the cutlery you'll need for it."

"But there is so much of it."

"And by the end of tonight, you'll know how to use every bit of it."

I wasn't sure, but I sat at the only seat at the table. Jenny stood next to me.

"You start at the outer cutlery and work your way in." She picked up a fork and handed it to me. "Hold it like this."

How was it possible I'd gone eighteen years and didn't know how to hold a fork correctly? Three hours later, I'd only just gotten the hang of what everything was for. My stomach gave a loud rumble.

"Oh, goodness me. Is that the time?" said Jenny, looking at her watch. You've missed dinner. I'm so sorry. You'll have to go down to the kitchen and ask the cook for something. Can you remind him that I'll need a bowl of soup for tomorrow's lesson?"

"Tomorrow's lesson is soup?"

"How to eat it correctly, yes."

"I thought we were learning important things? The ball is in thirteen days."

"My dear," said Jenny, ushering me out of the door. "There is little in life more important than knowing how to eat soup in a ten thousand dollar dress without spilling it."

I was going to ask what she knew about my dress for the ball when she shut the door in my face.

Charming! My stomach gave another growl, so I tried putting the dreadful-sounding dress to the back of my mind and headed to the kitchens. The "cook" as Jenny called him, was actually the head chef, Monsieur Pasqual, and he was one of a number of chefs, who as well as many other kitchen staff, fed the royal family each day. I'd only been down to the kitchens on a few occasions, but each time I had, it had been a hive of activity and filled with the most amazing smells. This time as I entered, only one person was there. A young man with curly hair stood with his back to me. To his side, was a mountain of dishes waiting to be washed. As I watched, each dirty plate flew through the air with a flick of his wand before dipping into the sink. He washed each one while humming to himself and tapping his toes. At the same time, on the pile of clean crockery, forks lightly tapped on glasses and plates, clinking as if they were drums, each moving through thin air thanks to the magic powering them. The whole effect was like a magical orchestra, filling the kitchen with a beautiful sound. I vaguely recognized the tune, but couldn't quite place it. And all the while, he danced to his own music, conducting the cutlery and crockery in a mesmerizing rhythm, oblivious to my presence.

I watched him enjoying his work for quite a few minutes unable to tear my eyes away. I took utter joy in watching the way he moved before I accidentally knocked over a salt pot on a counter to my right. He heard the noise and stopped humming immediately. His concentration lapsed, and the dish he'd been washing fell into the sink, splashing water everywhere.

"Please don't stop. I was enjoying it."

He bowed in the same way as all the servants did, his curls flopping over his eyes as he lowered his head.

"I'm sorry Your Highness. I didn't know you were here." His voice was much deeper and richer than his youthful face implied. He had the cutest dimples on his cheeks, and his curly brown hair was just a touch too long. His eyes were a shade lighter than his hair. Caramel to chocolate.

"Evidently," I said, and he blushed.

"Why do you clean the dishes individually?" I asked. "Wouldn't it be quicker to wave your wand and wipe them all clean at once?"

"Yeah, but where is the fun in that?" He grinned and then as if remembering his place, straightened up. "How can I help you, Your Highness?"

"I came down for something to eat, but I see I'm too late." The kitchen was clean with nothing left out.

"Sit down," he ordered, pointing to a huge oak table in the center of the room.

I arched my brow at his command. Having never been told what to do by a member of staff before, it took me by surprise. Nevertheless, I did as he said and took a place near the end of the table. He put a clean plate in front of me and an empty glass.

"What's this?" I asked, looking down at the plate.

"I'm going to cook for you. I can't have the princess go hungry."

"No, that's fine. I can't ask you to do that. I'll just grab some leftovers from the fridge." I stood as if to leave.

"I can cook. One day I want to be a chef. Of course, I've got a long way to go." He indicated the pile of washing up still to do. I didn't want to offend him, so I sat back down. He brought out a bottle of sparkling wine and poured me a glass.

"It's not as good as the stuff you guys drink from the wine cellar, but it's pretty nice."

I took a sip. The bubbles hit the back of my throat, and I began to cough.

"Sorry!" He looked stricken. "I thought it would be ok. I guess you aren't used to the cheap stuff, hey?"

I cleared my throat. "I'm not actually used to drinking at all. It's one of the few things I'm looking forward to at the ball—getting drunk for the first time and forgetting the whole thing."

I realized then that I had said too much. To talk in such a way in front of a servant was simply not done. He just laughed and opened the fridge, bringing out a host of fresh vegetables.

"Not looking forward to it, huh?" He brought a knife out and began expertly chopping up an onion into tiny pieces. His hands worked so quickly, I could barely keep up with them. I wondered why he didn't use his wand when he could so easily have done so.

"I didn't mean..."

"Don't worry. I'd hate to have to go in your position too. I totally get it."

Something about his manner put me at ease. Usually, any conversation with the servants, with the exception of Jenny and Agatha, had me reeling around in my brain to say the right thing.

"Maybe drinking should be in your lesson plan as well as soup! You don't want to get so drunk that you fall over." He turned and grinned at me again, showing off his dimples.

He moved from the onions to the carrots where he cut them julienne style.

"You know about the soup? I was supposed to remind Monsieur Pascal."

"He already knows. Look." He pointed at a huge white board, covered in barely legible text. I made out such words as *pheasant, 'lobster*, and in the top right-hand corner, *soup for Princess Charmaine's lesson.'*

I had never felt so ridiculous in my life. My cheeks burned as I realized that this cute guy knew that I needed lessons to eat soup. Whatever must he think of me?

"I can eat soup, you know. It's just that they don't trust me not to spill it all over my ballgown." I took another swig of the wine. This time, it went down the right way without me choking.

"I don't doubt it. I don't know why they are having this ball. There must be a hundred men already lining up to ask you for your hand." It was his turn to go red. If anything, it made him look cuter. He turned and threw the chopped veggies into a pan to try and hide it.

I gave a small smile and sighed. "It's not that. They have to be the right kind of men."

"Oh," he said. "And what's the right kind of man?"

I remembered what the reporter had said earlier. No Magi had been chosen. Something about it made me feel bad, although I really wouldn't have expected anything else. No Magi had ever been in a high position. They were usually to be found more in manual labor jobs.

"One who doesn't spill soup all down his tuxedo, I assume."

He laughed. "That rules me out then. I'm the clumsy one in the kitchen."

The way he'd deftly handled those veggies and the plates earlier, made me think he was telling a white lie to put me at ease. I'd never seen a man move in such an assured manner. Nothing about him was clumsy.

Even now as I watched him chopping up some meat, he moved quickly and with a dexterity I'd never seen before. He threw it all in with the veggies and added some other ingredients. With all the powders and creams he threw in there, it reminded me of the beauticians this afternoon except, this was not a face he was creating. Whatever it was smelled out of this world.

"Are you a sous chef?" I asked.

"I'm just a kitchen hand. I wash up when everyone goes home. I do errands, that sort of thing."

"Then how do you know how to cook so well?"

He sprinkled some black powder into the pan and sniffed it. "How do you know how well I cook? You've not tasted it yet."

"It smells so delicious. It can't possibly be anything but good."

"If only Monsieur Pascal could hear you say that."

"Haven't you shown him what you can do? One smell of that, and he'd be promoting you to second in command."

He gave a wry smile. "It's not that simple. People like me don't get those kinds of jobs."

"People like you?"

"You know."

And I did know. I felt awkward. While Magi took on many roles in society, they were widely regarded as suspicious because of their Magic. Because of that, they were rarely given any jobs in power, and I couldn't think of one that had a leadership role in the palace. If there were more of them, things would probably be different, their strengths obviously greater than the rest of us. But they were a small sect, who had been downtrodden for years. The few homeless people I'd seen were Magi, putting on magical puppet shows in the streets for a few coins.

Of course, I couldn't say any of this to him. I settled on asking him his name instead.

"I'm Cynder."

"It's nice to meet you Cynder. I'm—"

"Princess Charming."

"Charmaine," I corrected him.

"I know, but I always thought of you as charming."

I blushed again. He didn't notice as he was serving up food onto my plate.

"Aren't you going to eat with me?" I asked, noticing there was still a lot left in the pan.

"I can't eat with a princess. I'll finish it off when you leave."

Something about the thought of him eating alone made me feel sad. What rule was there that forbade a princess and a kitchen hand to eat together? There was none as far as I was aware. "Nonsense. Grab a plate and eat with me. You may as well pour yourself a glass of wine too. I don't want to be the only one drinking."

"I'm afraid I can't possibly." He looked nervous at the mere suggestion, but I was more nervous at the thought of him watching me while I ate.

"If anyone comes, I'll tell them I insisted."

He took out a plate and a glass and sat next to me. I picked up the bottle of wine and filled his glass to the top before refilling mine.

As predicted, the food was delicious. He'd made some kind of creamy white sauce that tasted like nothing I'd ever tasted before and poured it over chicken and rice. The vegetables he'd done before rested on the side.

"What is this?" I asked, wolfing it down in a very unladylike manner.

"It's an old family recipe. Do you like it?"

"Like it? It's the most delicious meal I've ever tasted. You need to serve this at the ball."

Cynder laughed.

"I'm not joking. I'll speak to my father and have Monsieur Pascal make this recipe."

"I don't think Monsieur Pascal will thank you for that. He's been planning the menu for this ball for months. We've already ordered all the ingredients."

I looked at the board again. "I hate lobster and pheasant. They are both so pretentious. I'd be much happier with plain old chicken."

Cynder laughed again.

"I can make this dish any evening you want, just for you. Just come down after ten at night because that's when everyone leaves."

"I'm sure no one will mind if you make me something before ten," I replied airily.

"If anyone found out that I had made a meal or eaten any of the food, I'd be fired. It's hard enough to get a job being a Mage in this kingdom as it is."

"Why would you be fired? You've only made me dinner."

"I have to play by the rules, and the first rule of working here is to know my place. My place is over there by the sink."

"But that's absurd!" His talent was wasted washing up dishes. Then I thought of the interview I'd had earlier. My mother had been so uneasy at the mere mention of the Magi that she'd cut an interview short because of it.

"I'm sorry. I shouldn't have spoken out of turn. I do love this job; I really do."

I heard him say the words, but I wasn't convinced he meant them. There was a sadness in his voice and an underlying note of anger. I'd struck a chord with him, but I wasn't sure how to handle it. As usual, I ignored that which made me feel nervous and instead threw the plate into the soapy water where I began to wash it.

"What are you doing?" Cynder ran towards me in alarm.

"I'm washing my plate. It's the least I can do."

"I can't let you do that! You're the princess."

"You made the dinner; I'll wash up. It's only fair. Here, give me your plate." I took his plate from him without even asking and threw that into the suds too.

"You are not at all what I imagined. Sure, I've seen you around, and you are nothing like the rest of your family, but I never expected..."

I could really feel the wine hit me. Between us, we'd finished the whole bottle. Maybe it was that, maybe it was something else, but having him close to me gave me an idea. An idea I'd never have contemplated if I were sober.

"Maybe you can do something for me in return?"

"What?"

"Teach me to dance the way you were dancing when I walked in earlier."

"I wasn't dancing. I was washing up." He looked perplexed, but I could see a hint of amusement in his face.

"Yes, you were. I saw the way your feet moved. There was such freedom in it. I'm having lessons, and I'm hopeless. I'll finish up this mountain of dishes while you dry, and then you can show me your moves."

He looked at me with a mixture of curiosity and something else I couldn't quite put my finger on, but he agreed nonetheless.

It took us a good twenty minutes to get it all finished, both of us doing the task by hand. As I'd been taking sips of wine from my glass, which had magically refilled itself before I washed each plate, I was very tipsy.

I stood to one side of the table and held my arms out the way my dance teacher had shown me only a few hours before.

"Shut your eyes and put your arms down by your side."

It wasn't what I was expecting, but I did as he asked.

He began to hum again, but this time picked a quicker tune than he had before. I could hear the tap tap tap of his shoes against the tile floor.

I expected his hand on my shoulder and one on my waist, but instead he took both of my hands in his.

"Feel the rhythm. Don't think about any fancy dance moves, just move your body whichever way feels natural."

"I don't know any dance moves. Nothing about dancing feels natural." I opened my eyes and looked right at him.

"Let me help you then." He grabbed my waist and pulled me towards him until our bodies were slammed together, shocking me. I opened my mouth to speak, but then he began to move. The same sinewy effortless moves he'd made before, but this time taking me along for the ride. I was so close to him, I could smell the cologne on his neck and feel the vibration of his throat as he hummed the sweet tune. I closed my eyes and let him take me with him into his magical world.

He spun me around effortlessly, our bodies molded together, and when he came to a standstill and the humming stopped, I opened my eyes. He gazed down at me, with those caramel eyes and then slowly took a step back.

"You are better than you think you are," he said. "You can move. You just have to learn to work your body in time to the music."

I'd never moved the way he'd just taught me. I think my father would have a heart attack if I tried anything like it at the ball.

"Will you teach me?"

"I just did."

"I mean every night until the ball. I promise to come after ten. No one will know."

"I guess neither of us has the freedom we'd like," he mused aloud.

He looked unsure as though he was doing something wrong. Indeed, it felt illicit to me too although I didn't know why.

"I'll help you with the washing up again."

"Then how can I say no?"

He smiled at me, showing off those dimples of his.

That night as I slipped into bed, for the first time in two days, I felt confident about the upcoming ball. With Cynder's help, I'd be the best dancer in the palace.

Cynder

The next morning, I woke up with a feeling of excitement as though I'd had a lovely dream but forgotten it the moment my eyes opened. It took me a few moments to realize it was because of last night and dancing in the kitchen. It was the first morning since Grace died that I hadn't woken up with pain being the first emotion I felt. Sure, I still hurt. Nothing could take away the anguish I felt at losing my sister, but at some point between ten o'clock last night and this morning, the crushing weight on my heart had lifted slightly, and my first thought upon waking was not of Grace or the upcoming ball, but of a servant who washed up in the kitchen downstairs.

I looked at my clock. Jenny would be along at any second to let me know what the day had in store. As if on cue, the door opened, and she appeared with a folio in her hand. At the very same time, the other door opened and Elise came bounding in.

"Is that what I think it is?" her eyes opened wide as she took in the folio in Jenny's hand.

"It's the list of men coming to the ball. Their photos and a little information about each of them are in there. It's for Charmaine's eyes only," she said, ignoring Elise's exuberance and passing it to me.

Elise, in turn, ignored her and jumped onto the bed beside me as I opened the folio to the first bachelor.

"Wow, he's ugly," remarked Elise. "Why does he only have three teeth?"

"You heard Jenny, you aren't supposed to be looking at this," I pulled it away from her prying eyes. I couldn't go through it with her commenting on the appearance of every guy in there.

"Why?" she sniffed.

"I don't know. Maybe they don't want anyone else falling in love with these guys before I do."

"I already am in love with them." She danced around the room with a silly grin on her face.

"You should go. I need to shower." It was a lie. I was sure to get scrubbed down in the marble room again later, but I wanted to look through the list in peace.

"Ok," Elise singsonged. "I'll see you later."

Jenny sighed as Elise left the room. "I'll be off too. I'll be testing you on their names after breakfast, so try and remember some of them, ok?"

She closed the door behind her, leaving me alone with a hundred photographs of men, one of which I was supposed to marry within the next six months.

I opened the folio and stared at the first photo. It was a grainy black and white picture that was clearly years old. I could see Elise's point. He did look like he only had three teeth. I read the name printed underneath.

Julius Darwin III

Landowner

Landowner? What did that even mean? Is that all he did? Own land? I put it down to my side, beginning a pile that would firmly be labeled, nope.

An hour later and my nope pile was getting ridiculously high. I'd put three photos on my maybe pile, and my yes pile was sadly deficient. I'd only included the three in the maybe pile because I thought Elise might like them.

There was a knock at my door.

"Come in."

Cynder walked in with a large silver tray containing cereal and fruit. My heart leapt when I saw him.

"The queen noticed you hadn't been down for breakfast, so she sent instructions to the kitchen to have something light brought up for you. I asked Pascal if I could bring it up."

I eyed up the bland looking cereal and sighed. "I'd kill for a bacon sandwich."

"I knew you'd say that!" He grinned, pulling a paper bag from his back pocket. Immediately, the aroma of bacon filled the air.

"You made this?" I asked in amazement. Was the guy a mind reader too?

"No," he admitted in a whisper. "You caught me. I used my wand."

I took the bag from his hand and pulled out the sandwich, stuffing it into my mouth. It tasted like heaven.

"I could just kiss you!" I said, between mouthfuls, not caring how unladylike I looked.

"I guess I will have to wait until you've gotten through this lot first," he replied, picking up the last photo I'd thrown down.

I rolled my eyes.

"I've still got about thirty to go through. Honestly, most of them are old enough to be my father. One of them, I swear was seventy years old."

Cynder grinned. "At least, you won't have to worry about being married to him for long. He'll be dead soon enough."

"Good point!" I said, "Now where was he? I'll put him on my yes pile." I began to rummage through the nope pile.

"What about this guy?" Cynder said, holding up a photo. "He seems nice enough. Handsome guy."

I took the photo from him and read his name out loud. Luca Tremaine.

He was good-looking. With dark, brooding features and a hint of a beard, he was quite the catch. Elise would drool over the guy.

"Prince Luca, second son of The King and Queen of Thalia," I read aloud. "My father would probably like me to pick him. He's all about strengthening relations with other kingdoms."

I put the photo on the maybe pile.

"I'm not sure," replied Cynder, picking the photo up again and putting it in the nope pile. "I've heard of him. He's not good enough for you."

"Whatever do you mean?" I wasn't used to servants offering their opinions.

"He's got a reputation as a bit of a playboy. There have been many women."

I arched my brow.

"What?" he shrugged. "The girls in the kitchen gossip. It's not my fault if I overhear."

I sighed. There was bound to be something wrong with all of them. "Maybe he just hasn't found the right woman to settle down with yet." I looked at the photo again. I could well believe the kitchen maids' gossip. He was a very good-looking guy. I put him back in the maybe pile. "At least, he has his own teeth."

"Just be careful."

I looked up to find Cynder gazing at me. The humor had gone to be replaced with concern. It unnerved me.

"What does it matter who I pick?" I asked honestly.

"I just think you deserve to be happy."

I placed the rest of the photos back down on the bed. The conversation was getting uncomfortable, and I couldn't figure out why. His familiarity with me was unnerving and yet exciting at the same time. I'd never had a member of staff talk to me the way he did.

Before I had a chance to think about it, I blurted out "Dance with me?"

"Here?" It was his turn to look uncomfortable now.

"Yes, here. I want to show my dance instructor that I can do better." I felt my cheeks redden at the audacity of asking a member of the staff to dance with me in my own room. Normally, I would never have dared to ask such a thing, but I wasn't ready for him to go.

"Ok, then," Cynder pulled out his wand and locked the doors. I could understand why. I could only imagine the trouble we'd be in if we got caught.

He took me in his arms as he had the night before and began to hum. It was the only music we had. This time, he hummed a slow song.

He held me tight while I rested my head on his shoulder. This was not a dance he was teaching me. We were doing little more than swaying together, and yet again, we had become one. His arms around me made me feel safe as we slowly moved around my room, our bodies almost meshed together with only the thin silk of my nightgown between his hands and my bare skin. It felt like an ending to something wonderful and an awakening at the same time

"We can't do this again," he said, pulling away abruptly.

Confusion abounded within me. Only a second before, it had felt so good, and now he was moving away from me with confusion in his eyes.

"Why not?" I asked, taking a step closer to him. He stepped back at the same time.

"I can't. I should go."

"Please. I need your help. I have to dance with these strangers, and I don't know how." I pointed to the pile of photos on the bed.

"You have a teacher."

"I like being taught by you."

He nodded slowly and kissed my cheek before unlocking my door and walking through it.

"Ok," he replied, closing the door behind him, leaving me alone with my thoughts, and with my heart beating at double speed.

I could still feel his lips on my skin when Jenny turned up half an hour later. She immediately saw the two piles of photos on my bed. A large one for no's, and a tiny one for maybe's. There were still no photos on the yes pile.

"Oooh, been making some decisions, have we?" She picked up the maybe pile. "Oooh, good choice."

She sifted through the photos, occasionally making comments such as "He's a tasty dish," and "I wouldn't kick him out of bed." This was Jenny's way of giving me her seal of approval.

"Where is Daniel Laurient?"

"Who?" I asked.

She picked up the pile of nopes and began to flick through it before pulling out one of the photos and handing it to me.

"He's the son of a friend of mine. I promised her you'd give him thought. He's a nice guy and would be a perfect match for you. He's a local lad too."

I picked up the photo of Daniel. A pair of piercing green eyes gazing out of a chiseled face stared back at me. He had blond hair and a wide smile. He looked nice. I must have missed him when I threw him on the nope pile. He looked honest and immediately I liked him. I threw him back on the maybe pile. I didn't like him enough to go on the yes pile. I didn't like any of them enough.

After another ten minutes of deliberation, I ended up with fifteen photos on the maybe pile and a whopping eighty-five on the nope pile. Jenny spent a good hour with me going over their names and titles of which I only remembered a quarter at best.

Later, she took me back to her room to learn how to eat soup. Part of me hoped I'd see Cynder again as it would surely be he that brought up the soup, but the large bowl of tomato soup was already waiting for us on the table.

Under Jenny's watchful gaze, I ladled spoonful after spoonful of the red soup into my mouth until I was bursting with the stuff, and not once did I spill it, much to Jenny's satisfaction.

After lunch (which I spent alone in my bedroom, going over the photos and names of the men) I proceeded to my dance lesson.

Stephan grimaced as I walked through the ballroom door, no doubt imagining all the horrible things I was about to do to his feet. He gave the signal, and the servant by the old record player pressed play.

I felt confident as he walked over to me, but as he took me in his arms, everything felt wrong. Everything Cynder had taught me went right out of the window, and the whole lesson ended up being just as disastrous as the one the day before. I couldn't understand why. Dancing with Cynder had been effortless. This was torture for both of us.

That night, I counted down the hours until I could go down to the kitchen to ask Cynder where I'd gone wrong. As soon as the clock turned ten, I raced down the stairs that would take me to the kitchen, making sure no one saw me. When I walked through the door, a wonderful aroma hit me. Two plates and two glasses of wine had been placed on the table.

"What's this?" I asked in wonder.

"I made sure it was ready for ten o'clock. I'll have to do the dishes after you leave." I looked over to see a huge pile of dishes, much larger than the night before, just waiting for him to clean up.

"You didn't have to,"

"No, but you secretly hoped I would, right?"

"I barely ate anything at dinner," I admitted, slipping into the seat beside him. The meal was amazing, even better than the one he'd made the night before and much better than anything Pascal had ever produced. It made me feel bad for his situation, and yet, I didn't understand it fully.

"You are too good for washing up. You could easily be the head chef here or at some other place."

Cynder sighed. "It's not that easy. I don't have a degree. I've never even been to university."

"But you are amazing. Surely, someone will hire you without a degree. Your dishes speak for themselves."

"You need a degree to get a job as a head chef, or you have to work your way up the ranks. I've been here three years and watched as people who don't know how to boil an egg, get promoted before me."

"But why?"

"Because I'm a Mage," he growled. "Magi don't go to university, and they don't get jobs as head chefs."

I was taken aback at his gruffness. I'd not seen him angry before.

"But why don't they?" I persisted. "Surely, with Magic, you'll be able to do things even better than the rest of us?"

"That's exactly the thing you non-Magi are afraid of, which is exactly the reason why we are kept out of positions of power, and why we are not let into university."

"I'm not afraid of magic," I replied, slightly put out by his tone.

"Maybe not, but your family is."

"That's not true," I said, but as I said it, the interview with my mother came back to me. Not a single Mage had been selected out of five thousand potential partners.

"Isn't it?" he replied bitterly.

I ate my meal quickly and stood up to leave.

"Where are you going?" he asked, sounding surprised that I was leaving.

"You obviously don't want me here."

"That's not true. I'm sorry. I'm out of order." He stood and pulled me into his arms the way he'd done the night before. I relaxed, feeling safe as he began to hum. As he spun me around the kitchen, I couldn't help but think that I was the one who should have been apologizing to him.

Afterwards, I helped him wash up, and he let me. Again, he didn't use magic.

Every day for the next two weeks went the same way. In the morning, I'd spend time with Jenny before going to the ballroom to have my dance lesson with Stephan. By the end of the two weeks, I'd managed to get through all the dances without stepping on him once, but it was nothing to the way I danced with Cynder in the kitchen.

The nights down there had become my only solace from a manic schedule of lessons and briefings. I counted down the hours and minutes until Cynder took me in his arms, and we'd weave around the kitchen furniture as though we were the only two people in the palace. Neither of us had mentioned him being a Mage again, and not once since he produced that bacon sandwich did I see him using magic.

On the night before the ball, he seemed subdued as he served up my meal. As usual, it was out of this world.

"What's the matter?"

"This is our last night together. I'm going to miss you, Charm."

At some point in the last two weeks, he'd started calling me Charm. In a world where everyone referred to me as Princess Charmaine, I liked it, a lot.

"Why?"

"Because you won't need lessons after tonight."

It's weird how I'd not thought about it before now, but he was right. In my mind, the lessons would go on forever, but in reality, how could they? My heart fell with a thud as I realized it was not the lessons I came down here for.

"I can still come and see you though?"

"In a few months, you'll be married. I doubt your husband will take too kindly to you coming down here and seeing another man."

In all the chaos surrounding the last two weeks, the reality of my situation had not really sunk in. I'd been concentrating on task after task, not looking forward to the reason I was doing it all. The ball had barely crossed my mind at all except for fleeting moments of panic, and my wedding day seemed like such a long way off that it could never come.

I almost said that I'd come down here anyway. After all, no one knew that I came down here now, why should they after the ball? But I knew it couldn't happen. The reality was that once I'd picked five guys to stay, my every moment would be recorded and my illicit trips to the kitchen would become a distant memory.

I laid my head on Cynder's shoulder, silent, listening to the music he made and the beat of his heart as we swayed around the room. We danced a slow dance, the one usually reserved for a special person at the end of the night. I wondered how I could ever find a special person by the end of the ball, especially when I was beginning to think I'd already found him.

The Ball

On the day of the ball, I was awakened by chanting. I opened my window to see where the noise was coming from. It got louder, but it was still indistinct as though it was coming from the front of the palace, and my room was at the back.

"Get away from that window!" Elise scolded coming into my room, "No one is supposed to see you today before your big moment."

"Can you hear that?" I asked, craning my head even further out of the window.

"There is some kind of demonstration against the ball," said Elise, pulling me in. "Apparently, the Magi are up in arms about the whole thing. I don't know why! It's not like they could ever realistically hope to become a prince."

"Why not?" I replied, thinking about Cynder.

"Because they are Magi! Can you imagine if they ruled? They'd do nothing but wave their wands around all day. It would be awful."

I'd never heard her talk this way before. Was this the way everyone thought of the Magi? Before meeting Cynder, I'd never really given them a lot of thought. They were just there, cleaning the palace and tidying the gardens. Before Cynder, I'd not talked to many of them. Agatha was the only one I really talked to, and she never mentioned it.

I was just about to tell Elise my own thoughts on the subject when Jenny walked through the door to take me to breakfast. After that, I would be escorted to the dressing room.

Xavi was ready with her crew, all waiting in a line to turn me into something amazing. I'd already been told I wouldn't be waxed that day (I'd had that pleasure the day before) and a dress had already been made for me specially for the occasion, so I wouldn't have to choose. But I was still scheduled five whole hours in the dressing room. I had no idea what they could possibly do to me that would take five hours, but as I predicted, it began with a thorough scrub down in the marble room. The ladies were much chattier as they moved the soapy sponges over my skin, deliberating about who they would pick if they had the chance. Very few people knew the official list of men who had been invited, but there had been a lot of speculation throughout the palace and on the national news. Most of the candidates, they had gotten right, some, not so much.

The wash girls asked me whom I favored, but I mumbled noncommittally. I wasn't allowed to say anything even if I wanted to, but the truth was I had no idea who I would pick. Daniel Laurient flashed through my mind. If Jenny supported him, I knew he would be one of the first I scouted out. Usually, when I left the marble room, the girls began to clean up, but I'd put a special request in for Elise to have the same treatment as me, so instead, they began to get the room ready for her. She came through the door as I was just about to leave.

Giving me a huge hug, she squealed with excitement at the waterfalls around the room.

"I'll see you later on," she giggled nervously, and, not for the first time, I thought that she would be so much better at this than I.

Jon was the first to see to me, and I luxuriated in his expert hands as he washed my hair thoroughly, massaging the shampoo into a lather. I noticed he used a different shampoo than usual. This one smelled delightfully of oranges. As he worked the shampoo into my scalp, I closed my eyes. This was the only part of the whole makeover that I truly enjoyed. I was sad when it was over, and Alezis took over to create, in his words, a masterpiece. He was wearing even more makeup than usual today, and I wondered if it was in anticipation of the ball tonight. A lot of the palace staff would be in attendance, and some of the higher staff had been invited to dress up.

He spent a whole hour teasing my hair, braiding parts of it and moving it around until he was happy with the result. It didn't look like anything too special until he brought out a large diamond tiara and placed it on my head. Instantly, I could see the look he was going for, and it was magnificent. I didn't look like me at all. I looked like Grace.

When the three makeup artists had finished making me flawlessly ready for Louis, the similarity between Grace and me had strengthened. I could barely look at myself in the mirror.

"I want red lipstick," I said when Louis appeared at my side with his bag of tricks. He looked taken aback as if I'd asked him to cover me in war paint.

Without saying a word, he walked over to Xavi and whispered something in her ear. She walked over to me.

"Louis tells me you want red lipstick. May I inquire why?"

How could I tell her that it was because I didn't want to look like Grace? A thousand eyes would be staring at me tonight, and I didn't want them comparing me to my dead sister. I knew they would anyway, but if I looked different from her, then the comparisons would be harder. Grace had always worn pale pink or nude lipstick. I never wore any. Red was as far away from her as I could imagine.

"I'm afraid the dress we picked out for you will not go with red. How about a subtle pink color? It will compliment your skin tone."

"No!" I shouted a little too loudly. "I'll wear another dress."

I knew I was making a scene and that the dress had been specially selected for me, but I couldn't stand it.

"I'm afraid that is not p..."

"She said she'd like a new dress," butted in Jenny forcefully. She could see the tears that were threatening to fall down my face.

"Ok, Fine." Sniffed Xavi, clearly not used to being bossed around. "I'll go and see if I can find something suitable."

"Don't worry, I'll go and find something for her."

"I'll help too," chimed in Elise, who had just appeared, freshly scrubbed from the marble room.

The three of them drifted away into the dress wardrobe, leaving me with a clearly disgruntled Louis.

To give him his due, he did a marvelous job with my makeup, including the red lipstick I'd asked for. It was so much more dramatic than I had expected, but I could hardly complain after I'd asked him to change his whole palatte. My eyes had been swept with browns and beiges, and he'd brought out cheekbones I didn't even know I possessed. I looked so elegant, regal, and sure of myself. More importantly, I looked nothing like Grace.

"Charmaine,"

I turned to find Elise waving at me from the dressing room.

I thanked Louis and went to her.

"Close your eyes," she giggled.

"Why?"

"Because I know you'll say no to the dress, but I think once you see yourself in it, you'll love it."

I doubted it, but I did as she asked. The dress felt heavier than I expected, and I began to worry that they had decided to turn me into a meringue. Elise would pick the fluffiest most over the top dress imaginable, but I was hoping that Jenny would rein her in a little.

"Shoes!" said Elise, picking up my feet and putting them into a pair of shoes with more heel than I was used to.

I stumbled as she dragged me back into the main room.

"Open your eyes."

I did as she asked, and as I did, there was applause. Behind me in the mirror, I could see Xavi and her team clapping and cheering. I could see Jenny crying and Elise jumping up and down with excitement. In front of them all, I could see me. At least, I thought it was me. My dress shimmered with a hundred thousand diamonds, all sewn onto a nude-colored dress. Light bounced off in sparkles, dazzling my eyes. I looked stunning. I watched as my reflection opened her mouth into a perfect "o" shape. I could barely believe it was me standing there. A princess had never looked so beautiful. I lowered my gaze down to my shoes. Elise and Jenny had picked out some glass slippers to go with the dress and, uncomfortable as they were, they matched perfectly. For the first time, I thought I might actually be able to pull this off!

I was under strict lockdown until I was to make my grand entrance at the ball at ten minutes past seven precisely. After all the time it had taken me to get ready, I still ended up with over an hour to spare. As my parents didn't want anyone to see me until the correct time, I was told to go to my room.

As I closed the door behind me, glad to have the time to collect my thoughts, I noticed a small envelope on my bed. I picked it up and read my name on the front. Inside there was a scrap of paper on which was written: "A lucky charm for a Lucky Charm" in a hurried script. It was signed with a C. It could only be from Cynder. I turned the envelope upside down and out fell a silver bracelet. I held it up to the light. It was a simple silver chain with a charm in the shape of a carriage. I fell instantly in love with it, preferring its beautiful simplicity to the ostentatious diamond earrings and tiara I was wearing. I slipped it onto my wrist, just as Jenny walked through the door.

"I know you'll be eating a huge banquet later, but I thought you'd want something to keep you going." She threw me an apple. "Try not to smudge your lipstick."

I gave her a grateful grin and bit into the apple.

I spent the last hour going over the photos one last time with Jenny, and then the sound of music told me it was time to go.

"Ready?" asked Jenny

"As I'll ever be."

Even though it was Jenny who would take me down to the back entrance of our huge ballroom, it was my mother and father who would escort me out to the masses.

The room next to the ballroom was tiny, no more than a place to get oneself ready for a grand entrance. This royal family was big on grand entrances! Mother and father were already there with my father's chief of staff, who was busily consulting his watch and checking his clipboard.

"Ah, here you are. You look perfect," smiled my mother, giving me the lightest peck on the cheek. If only she could see the utter dread I was feeling inside me. Louis' makeover had me looking a lot more confident than I felt.

From here I could hear the chanting outside the palace. They were still protesting. I briefly wondered if Cynder was with them. He was a Mage after all.

"Right, you go here," said the chief of staff, grabbing my arm roughly, and positioning me beside my father. I linked my arm with his and waited for my mother to join us. Instead, she stayed back.

"Elise will walk in with you, Your Majesty," he said to my mother. So Elise was going to be formally presented too. That was fine by me. It took some of the heat off. As if she had been summoned by magic, Elise appeared at the door behind us. She looked stunning in a long, pale blue dress, her hair bouncing around her shoulders in large curls and the daintiest tiara on her head. She gave me a thumbs up and linked arms with our mother behind me. A fanfare sounded signaling that the double doors were about to open. I gulped and snuck a look at myself in the mirror. I looked exactly how I felt. Absolutely petrified. I tried to rearrange my features into an expression more benefiting the occasion and waited. A loud voice on the other side of the doors shouted out.

"Lords, ladies and gentlemen, please be upstanding for His Majesty, King Aaron, and Her Royal Highness, Queen Alice."

The chief of staff looked down at his clipboard in confusion.

"Change of plan," he said, pulling me quickly to one side so my mother could take my place. She took my father's arm just as the doors opened to the applause of the congregation.

When the doors had shut behind them, Elise ran forward.

We both looked to the chief of staff for instruction, but he just shrugged his shoulders.

"Lords, ladies and gentlemen, please stay upstanding for Her Royal Highness, Princess Elise."

Elise clapped her hands together and gave me a kiss. The chief of staff seemed to have recovered from the shock of not knowing what was going on and pulled me back out of the way.

Elise turned and placed something in my hand.

"I thought you might like to wear this," she whispered before turning around and stepping through the doors. The applause was louder this time. There was no denying that the people loved her. I wondered if anyone would even notice when I walked through the doors. Elise was a tough act to follow.

I looked down at the small object she'd given me. A small silver rose glinted in my palm. It was a small pin that Grace had worn on some of the more important occasions. She called it her good luck pin. If I ever needed good luck, now was the time. I carefully pinned it to my dress, just as the doors opened for the last time, and I walked out to my future.

Bright lights stunned me, and the noise was deafening as I stepped out into the grand ballroom. I'd not been expecting photographers, but judging by the flashes, they were out in force. I blinked a few times and tried to see the people. Before I'd had time to figure out what was going on, a rough hand guided me to a spot near the front next to my parents and sister. A long line of men stood waiting to meet me.

The first stepped forward and reached out his hand. He was a small man with a curled mustache. I wracked my brain to come up with his name, but I couldn't even remember his photo, let alone what he was called.

"Lord Jonathan Ashbury of Ratterham." The chief of staff said beside me. I breathed out in relief. If he was introducing them all, I wouldn't have to remember any of their names.

"It's a pleasure to meet you Lord Ashbury," I said, reciting the words I'd been practicing with Jenny. "I do hope your journey was a good one."

"All the better for meeting you at the end of it," he replied smarmily and kissed my hand, leaving a wet mark on it. I wished I'd have thought to wear gloves if they were all going to do this. I couldn't help but think how unsanitary it was going to be, being slobbered over by a hundred different men. I was supposed to spend a couple of minutes with each one, asking a polite question and deciding whether I liked them enough to ask them to stay. After twenty seconds in his company, I knew Lord Ashbury would not be staying. He bowed and moved over to kiss Elise's hand. I had placed my own hand behind my back to surreptitiously wipe his drool on the back of my dress when someone passed me a handkerchief. I glanced over my shoulder to find Jenny standing there. She must have dashed up to her room to get changed because now she was wearing a lovely violet dress with flowers along the neckline.

"Sir Barney Drake."

I remembered him if only for his name. No one called Barney should ever be a sir. I held out my hand and smiled. It was going to be a long night.

After meeting about twenty of the men, one of them on my maybe pile was introduced. Daniel Laurient's smile was as beautiful and genuine as it had appeared in his photo. He moved up towards me as his name was called and took my hand in both of his, shaking it with exuberance. He was the first not to try and kiss it. I liked him immediately, and I could almost feel Jenny grinning behind me. I was surprised she'd not prodded me in the back.

"How was your journey, Mr. Laurient?" I asked politely.

I'd asked the same question to all of the men so far because it was the only question I could think to ask. They had all responded with variations of "good."

"It's was awful, Your Highness. I had to fight bears and climb mountains. At one point, I thought I was never going to make it when I slipped into quicksand."

"That's awful. How far away do you live?"

"My house is just outside the palace gates, Your Highness."

I looked to see if he was being serious. The sparkle in his eyes told me he was not. I couldn't help but laugh. Daniel Laurient had firmly taken himself from the maybe pile and landed in the yes pile. Now, if only I could find four more to add to it.

I didn't have to wait long. The very next guy was also one of the ones from my maybe pile. I remembered his name, Leo Halifax. He was also a local in town and the only one I'd actually heard of. He was an entrepreneur and philanthropist, and his name often cropped up in talks about charity events. He was also one of the most attractive men I'd ever laid eyes on, with the most stunning amber eyes. He didn't make me laugh in the same way Daniel had, but he was attentive and the first to ask me questions about myself. As I placed him into my yes pile, and he moved forward to talk to Elise, I began to feel much better with how the evening was going.

Unfortunately, my run of good luck didn't hold out. By the time I was at the ninetieth man, I'd not picked another. No one else had stood out the way Daniel or Leo had. My feet were also hurting in my glass shoes, and my stomach was rumbling from eating no more than an apple since breakfast. I wanted nothing more than one of the dishes Cynder made for me, but that was not going to happen.

As Mr. Instantly Forgettable Ninety-One was introduced to me, I did the unforgivable and yawned. Thankfully, he didn't notice. He was too busy staring at my breasts. Next!

I smiled and nodded politely to the last few, noting Luca Tremaine, the prince I'd had a conversation with Cynder about earlier. He was as good-looking as he had been in his photo, but I only flipped him over to the yes pile because I was seriously running out of men. I was supposed to pick at least five, and I'd only managed three. As my father came towards me to take the names of the men I'd chosen, I quickly scrambled around in my brain for two more names. As I recited the names of Daniel, Leo, and Luca, to the chief of staff who wrote them down to pull them out of the crowd to sit near me at the table, I tried really hard to think of two more. "Alexander DeVille," I blurted out. I couldn't really remember the guy at all, but I liked how his name sounded. "And... um..."

"Xavier Gallo," My father said to the chief of staff who took it down and then left to round up the men.

Xavier Gallo? I remembered the name, but his face hadn't stuck in my mind. I vaguely remembered him as having jet black hair with too much product in it, but beyond that, I had nothing.

I wondered why my father had picked him out. He wasn't one of the princes, I knew that much. There were a total of five princes in attendance, and I'd already picked one of them—Luca. The others were all at least twenty years older than me, and I'd dismissed them immediately.

Thankfully, dinner was to be served before dancing, something I was grateful for. My feet were already chafing inside the glass slippers, and my stomach was tying itself in knots with hunger. The meal was a chance for me to get to know the five men I'd picked in more detail. After the meal, I could choose to dance with them or choose some others if I didn't like them.

We moved from the ballroom to the banquet hall where a dozen tables were set out to seat over two hundred guests. Hundreds of items of the royal silver cutlery were laid out in perfect formation with crystal glasses at each setting and thousands of white lilies providing centerpieces for the tables.

I had never felt so nervous as I was seated in the middle of the head table. Elise was to my right and my mother to my left with father next to her. The five men would be seated nearest to me, while still keeping a boy-girl formation.

I noticed that Elise turned a deep cherry red as Leo was seated next to her.

Luca was directly in front of me with Xavier two seats to the right of him (with a young lady between them) and Alexander two seats to his left. I was disappointed to see Daniel sitting the furthest away. He was too far for me to make conversation with him without raising my voice, and of the five, I thought he'd be the most fun.

The first course was brought out straight away. It turned out to be soup, and all those lessons about how not to spill soup on a ball gown would come in handy seeing as the choice was tomato.

I slipped my aching feet out of my glass slippers, confident that no one would notice under the table and began to relax as the bevy of waiting staff brought out large tureens of soup. The first was placed on our table in front of my father. As with every royal occasion, he was the first to be served, then my mother. Once Elise and I had been served, everyone else would get their soup. The waiter ladled the soup directly into my father's bowl.

After filling my mother's bowl, he moved along the table to me.

"How are you holding up?" I recognized his voice immediately— Cynder.

"My feet are killing me," I replied so quietly that only he could hear. "Glass slippers."

"You look beautiful. Any man here would be lucky to have you."

He whispered it closely in my ear as he bent forward to ladle the hot soup into my bowl. His breath tickled my neck, giving me goose bumps right down my arm, and then he was gone. He'd moved on to serving Elise. It was then that I realized I'd not thanked him for the charm bracelet.

I picked out the correct spoon, thanks to Jenny's meticulous teaching and began to sip at my soup in the most ladylike fashion I could muster. I was so hungry, I'd have happily picked up the whole bowl and drank it from there, but I didn't. I hadn't said a word to anyone in ten minutes, and I was beginning to get the feeling that people were wondering why not. Jenny had taught me to listen politely to people and then ask more questions. The problem was, everyone was already involved in conversations with other people. Elise was chatting with Leo. My mother was currently laughing over a joke Daniel had just told, and Luca and Xavier were chatting with the women on either side of them, whom I recognized as staff members at the palace. This had been set up by the chief of staff who had handpicked young ladies from the staff to sit at the head table with us. This had two benefits: The ladies were told to be friendly but not overly friendly to the men, so the focus of attention stayed on me, thus eliminating any chances of the men deciding on someone other than me, and it gave the staff members who worked hard a reward for their service. I couldn't help think it was all rather unfair to the male members of staff, who still had to work. It looked like one of the women hadn't got the memo as she was flirting shamelessly with Prince Luca, who was lapping it up. The only member of my five not chatting was Alexander, who, like me, was paying more attention to his soup than anyone around him. I scoured around for something to say.

"Are you enjoying your soup?"

He looked up, startled to have been spoken to. I remembered him from the line up now. He'd mumbled an incoherent answer to my question and stared at his shoes the whole time. He wasn't the worst of the bunch by a long shot, but I couldn't see any kind of lasting relationship between us if he couldn't even speak to me. Not that I was doing any better myself.

"It's nice," he said and then went right back to it, leaving me yet again with no one to talk to.

Here I was, the star of the show, and I couldn't get anyone to talk to me. I couldn't think of anything in my training that would help me in this situation. I began ladling the soup into my mouth faster now, desperate for the first course to end just so the bustle of changing courses would cover up the anxiety I was beginning to feel.

Just then, I felt a pair of eyes on me. I looked up to find Prince Luca staring back at me with a sly smile on his face.

I smiled back shyly. He was definitely a good-looking guy and marrying someone who was already a prince would be a bonus, and yet, I couldn't get Cynder's words out of my mind. Nor could I rid myself of the image of him flirting with the lady next to him, who I was sure worked in the kitchens.

Talking politics had never been my strong point, but asking him about his country seemed like a good place to start a conversation. With us both being members of royalty, at least we had something in common.

"Prince Luca," I began. "How are things in Thalia these days?"

"They are as well as can be expected, Your Highness; however, a bond between our countries could only cement relations between your kingdom and mine."

To his right, I saw the kitchen maid scowl as her talking partner was now ignoring her. She folded her arms and pouted.

"Quite!" I answered, feeling myself redden. He was right, of course, but that didn't mean I was going to choose him for a partner.

"And how are the king and queen? Both doing well, I hope."

"They are looking forward to the day I settle down and marry a beautiful young lady. A princess, perhaps."

"You are rather forward if you don't mind me saying so," I replied feeling flustered.

His smile widened, and he leaned forward so no one else could hear. "I'm in competition with ninety-nine other men. I would say I'd be a fool not to be forward." He winked.

"I've always wanted to visit Thalia," said the maid, thrusting her breasts forward and leaning in towards Prince Luca. I watched as she ran her fingers up his arm to get his attention.

He turned to her. "It's beautiful this time of year. You should visit. The flowers are all in bloom."

"Sound's delightful," she purred. "Maybe you could give me a tour?"

And with that, I'd lost the only person who'd bothered to speak to me.

To my right, I heard Elise laughing over something Leo had said and, not for the first time, I wished it was she, who was sitting here in my place. She found it effortless to talk to strangers, whereas, I was feeling like a fish out of water.

The waiters came to take away our dirty soup bowls and serve us with our dinner. Cynder was one of the first out with a number of silver crested plates in his hand. He headed straight up to the top table, placing the first plate in front of my father, who began to tuck into his lobster straight away. My mother was next, and then he came to me. When he placed my plate in front of me, I could see it was different from my parents. Where they had lobster and pheasant with their potatoes and veggies, mine held a plate of plain chicken. He'd remembered our very first conversation in the kitchen! Beside me, I heard something drop on the floor. When he had finished serving and left to serve Elise, I looked down to find a pair of sneakers lying beside my feet.

As I gratefully slipped my feet into them, I grinned. Cynder was turning into my fairy godmother. I watched as he sneaked my glass slippers under the silver platter he was holding.

"I'll get them back to you later," he whispered into my ear, and then he was gone.

The Men

I felt sick as I led the way back into the ballroom. Even with Cynder teaching me, plus all the hours I'd put in with Stephan, I still didn't feel comfortable dancing in front of hundreds of strangers. With my dress flowing down to the floor, I was confident that no one would see the sneakers Cynder had given to me, which was my only solace.

In the corner, an orchestra played soft music as we all entered, and the photographers and camera crews that were there earlier, now stood around the edge of the ballroom, all lenses trained on me.

My first dance was to be with my father so as not to show preference straight away. I was also instructed not to dance with any of the five that I'd already picked so that all the other men felt like they still had a chance. I had to dance with at least two others before dancing with one of the five.

My father took my hand and led me out into the center of the floor. Hundreds of flashes went off again as the orchestra struck up a waltz I'd learned with Stephan.

My father guided me skilfully, and, to my relief, a minute or so in, all the other couples took to the floor until I was hidden amongst two hundred other dancers. When the music changed, and my mother took my place, I picked a couple dancing nearby and cut in. At any other occasion, I'd have felt incredibly rude, but here, it was something I was expected to do. Both the hundred men and the hundred young ladies had been briefed, and the girl in question curtseyed as she let me take her partner. Her partner, I remembered from the lineup as being polite enough although bland in the looks department. He seemed quite surprised to find himself dancing with me which put me at ease. He wasn't the best dancer in the world, but between us, we managed a few turns around the dance floor without crashing into anyone.

When it came the time to find one of the five I'd already picked, I had to look closely. The hall was filled with the movement of couples and colorful dresses, all spinning around to the music. I caught sight of a blond head that I immediately recognized as Daniel. He was dancing with Agatha, who had been chosen to attend. I watched them both for a second and felt jealous as they moved together exceptionally well. It seemed my maid was something of a dancer. I'd have to ask her about it in the morning. I cut in between them and saw Agatha give me the thumbs up as she disappeared into the crowd.

"Oh, no. Now I have to dance with a stunning princess after eating the best meal I've ever had," he said with mock sincerity. "My life sucks right now."

I grinned up at him. "I can leave if you like."

"Nah, I've already missed the match. I may as well stay."

"Match? You follow football?"

"No, I hate it. I just thought it might be more preferable to coming here tonight. Dancing around with the most beautiful woman I've ever seen is so boring."

"It is, is it?" I tried not to fixate on the part where he'd called me beautiful.

"Utterly dull. I'd rather watch paint dry."

"Watching paint dry can be rewarding if you have the right paint."

"I always buy tartan paint. It does so set off my collection of chocolate teapots."

I laughed. The guy was a goofball, and my conversation with him was nothing like I expected.

"I'm glad to see you've gotten over your trials and tribulations."

"Tribulations?"

"Fighting those bears," I continued. "You must be very strong."

"With these puppies, I could fight off anything." He stopped dancing and posed with his arms flexed. He had such a cheesy grin on his face; I couldn't help but laugh.

"Tell me about yourself," I asked, pulling his arms back around me.

"I live in town and work with my father. We are carpenters."

"Oh, and what do you make?"

He pointed to the throne at the top of the room. "You see that chair over there?"

"You made that?"

"No, It's nice though, huh?"

I swiped him playfully on the shoulder. "Are you ever serious?"

"Not if I can help it. I am a carpenter though. We have made a lot of furniture for the palace. I think the biggest thing was your father's desk."

"You made that? It's beautiful." And it was. It had been hand carved out of mahogany with the royal crest in marquetry on the top in the most extravagant style.

"Thank you. Hold on!"

"Hold on?"

He grabbed me tighter and spun me around faster and faster to the music until I was dizzy and then ended it by dipping me down. I heard people clapping around us and the popping of more flashbulbs as the camera's captured the moment.

He pulled me back up and gave me a hug. It should have been inappropriate, but it felt nice. He'd firmly cemented himself as one of the five I chose to stay on after the ball.

"That was a blast," he whispered, and then he disappeared into the crowd.

I was still feeling wonderfully light when Xavier came to me. He took my hand and waist and guided me as the music started again. Unlike Daniel, his style was polished and much less fun. However, he was impossibly beautiful, and my father had thrown him into the mix for a reason. I just had to figure out exactly what that reason was.

"Thank you for choosing to dance with me," he said although it had been he that had come to me and not the other way around. He spoke with an accent that I couldn't quite place. I wondered if he was a prince like Luca although it hadn't said so on his form. It would explain why my father had favored him. I noticed he had a dimple in his chin. On most people, it would look cute or charming, but "cute" didn't fit him at all. He was stunning. There was no other word for it, and to call him cute underestimated just how beautiful he was. Despite his good looks, he also had a hard look to him. Not manly, as such, although he was; but as if there was a lot going on under the surface. Just what, I had no idea, but I wanted to find out.

"Thank you for coming," I replied, feeling awkward. For all my lessons with Jenny, nothing had really prepared me for this. None of the memorized questions really seemed fitting, and Xavier's obvious beauty was off-putting. Maybe I should have picked someone ugly. I might have found it easier to converse with them. "What brings you to Silverwood?"

He looked surprised at my question. "I'm from here. I came to the ball to meet you."

Now it was my turn to be surprised. "Your accent isn't from around here."

"I've traveled a lot. My mother died when I was young, and my father moved around a lot for his job. I picked up my accent from the places we stayed. We were never in one place longer than a few months, so it has a little bit of everything in it."

I didn't believe him. At least not the accent part. I'd heard the accent before, probably at some royal function or other. I just couldn't place it. "I'm sorry to hear about the loss of your mother. That must have been hard for you."

"It was a long time ago. I barely remember her. Let us not talk of such dark things. Now is the night to dance and have fun."

And so we danced. He was an elegant dancer, with not a single misstep, and although I struggled to keep up with him, he expertly led me around the room, not staying in one place, but guiding me so that everyone saw us together, which was probably his intention.

When the song ended, he reluctantly let me go, before bowing down to me curtly. Despite myself, I liked him too. He had depths I wanted to explore and, even though he was like no man I'd ever met before, there was something about him. The next song was just about to start, and I was without a partner. As the orchestra began, I saw Prince Luca dancing with the very same kitchen maid that had flirted with him earlier. Even though I was beginning to think I should mentally move him from my maybe pile onto my nope pile, the thought of coming between the two was just too good to resist. With Alexander and Leo lost in the crowd somewhere, he was the only one I could see to dance with anyway.

I cut in between the two, giving the kitchen maid my widest smile. She curtseyed reluctantly and smiled, but before she turned away, I saw her smile turn into a grimace.

"My lady," he said.

"I'm not your lady yet," I said.

"Yet!" he said, picking up on my unfortunate choice of words.

"That remains to be seen," I replied coolly. His dancing technique was not as refined as Xavier's, but he knew the moves alright. He pulled me close to him, much closer than I felt comfortable with, and led me around the dance floor. I had no choice but to rest my head on his shoulder, although it gave me a crick in my neck as he was so tall. As we spun around, I could see the jealous looks of scores of the women. I tried to ignore them; after all, I really wasn't sure about Prince Luca. Sure, he'd be a good political match and marrying him would be good for the kingdom. But the things Cynder had said about him kept swirling through my mind. With my head on his shoulder, I couldn't tell if he was looking at other women or not. I felt his stubble on my cheek. It had looked sexy on him, but at such close proximity, it just hurt my cheek. At one point I saw Leo dance past, and I was surprised to see Elise in his arms. She had her eyes closed and a look of bliss on her face. At the end of this dance, I'd go and find Alexander to dance with. I couldn't be the one to wipe that smile from my younger sister's face.

I didn't have a chance to finish the thought because just then, a huge boom sounded, and rubble began to fly through the air. The room went dark, and in the panic, all I could hear were the screams of the people around me.

The ballroom had exploded.

The Explosion

The force of the explosion knocked me to my feet and sent Luca flying over me. His body hit the floor with a crash, tumbling over mine. He recovered quickly and turned to me.

"Are you ok? Are you hurt?" He looked as shocked as I felt. The sound of the explosion was still ringing in my ears, and the pair of us were covered in dust and debris.

"I think so," I said, feeling anything but ok, but, at least, I wasn't injured.

He helped me to my feet, pulling me through the crowd until we were away from the ballroom. One of the palace guards in the entrance hall ran over to us.

"What is happening?" I asked in shock as the sound of screams hit my ears, which only added to the ringing sound that the explosion had caused.

"I don't know, Your Highness, but I need to get you to safety."

Luca followed us as the guard navigated a path through the screaming crowd that had followed us, and led us down to the basement through a door under the main marble stairs in the entrance hall. Another guard at the door to the vault was poised and ready. The huge steel door was already open to admit me.

"The princess only!" he commanded, as Luca tried to follow.

"Let him in. He's with me."

The guard reluctantly let him in, and the three of us ran through the warehouse-sized room past shelves of antiques and treasures.

"This room is the safest in the house," said the first guard as he guided us through the corridors of shelving units. "It's where we have been trained to bring you in the event of an emergency."

At the end of the vast room were a sofa and a number of chairs. Along the wall were five bunks, one for each member of the royal family. I could see a neat pile of canned food and a small stove and fridge to my right.

"What is this?" I asked. I'd never been down here before.

"It's a safe room. The whole room is bomb and fire proof. The King, Queen, and Her Royal Highness, the Princess Elise will be down here in a minute. I must leave you to go help find them."

"You can't leave me!" I cried, but he turned and left.

Luca put his arms around me and comforted me. My whole body shook with the shock of what had happened. A bitter burning smell lingered in the air as I breathed in the dust from Luca's jacket.

"You are ok; I've got you." Luca held me tight in the protective cocoon of his arms as he spoke to me soothingly. Because of his height, I felt like a child in his arms, a thought which was only compounded when he began to stroke my hair.

At that instant, there was a noise at the other end of the room. I jumped and pulled myself away from Luca, but it was just my mother and father with Elise and a couple of other guards.

Elise and my mother ran over when they saw me, whilst my father stayed at the entrance to talk to the guards. Luca went over to him, presumably to offer his assistance. It felt weird that I missed the comfort he'd given me when he was gone.

"What happened? Where is everyone?" I asked my mother.

"We don't know. Some kind of explosive device has gone off. Other than that, I don't know any more than you."

"What about everyone else? The staff, the guests?" Cynder?

"They are being evacuated via the safest route. The guests will be counted in the front courtyard whilst the staff will be taken to the back courtyard. They all know the drill and the quickest route from the palace. The guards are well trained and know what they are doing. They will keep everyone as safe as possible."

"But why can't they come down here with us? The room is big enough to hold hundreds of people."

"Because we don't know if one of them planted the bomb."

It was a sobering thought that one of our guests or one of our own staff could have done this. I looked over at Elise, who was still sobbing loudly. It was then that I noticed her dress was covered in blood.

"Elise, Are you alright?"

She looked down to where I was staring, and her eyes went wide. A second later she had dropped to the floor in a faint.

"Aaron," called my mother, dropping down to see to Elise. "Get someone to fetch a doctor down here immediately."

I peered down at my younger sister. She looked so beautiful and so deathly pale. A vision of the last time I'd seen Grace came to me. She'd looked exactly the same. I couldn't bear to lose another sister. I bent down to Elise's side and, along with my mother, we both tried to awaken her. There was so much blood, and yet, she was still breathing. The palace physician was summoned quickly, and he ran straight over to us. He must have already been on his way as he was so quick to get to us.

He barely looked at her. "She's fainted."

"Of course, she's fainted," replied my mother abruptly. "Look at how much blood she's lost."

"That's not hers," he replied, after examining her. "She's fine, but she's had a shock."

So whose was it?

"When this is over, I'll take her to the palace infirmary where I'll keep an eye on her for a few days. The rest of you should get checked out too."

We washed up as much of the blood as we could in the small sink at the side of the room, and when she awoke, we let her lie on the sofa.

The hours that passed seemed to go on indefinitely without word. My father and Luca had left hours ago and not returned. When my father eventually did come back with a number of guards, I was escorted up to my room. The physician tried to get Elise to go with him, but my feisty sister was having none of it, so she came back upstairs with us.

I collapsed onto my bed, feeling utterly exhausted. The ball had been due to finish at midnight, and yet, it was nearly five in the morning. The dawn light was beginning to stream through my window, and I could hear the low voices of the guards outside my door. I kicked my shoes off and tried to unfasten my dress. With the zipper at the back, it was impossible.

I padded over to Elise's door and knocked lightly. She opened it, her face puffy from crying and dried blood still clinging to her dress. I pulled her into a hug.

"I can't believe this happened." She broke down in tears, so I guided her to the bed. "After all that we've been through. Why would anyone do this?"

"I don't know," I answered truthfully, "but Father will find out. Come on; let's get you out of those clothes."

I helped her into her pajamas, and she did the same with me. I felt filthy and desperately needed a shower, but I knew there was no way I'd get past the guards without them noticing. When Elise was in bed and asleep, I went back into my own room, taking my spoiled dress with me. I threw it on the floor almost covering the sneakers Cynder had given me. Without knowing it, he'd probably saved my life. Without running shoes on, I'd not have been able to run so fast. I only hoped he was alright. I'd been told that the ballroom was the target, and the rest of the palace was intact, but I had no way of knowing if Cynder was in the ballroom at the time of the blast.

I opened my door to the corridor and stepped out.

As soon as I had, the guard at my door blocked my path. "I'm sorry, Your Highness, but you can't come out here. The palace is still being checked over for more devices, and the king has explicitly forbidden you or The Princess Elise to leave until we know it's safe."

I sighed and headed back to my room. Getting past the guards was going to be impossible. There was no way that they would let me past, but I had to get to Cynder, to know he was still alive. I couldn't wait until a thorough head count was done. We had a thousand staff on top of all the guests at the ball. It could take days to count everyone. It could take weeks to identify the bodies.

My heart lurched at the thought of it, and yet, it spurred me into action. I had to know. I ran to my window and looked outside to see if there was any way I could climb down. I was on the fifth floor and looking out, I could see that the face of the palace was sheer with no way to climb down. No ivy, no ledges, and no drainpipes. At least none I could reach. I could see a climbable pipe, but the only way I could see to reach it was through a room at the other end of the palace. As my room was being guarded, I couldn't see how I could get to it. I ran back to the bed and threw myself on it, feeling frustrated.

It was then that a plan came to me. Adjoining my room was Elise's and at the other side, the door that led to Grace's room. It hadn't been opened in weeks, and I'd not wanted to go through it. What was the point? She wasn't in there anymore. More to the point, there would be no one guarding it from the corridor. Of course, the guard might see me leave, but if he was distracted, there was a chance I could get into the corridor unseen. From there, the corridor bent slightly. If I could get round the bend and out of view, I'd be able to run to the end and out through the window to the drainpipe. It was incredibly risky, but I couldn't get thoughts of Cynder lying in the rubble somewhere out of my mind.

I fitted the sneakers he'd given me back on and went to wake Elise. I hated to do it after the trauma of the evening, but I had no choice.

"Hmm?" She jumped up out of bed in alarm. "What's the matter? Has another bomb gone off?"

"No. Nothing like that, I just need your help."

She wiped her eyes and yawned. "What do you need?"

"I need you to talk to the guard. Distract him."

"Why?" Her eyes widened in shock. "You aren't planning to leave your room, surely?"

"I just need to get a shower," I lied. "I feel disgusting."

I certainly looked filthy enough to warrant one. Dust clung to my hair and my skin was so black with dirt that it had stained my bed sheets. As the bathroom was just a little way along the corridor, I knew she'd not see any danger in it.

"Ok, but be careful."

"I will. Give it a couple of minutes and then go and ask him a question."

I ran back into my own bedroom and then straight into Grace's. My heart stopped for a second as I took it in. It was the same as it always had been except now there was no Grace; it seemed empty without her.

I swallowed back my tears and ran to the door that led out to the corridor. I waited until I heard Elise's voice and then slipped out as quietly as I could. The guard was closer to my door than Elise's, but as he had his head turned towards her, it was easy to slip along the corridor unnoticed. Once around the corner, I ran the full length of it, trying to judge which door to go through to get to the drainpipe. This end of the corridor was usually reserved for guests, but after the bomb, almost everyone had elected to go home to safety. I'd been told that only Luca, Leo, and Xavier had decided to stay and they had been given their own guest houses in the grounds. Daniel had gone home, not because of the bomb, but because it had always been his plan with him living so close by.

When I thought I'd gotten to the right place, I opened the door. The suite had been made up for a guest that would not be staying. Fresh flowers sat in a vase by the four-poster bed along with a basket of fruit, and some chocolates had been left on the pillow.

I ran past and opened the window. The acrid smell of smoke lingered in the air. I ignored it and looked for the drainpipe. It was there, about two feet away. It would be a stretch, but I was confident I could reach it.

Grabbing it with my right hand, I pulled myself out of the window and swung around until I had hold of it tightly. From there, it was pretty easy to shimmy down it until my feet hit the stone pathway at the bottom.

The sound of sirens had long since stopped, but I could still hear the noise of the fire crews as they sifted through the wreckage of the ballroom at the right side of the palace. Going past them was not an option, not unless I wanted to get caught, so I slowly crept around the side of the palace to my left, past the staff entrance and the stone steps that led down to the driveway. The lights were still on in the kitchens even though the sun was almost fully up in the sky. I peeked through the window, surprised to see the kitchen full of staff, washing up and cleaning after the big night. My eyes went straight for the large sink where I'd usually find Cynder, but instead, there was someone else there. In fact, there were a number of other people there, scurrying around and making the place tidy. I scanned the rest of the kitchen, trying to pick out his curly hair in amongst all the others, but I couldn't see him. I also couldn't see anyone else dressed in the smart uniform of the wait staff as he had been, so perhaps he'd been allowed to go home early. It was my only hope as the alternative was unthinkable. I knew there were many members of staff serving drinks when the bomb went off. Had he escaped like I had, or had he been too close to the explosion? A sob escaped my lips and the sound cut through the air. In the distance, at the end of the long staff driveway, I noticed someone talking to the guards at the gate. I got a shock when I realized it was my father. I had to get back inside before he saw me!

I turned and made my way back to the drainpipe. As I passed the staff steps, something glinted in the sun, catching my eye. It took me a couple of seconds to register what I was seeing, but when I did, I couldn't make sense of it. There, about half way down the stairs was a sparkling glass slipper. My glass slipper.

The Aftermath

etting back inside the palace was easy. Instead of chancing the drainpipe again, I walked in through a back door and headed towards my room until one of the guards saw me. For the second time that morning, I was escorted back up to the fifth floor. The guard outside my room looked surprised as I walked back into my room, but neither of us said anything.

I never thought I'd sleep again, but after the adrenaline and shock wore off, I slept all through the day and into the next night. No one came to wake me or to bring me food. It was the heel of the glass slipper, digging into me that finally roused me from a nightmare-filled sleep.

I pulled it out from under me, where it had fallen. I'd slept with it, not knowing if Cynder was alive or not, and it broke my heart. The pain I felt was indescribable and so raw it eclipsed the ache left behind by Grace. I had never felt more confused in my life, nor as low as I did now. My heart felt like a lead weight in my chest, threatening to pull me under. When I saw the light of day, I realized just how long I'd slept.

I jumped out of bed as Agatha walked in. She seemed surprised to see me awake.

"Morning, Your Highness." Her voice was flat and her face expressionless.

"You're ok!" I ran to her and gave her a hug. She hugged me back tightly.

"I'm fine. I was at the other side of the room when it happened. The king kindly gave me the day off work yesterday and for the rest of the week. He even offered those of us who live in the staff quarters money for a hotel in town, but I couldn't bear to stay away. This is my home."

"Of course it is. Do you know what happened?"

"You don't know?"

"No, I've been here since the morning after the explosion. No one has told me anything."

"That was yesterday morning. I can't believe no one has been to see you since then. You must be starving."

"I slept through it." I yawned as if to prove my point.

"Let me get you something to eat."

She turned to leave, but I caught her arm.

"No. I'm not hungry. I just want to know what happened."

"I don't know much," she said, suddenly looking fearful.

"Then tell me everything you do know."

"The investigators seem to think it was a bomb planted by the Magi who were demonstrating."

She was so quiet when she said it that I almost didn't hear her at all. I wasn't surprised. She was a Mage too.

"They couldn't have!" I cried, sounding more outraged than I had planned.

I watched Agatha's expression turn from one of fear to one of relief. "You don't think so?"

"No, do you?"

"Of course not. We are not a violent people. I knew people in that demonstration, and none of them would hurt anyone."

"Of course, they wouldn't." Would they? I remembered Cynder's anger as he spoke about his people being treated unfairly. Were the other Magi as angry as he? Were any of them angry enough to kill?

"Agatha, I need your help. I need to go and have a shower. I feel disgusting, but there are guards outside. Can you tell my father to tell them to go, so I can go use the bathroom?"

"There is no one outside the door, Your Highness."

I peeked out, and she was right. I ran across the corridor and used the toilet before jumping into the hottest shower I'd ever had. The burning water washing over my skin was a relief, taking my mind from everything that had happened in the past few days and cleansing me of the dirt and spots of blood that had caked on me.

Agatha appeared ten minutes later with a large white towel and some clothes for me. I let her dry me and help me into the black dress. Another black dress. Were we still in mourning for Grace or were we mourning someone else now?

"How many people died in the blast?" I asked as she buttoned up the dress.

"I don't know," replied Agatha. "There hasn't been an official total, but the newspaper said that there were more than twenty. The Prince of Aurora was killed."

I remembered the prince of Aurora was one of the older princes. I'd not spoken to him apart from saying hello at the beginning of the night. His death would cause a huge impact for our already floundering kingdom.

"Who else?" I asked thinking only of Cynder.

"No other names have been released. I do know that Jenny is in the palace infirmary."

Jenny! I'd not thought of her at all, and now I felt terrible.

"Is she ok?" I demanded urgently.

"I think she was hurt pretty badly, but she's alive."

I ran out of the bathroom, with my dress not buttoned up all the way to the top and with no shoes on my feet. Not that I cared what I looked like. The palace was subdued. There were guards on every corridor, but none of them made any attempt to either stop me or speak to me. When I got to the infirmary, I found that it too was guarded.

The two guards stepped back when they saw me to let me pass.

The small ward of ten beds was full. I recognized some of the staff as well as some of the men from the ball. Jenny was in the last bed. I ran straight over to her. Her right arm was in a sling, and she had cuts and bruises on her face, but she was alive and awake.

"Jenny. I'm sorry I've not been down to see you. I was asleep. I only just found out."

"Don't you worry about it. The king has been sitting with me."

"My father?"

"Yes, he was down here most of yesterday making sure that everything was being done that could be done. Most of the injured went to the hospital in town, but those of us with only superficial injuries were treated here."

"Superficial injuries?" I eyed her arm.

"Just a hairline fracture. Nothing to worry about. It will be in a cast for six weeks then back to normal."

"Can't they fix you with magic?" Even though Magi were not permitted to become doctors, we did have a Magic nurse on staff. I knew she could mend bones; she mended a broken finger of mine a couple of years back when I fell out of a tree.

Jenny beckoned me closer and talked to me in hushed tones.

"There has been talk that the Magi set off the bomb and the police seem to think it was an insider. All the Magi in the palace have been suspended for a week while the police carry out their inquiries."

"But that can't be true!" I'd only just left Agatha. She was a Mage, and she was still working.

"Shhh!" Jenny nodded her head to the bed opposite where a Mage was sleeping. It was one of the cleaners.

"Agatha is still here," I whispered.

"Your father, along with the chief of police, called for it, but I know there were a few that were asked to stay. Agatha was asked to stay because they thought you might need the support. June, Elise's dresser was also asked to stay, but the majority have left."

"But that's madness."

"Your father has to be seen to be doing the right thing, plus the police demanded it."

"But my father is the king!"

"Not even the king is above the law. Some very important people were killed here the other night. He has to be seen to be doing what is right."

"How is it right that half the staff have been taken away? Why do they think it was a Mage anyway? Just because they were demonstrating, doesn't make them murderers."

"Keep your voice down!" Jenny hissed. "There was a shoe found by the site of the bomb blast. A glass slipper. It was melted beyond recognition by the heat of the blast, but one of the guests said they'd seen a member of our staff carrying glass slippers just before the blast. The police seem to think that whoever set the bomb dropped the slipper just before they ran away. They are now scouring the kingdom for the other one."

My thoughts went up to my bedroom. I knew exactly where the other slipper was. It was lying on the floor next to my bed.

"I need to go and see my father," I said hurriedly, kissing her cheek. I hated to leave her after such a short visit, but I needed to find out why they were looking for Cynder. A melted shoe was hardly enough evidence to mount a kingdom–wide manhunt.

I found him in his study surrounded by people.

"Father, I need to speak to you. It's urgent."

Normally, he'd call me on my rudeness for barging in, but he must have seen the panic in my expression.

"You heard her gentlemen. My daughter needs me. We'll resume this conversation after lunch."

The men filed out until there were only myself and my father left in the room.

"Charmaine. What is it?"

"Who do they think planted the bomb?"

"Have you had breakfast yet? You look so pale. You must still be in shock. I must say the last few days have been shocking for all of us."

"I'm fine. I'll eat later. I just want to know who planted the bomb."

My father sighed. "Sit down. I was hoping to be able to brief you and Elise together, but as you are here asking, I'll tell you all I know."

I sat in the leather chair opposite him and waited.

"At ten fifteen one of the guests saw a member of staff acting strangely in the outer corridor. He was carrying a pair of glass slippers and something else. The guest thought it odd that one of our wait staff was carrying something so out of place as glass slippers, but he shrugged it off and carried on his way to the bathroom. It was there he heard the explosion. The center of the explosion was found to be right at the exact spot where he'd seen the member of staff. The boy's description matched one of our kitchen hands who'd been working as a member of the wait staff that night. The boy escaped, but don't worry, the police are after him."

So Cynder escaped. The relief that I felt knowing he was alive was overshadowed by the fear I felt that the police were after him.

"Why do they think Cy...the kitchen hand did it? I'm sure a lot of the wait staff used that corridor."

"A few reasons. Firstly, he dropped one of the shoes right in the spot where the explosion was. The police think he would only have done that if he was in a hurry. They also think he might have stolen the shoes from a guest because they were expensive. Way beyond the means of a kitchen hand. Secondly, the boy in question had links to the protest group. He was a Mage and was known for protesting for Magi Rights. Thirdly, he ran away. If he was innocent, he'd have stayed like the other Magi."

"So they know he ran away and wasn't caught up in the blast?"

"He was seen a couple of hours later on the outskirts of town, but by the time the police got there, he'd escaped."

So Cynder was definitely alive. He was also wanted for murder. I thought back to the man I'd come to know. Could he really have done this? I didn't think so, but at the same time, I realized I didn't know him as well as I thought I did. I didn't know he was a member of the protest groups. He'd never mentioned it, but on the one occasion we'd talked about the treatment of Magi, he'd become angry, before changing the subject.

"If they know...think they know who did it, why have they rounded up all the Magi in the staff?"

My father sighed and massaged his temples.

"We are living in difficult times. I argued with the chief of police, but he got the mayor involved, and from there, word got out that it was a Mage that had done this. We had to be seen to be doing something."

"By rounding up innocent people? You are the king. You have final say on everything."

"The people need to see that things are being done. I did what I had to do. The Magi will be ok. In a couple of days, they will be let off without charge and sent home."

"Sent home? You mean they won't be coming back here?"

"No. We are in the process of hiring new staff. Non-magic staff. When we have filled the positions, we'll be doing the same for the remaining Magi."

I stood up. "You are firing the Magi?"

"I have to. There would be an uprising if I didn't. They have caused enough trouble. Don't worry. I'm sure they'll get jobs elsewhere."

"How are they supposed to get jobs elsewhere when our very own king won't support them?" I screeched.

"Calm down, Charmaine. Why is this so important to you? You've never shown any interest in politics before."

"This isn't politics, this is people's lives. Innocent people who will now not be able to put food on their table."

His level of anger rose to match my own. "And what about the innocents who were killed here on Saturday night? Twenty-three people lost their lives, Charmaine. One of which was a member of royalty. I have spent the last twenty-four hours trying to persuade the Prince of Aurora's parents not to declare war on us. I had to explain to them why I let Magi into the palace at all when they are so obviously volatile. I had to fire them. I had no choice."

"But..."

"This discussion is closed. I did what I had to do, and I don't want to hear any more about it. Now go and see your mother about breakfast."

Every part of me wanted to argue right back at him, but I knew there was no point. I stood up and stalked out of the door.

One thing my father was right about—the only thing. I needed food. I'd not eaten in over thirty-six hours, and I was beginning to feel lightheaded. I headed for the breakfast room.

My mother and Elise were there eating. I took my usual seat. Within seconds, one of the staff brought me breakfast. The food smelled lovely—poached eggs and salmon, but I felt so miserable, I wasn't sure I'd be able to eat it.

"Charmaine, it's lovely to have you with us. How are you feeling today?"

I looked at my mother. She looked worn and tired, but, as usual, she had a smile on her face. I wanted to tell her how angry I was with everything, but she held no sway over my father. Shouting at her would solve nothing. I tucked into my eggs. "I'm fine."

"Good. I'm glad your long sleep did you some good. I've set up your first official date. I know you were supposed to choose five men at the end of the ball, but obviously, that didn't happen, so I went with the ones you'd picked earlier in the evening. Alexander decided to go home after the explosion and have no more to do with the competition, but the others stayed. I'd like to have fixed you up with the dates in alphabetical order to show no preference, but that lovely Leo never got to dance with you, so I thought it would be nice to let him go first."

I nearly choked on my eggs. Was she being serious? Elise looked up in surprise too. I guess she, like I, had thought that the men would be allowed to leave and this whole marriage thing would quietly go away on its own.

"This ridiculous charade is still going ahead? After everything that's happened?"

My mother clucked impatiently. "Of course, it's still going on, and please don't call it a charade. We need this now more than ever."

"People have died, and innocent people are being thrown out of their jobs, and the people need me to go on dates with men I don't even know?"

"It's important we keep going as we were. Our people expect strong leadership. Now how would it look if we decided to drop everything just because of a little incident?"

"Little incident? Twenty-three people were killed, and the police are looking for an innocent man."

I didn't mean to say it, but my mother didn't seem to notice. Elise, however, gave me an odd look.

"And that's exactly why we have to carry on as before. Now I've set your date for seven o'clock this evening. Leo has already been notified. I just need to know exactly what you want to do for your date."

"I don't want to go on a date."

My mother ignored me. "I'll tell him you'll meet him in the gardens at seven precisely. Xavi will be informed so she can dress you for the occasion. I'd like to have invited the press, but security is high at the moment, so it will be just the two of you. Don't worry though; guards will be keeping an eye on you from a distance. You'll be perfectly safe."

And just like that, the nightmare I'd woken up to got a whole lot worse.

The First Date

Leo was waiting for me by the front door of the palace at exactly seven. Two guards at the door let me through, and I could see others in the distance at the end of the long drive by our large wrought-iron gates. No doubt, there would be even more in the gardens.

Leo had dressed in cream trousers with a smart cream shirt, which showed off his dark skin to perfection. He'd left the top button of his shirt undone, which showed just a hint of chest hair beneath it.

We walked in silence down to the lawn. The gardens were a marvel of engineering, as well as horticulture, with a large pond served by a stepped waterfall and hand-sculpted statues dotted around the abundant greenery. A large lawn, neatly cut into a striped pattern, circled around the house, edged with beautiful flowers and shrubs. At the very back was the tall wall that surrounded the entire property. Although I could see no guards at the moment, I was sure there would be plenty on the other side.

After a few minutes of walking, when it had already gotten past the point of politeness, I spoke.

"Thank you for staying on, Leo. It must have been a difficult decision for you."

"Not really. Now, don't get me wrong. The explosion was a horrible, horrible thing, but we should stand with our backs straight and carry on as usual in the face of adversity." His words reminded me of my mother, but I let him continue. "If I may be so bold, I've set up a charity to aid those who were hurt in the blast."

"That's a nice gesture. And what about the Magi that have lost their jobs because of this?"

He seemed surprised by my words.

"Some say it is the Magi that are the cause of this. Now I don't believe it myself, but until the perpetrator is caught, there is nothing I can do to help them."

"So you don't believe it was a Mage?"

We rounded the corner of the house. The sun was low in the sky, but still pleasantly warm and the smell of freshly cut grass filled my nose. It would have been perfect if not for the huge hole in the side of the palace, now covered with tarpaulins.

"I run a lot of charities. In my time, I've made a lot of money, thanks to some wise business deals, and I like to give back where I can. I've worked with a great many magic people in my time, and I've not met a single one who would do something like this."

He gestured to the mass of debris and rubble we were currently walking past.

I didn't want to argue with him because I happened to agree, but there was a flaw in his logic. "Just because you know nice Magi, doesn't mean there aren't some that are capable of doing something like this."

"That's very true, but there are good and bad people everywhere, both magic and non-magic. My thoughts though, if it were a Mage that did this, why would he or she use a bomb? The police have reported that a device was found. Why would a Mage go to such lengths when they could use a wand to do the same damage. It doesn't make sense."

And there it was. The argument I needed to stop this madness.

"Do Magi have enough power to make such a blast?"

"While I believe Magi hold a lot of power, they are not all powerful. A blast this size would be too much for the average Mage, but there are some that could do it. Oh, look. They have set a picnic out for us."

I looked to where he was pointing. The gardens at the back of the house slanted down so we could see the tops of houses over the wall. On this side of the wall, was a large rug filled with food. To one side, was an ice bucket with a bottle of champagne in it waiting for us. Two long-stemmed glasses stood next to it.

I sat down and let Leo uncork the bottle, before pouring the bubbly into both glasses.

I felt at ease with Leo, but I had no spark with him. He was polite, great-looking and a good catch, and yet, he didn't possess the wit of Daniel nor the intrigue of Xavier. I liked him though. He was honest and according to his bio, was generous to boot.

"Tell me about your charities, Leo."

As he told me about the good work he had done, of which there was a lot, something glinted in my eye.

I blinked, trying to make out what it was, but I could only see the sunlight reflecting back from the windows of the houses beyond the palace grounds. Leo picked up on my staring and turned around. Whatever had caught the sun had now stopped.

"What was that?" he asked, turning back to me.

"I don't know. Something shone in my face. Never mind. It's gone now."

Leo kept on talking as I ate. Whatever had shone in my eye had gone, but by the end of the date, it was still on my mind.

"Shall we pack all this up?" asked Leo, indicating the left-over food.

"Hmm?" I was miles away in my thoughts. "Sorry, no. Don't worry about it. The staff will take it."

"Do you think they would mind me wrapping up some of the leftovers?" He'd put some of the uneaten food to one side.

I looked down at our half-eaten picnic. I'd barely touched it even though it was delicious. Immediately I felt bad. I'd been the worst date ever, barely saying a word and barely eating. Leo was a great guy. He deserved more.

"If you are still hungry, we can stay a while longer."

"It's not that. I just know a lot of homeless people, and I like to take food to them when I can. Unless you want more?"

He would make a wonderful partner, I mused. Not just for me, but for the nation. He was perfect in every way. I could quite clearly imagine him standing beside me as we ruled Silverwood. The people would love him, but could I?

"No, I'm fine. Go ahead and take it. I'll ask the kitchens to wrap it up for you."

We walked back up to the palace. Once back, I asked a guard to tell the kitchen to wrap up the picnic leftovers and give them to Leo. He gave me a peck on the cheek and thanked me for my generosity.

I'd barely made it back to my room when Elise came rushing in.

"What was the date like? Do you like him?"

I laughed at her exuberance. It was weird that she was more excited by my date than me, but nice too.

"He's very nice."

"Very nice? Is that all?"

I tried to think of something else to say but 'very nice' was all I could come up with.

"Yep."

"Don't be coy. He's gorgeous. He told me about all the things he has done for charity. Did he tell you about the time he flew over the jungle, dropping food to people who had been cut off by a flood? Or about the time he nursed a sick orphan back to health before finding him a forever family to live with?"

It turned out that Elise knew more about the guy than I did. Of course, she did. She'd sat next to him at the ball. She would have asked him all the right questions and remembered every detail. The main thing I took from my date with Leo was his thoughts on the bomb. It had been plaguing my mind ever since, and after that, I'd not really taken much in.

"He talked about his charity work a bit."

"Did you kiss him?"

The thought of kissing him hadn't crossed my mind. For a start, the opportunity hadn't really presented itself, and secondly, I didn't feel that way about him.

"Shouldn't I wait until I fall in love with one of them before kissing them?"

"But how will you fall in love with them if you don't kiss them?"

How indeed? Later, when Elise had left, I peered out of the window. I watched Leo walking down the driveway from the staff entrance with two bags. He walked right to the gates where a guard let him through. I had to give it to him. He could have gone through the main gates where a thousand photographers would take his picture to publish in the press. It was refreshing to see someone who would do something so lovely without reward or recognition. I vowed that on my next date with him, I'd put in more effort.

Just as I was about to turn around, I saw the flash of light again. As it was so dark, it must have been a flashlight this time. It was pointing up near my room. Was I being spied upon? It wouldn't surprise me if a member of the paparazzi had rented the townhouse just to get photos of me. They'd been known to do worse. I hid behind my curtain. When I peeked out again, the light was gone.

The Interview

"Time to get up. rise and shine!" A bright light, which could only have been the sun pouring in, thanks to the curtains being opened, hit my eyes. I blinked carefully.

"Jenny?"

"Of course, it's me. Who did you think it was? The press have gotten wind of your date with that rich fella, and they want the scoop. Your mother has told me to drag you out of bed and get you down to the sitting room. Leo is already there, and I must say he looks smart for the photo."

"Photo?" I mumbled as I dragged myself out of bed, rubbing the sleep out of my eyes as I did.

"Yes, a photo. They want one with you and Leo. There's no time to go and see Xavi, but she did give me this dress for you to wear and instructed me to tell you to put your hair in a ponytail. I think she called it damage limitation."

Jenny thrust the dress into my hand. I was glad to see it was understated and plain.

"How are you?" I asked as I pulled the dress over my head. Her arm was still in a sling, but she wasn't letting that stop her from being her usual bossy self.

"Never better. Now get a move on."

Suddenly I became aware that Agatha wasn't here to help me. A feeling of dread descended. "Where's Agatha?"

"Don't worry. They wouldn't let her go without saying goodbye to you. She was told she wasn't needed this morning that's all."

Phew. I was so relieved, I almost didn't catch Jenny's eyes go wide.

"What's this?"

I looked to where she was pointing. My glass slipper lay where I had left it on the floor next to my bed. I'd forgotten to hide it.

"It's the slipper from the ball," I replied as nonchalantly as possible.

I knew what she was thinking. The slipper by the bomb blast had been melted beyond recognition. No one had connected it to me. Not before now, at least.

"Where is the other one?" her eyes gazed at the floor, searching for my slipper's wayward partner. I loved Jenny with all my heart and had done so since I was a small child. In all the years of knowing her, I'd not lied to her once. It was a habit I was about to break in the biggest possible way.

"Thanks for finding it. I've been looking for it. The other is in my wardrobe." I took the glass slipper from her and smiled. I could see her searching my eyes for the truth. Either she believed me or didn't want to dispute it because she handed the shoe over to me without any more questions. I felt that, in that moment, something had broken between us.

I was surprised to find only one photographer in the sitting room. My mother was there as was Leo. Jenny had been right. He was looking very smart in a tailored suit. There was also a woman with a microphone, no doubt to interview us, and Louis with his box of tricks.

He sidled over to me and spent a few minutes "freshening me up" for the camera before the interviewer came over and introduced herself.

"Hello, Your Highness," she had a nasal voice, but a genuine smile. She shook my hand warmly. "I'm Sadie from Silverwood News. We want to run a feature on each of your dates. As you know, we aren't permitted to actually come on your dates, but her majesty has asked us to mock them up after you've had them. I hear you two love birds had a lovely picnic yesterday afternoon?"

"I wouldn't say we are lo..."

"We did, Sadie," cut in Leo. "The food was magnificent, the weather glorious and the company ravishing."

"And was there any ravishing going on?" Sadie appeared visibly more excited as she asked the question.

"A gentleman or a lady never kisses and tells." Leo laughed. I turned red. Now the whole Kingdom would think we had started some kind of torrid love affair, but we were keeping it to ourselves. "Shall we go outside?" Leo held his hand out towards the door. Sadie ushered her cameraman to follow, and the four of us left the palace. I noticed the cameraman got a good shot of the building work that was now going on to repair the palace wall. It had been quiet yesterday, but now the peace was interrupted by the sounds of hammers and drills and other machinery, not to mention the sheer number of people working there.

In the exact place we'd eaten yesterday, another picnic blanket had been laid out. This time, instead of the massive spread from the day before was a cooler. Inside was a punnet of strawberries and a carton of cream. There were two bowls and two spoons next to the cooler. I filled both bowls and passed one to Leo.

"Just act naturally," said Sadie. "I'll ask you some questions, and Martin here will take some pictures. Ok?"

"Go ahead," I replied nervously. At least, the strawberries were delicious.

"Leo Halifax is one of Silverwood's own eligible bachelors. Would you say you were attracted to him right from the start?"

I looked over at Leo. I could see he was as interested in the answer as Sadie was.

"He was one of the five men I picked to sit with me at dinner, yes." It was no more or less than the truth.

"I hear that you are now down to four men. Is that correct?"

"As you know Sadie, the ball didn't end very well. One of my potential suitors decided to go home. No one was brought in to replace him, but that is ok. I've got four wonderful young men to choose from. I hope to pick a match that will be good for our kingdom."

"You are a lucky girl dating such handsome young men." Sadie glanced over at Leo and grinned. If only she knew how much I'd rather be anywhere else but here right now.

"Or maybe they are the lucky ones to be able to date me." It sounded pretentious, but I was sick to death of being called lucky.

"Of course. Who wouldn't want to date the hottest young princess in the kingdom? I know Leo is here, but just between you and me and our thousands of viewers, do you have a favorite picked out yet?"

I tried to act demure. "I couldn't possibly give away anything at this early stage, Sadie, but I can tell you that my date with Leo was wonderful, and I'm looking forward to the next one."

Sadie turned back to the camera. "You heard it here first folks. Now stay tuned for a rundown of the princess's finalists. We're the only station in town that has access to the palace, and we'll keep you updated as things progress. For now, this is Sadie Black, signing off."

She turned to me

"Thank you, Your Highness. We'll be back in a couple of days to find out how your next date went."

She gave me a wink and then stood up, taking a strawberry and her cameraman with her.

Leo popped the next to the last strawberry in his mouth before passing the punnet to me. "I'm glad that's over."

"Me too," I agreed, watching the juice from the strawberry stain his lips. They were definitely kissable, that was for sure. I thought back to what Elise had said earlier. I'd only know if I'd fallen in love with someone if I kissed them. Could I kiss him? His lips looked so sweet to me right now, and yet there was something inside of me saying no. I knew I wasn't in love with him. Maybe it would change in time, maybe it wouldn't, but kissing him on my first date would not be fair to the others. Nor would it be fair to him. Instead, I leaned forward and wiped his lips with a napkin. It was as intimate as I could deal with and for a second, when he gazed at me with those amber eyes, I did feel the beginnings of a flutter.

"Let's pack this stuff away." I picked up the empty carton and spoons while Leo folded the blanket.

As I was looking at him, something flashed in my eyes again. When I tried to see where it had come from, it had already gone.

The Second and Third Dates

Once again, I found myself having to choose between the three men left for my next date. Without hesitation, I picked Daniel. Yeah, Xavier and Luca were gorgeous; but Daniel made me laugh, and if there was anything I needed right now, it was to laugh. I'd found little to laugh at in the past month or so, and Daniel seemed like just the person to lift my spirits. Prince Luca was at the bottom of my list. Unfortunately for me, according to the local newspaper, he was quickly becoming the firm favorite to win my heart. So much so, that they were running a competition with entry into a big prize drawing for those that chose the winning bachelor. I considered entering for myself and running away with the winnings, but to do that, I actually had to pick someone, and I was no closer to that than I was before the ball.

After picking Daniel for the next date, I was also expected to pick the venue. That is as long as it was somewhere within the palace or grounds. Going outside in the current political climate was an absolute no-no. I'd already done the garden, and although I'd be quite happy to sit in the garden for every date, I was told that this was also not an option. I had the choice of the cinema, bowling alley, or swimming pool, all of which the palace possessed. Sitting in the dark watching a movie was the easy way out. I wouldn't have to think of anything to say, but somewhere, in the back of my mind, I'd earmarked that for Prince Luca. I ended up choosing the bowling, thinking that Daniel might think it the most fun. The bowling alley was situated on the ground floor at the opposite end to the ballroom. That meant that the noise of the workers wouldn't reach us and we could bowl in peace. It also had a sound system, which would cover any sounds that did get through.

Of course, I had to have the obligatory primping and preening with Xavi and her crew. As we were doing something active, I got to wear a pair of pants for the first time in months, something that I was extremely happy with.

Like Leo had been, Daniel was on time. In his hand, he held a box wrapped in pink paper, which he handed to me as I entered the bowling alley. Upon opening it, I found a beautiful carved statuette, a tiny replica of me in my ball gown.

"You made this?" I asked, marveling at the beauty of it, and the skill involved. He'd gotten my features down perfectly.

"I've been carving it since the night of the ball. I finished it last night."

"It's beautiful, thank you." Then I did something that surprised the both of us. I kissed him on the cheek. It was a kiss of friendship, but the significance of it was not lost on either of us. It was my first kiss with one of the bachelors. I thought of Sadie and whether she'd ask me if I kissed him in tomorrow's interview.

I could say no. A kiss on the cheek didn't count for anything.

"I took the liberty of ordering us some drinks," Daniel said, pointing towards a table at one end of the alley. On it were two glasses and about fifteen different bottles, filled with different colored liquids. It was more alcohol than I'd drink in a lifetime.

"Follow me," He took my hand and led me to the table.

I arched a brow at the sheer quantities. "Are you trying to get me drunk?"

He gave a laugh. "I'm going to make you a cocktail. What do you fancy?"

"You make cocktails as well as furniture?"

"Wait til you see me bowl!" he winked and picked up a cocktail shaker. "So what will it be?"

I looked at all the bottles with names that were foreign to me. I'd never had a cocktail in my life.

"How about a mojito?" he asked, without waiting for me to answer.

"Sure."

He picked up a couple of the bottles and threw them up in the air. I watched as he spun them around before expertly catching them. The way he used his hands to manipulate those bottles through the air was mesmerizing. He threw them from behind his back and juggled them, and somewhere in the show, he managed to make two cocktails. He finished his show by garnishing them with a sprig of mint and then handed one to me. The first sip hit me like a truck. It was so strong and yet had a refreshing minty lime taste to it. I'd never drunk anything like it in my life before.

"This is amazing!" I said, and I meant it.

"Great. Let's bowl."

I sipped on my mojito as he programmed our names into the screen that would record our scores and then picked up a green bowling ball. With his first move, he scored a strike, knocking all ten pins over.

"Are you naturally good at everything?" I asked, rolling my eyes.

"Not everything. I've still not mastered the unicycle. Here,"

I laughed as he passed me a bowling ball. I rolled it down the lane and watched as it fell into the gutter.

"You are not standing right." He picked up another bowling ball and handed it over. He then moved behind me and held my wrist. His intentions might have been to help me bowl, but I could feel his hard lean body against mine as he pulled back my arm. I'd already danced with him, but this felt different. We were alone for a start, and this simple act of bowling felt much more intimate. I let go of the ball and watched as it knocked over seven pins. My turn was over, and he had no excuse to hold me anymore. It felt cold as he moved away.

The game continued although he didn't touch me again. With each round, I was getting tipsier as he poured cocktail after cocktail, each with a more imaginative name than the last. By the time the first game was finished, I was already quite drunk.

"Why did you apply to be one of the hundred?" I asked, trying not to slur my words.

It was a question that had been nagging me since the ball and one I wanted to ask all of the men but hadn't dared until now. The alcohol had loosened my tongue. As he'd been drinking the same amount as me, I hoped his answer would be truthful.

"I want to make my father proud."

"He isn't already?" I asked.

"Not really." He sat on one of the chairs at the table and nursed his drink. I took the seat opposite. "I used to have an older brother who was brilliant at everything. He was one of those guys that everyone liked, and he could turn his hand to anything. He just knew things. You could give him a task, and he'd figure it out straight away without any training. As a child, he was my idol. About five years ago, there was an accident in my father's workshop. Kyle was caught in a machine and killed instantly. I was seventeen at the time. I was the only one there. I tried to help him, I really did, but there was nothing I could do. My father never really forgave me. Ever since then, I've been trying to be better, to be more like Kyle. I hoped that marrying a princess would change things. He was so proud when I was chosen to attend the ball."

I looked at him, not knowing what to say. His story was heartbreaking. I could see the sadness in his eyes. He looked lost. He was so good at everything, how could he not see his worth?

"You are a great man, whether you marry a princess or not."

"If only my father could think that."

I had no idea of the protocol, but the cocktails had made me feel bold. I walked around the table and held him. He didn't weep, he was too strong for that, but he clung to me as I did my best to soothe him. After that, the second game of bowling never happened. We sat and chatted. He told me about his home life, and I told him that I never really wanted to be queen. It was an afternoon of brutal honesty, and at the end of it, it was apparent that neither of us wanted to be involved in this silly contest. Yet, despite that, we were both glad that we were in it together.

A week later, after more interviews and makeovers, I had my date with Xavier. Xavi had an easy time with me as we were going to go swimming, and so no makeup or dresses were involved.

I was the first to get there, so instead of waiting, I jumped into the cool water and swam a lap under water. When he still hadn't shown, I did a few more, loving the feel of the water as I glided through it. As my head crested the surface, I heard a splash at the other end. Xavier swam towards me at a speed I wouldn't have thought possible, and I thought of myself as a good swimmer. He reached me quickly, but instead of saying anything, he pulled himself out of the pool and positioned himself to dive in again.

I opened my mouth as I took in the detail of his perfectly sculpted body. Water formed rivulets over his muscles that cut so deep they looked to be cut from stone. I'd never seen anyone so perfectly built, and I'd never seen anyone so naked before. His choice of swimsuit was barely-there. I gulped as he performed a perfect dive, cutting through the water as if he was born to it.

If I'd felt nervous about my dates with Leo and Daniel, it was nothing to how I was feeling after seeing Xavier in all his glory. I knew I had led a sheltered life, and men were not something I was really used to which was one of the reasons this contest had been such a difficult pill to swallow. I knew I'd have to come out of my comfort zone, but this was so far out, I couldn't even see my comfort zone anymore. I was speculating on just taking my towel and leaving when his head appeared beside me. He gave it a shake, wetting me with drops of water from his hair, and smiled.

I smiled back, although inside my stomach was squirming with nerves. Perhaps the swimming pool had not been a good choice after all.

"I've been waiting for this day for a long time. I hope I can make it as special for you as the others did."

I tried to concentrate on his words, but I was all too aware that beneath the surface of the water, he was practically naked save for a tiny pair of swim trunks.

"I don't think it would be fair to comment on my dates with Leo and Daniel," I gulped.

"No, of course not. That was insensitive of me. I merely wish for you to have a good time with me."

He raised his eyebrow. It should have been cheesy, but on him, it worked. I felt my stomach flip again, and this time it had nothing to do with nerves. He had to be the best-looking guy I'd ever met.

"Shall we swim?"

I nodded eagerly. Anything to get me out of talking to the guy. There was something so worldly and exciting about him that made me nervous and put me at a loss for words. I pushed off the side, confident, at least, in my ability to swim well.

I pushed myself to the limit, feeling my muscles burn as I swam. Even at top speed, he swam past me, beating me to the other side. As I caught up, he ducked under the water. I thought he was going to swim right under me in the opposite direction, but a tug on my feet told me otherwise. I'd barely gotten my breath back when my head submerged. The chlorine stung my eyes, but I could see Xavier, swimming through my legs. I pushed against the tile at the bottom of the pool and hit the surface at the same time as he did. He had a broad smile on his face. Not a grin as such, but the look of a playful puppy. He even managed to make that look sexy. He wasn't trying to drown me at all. He was playing.

"You think that's funny, huh?" I said, trying to look angry and failing. I jumped forward, knocking him off his feet and pushing him under the water. He took it in his stride, pushing down on my shoulders, so he could get back to the surface first. I tried grabbing his feet as he swam past, but he was too quick. I had to be content with coming up for air second. It was a fight I could never win. He was bigger and stronger than me in every way, and yet I was beginning to loosen up around him and enjoy myself. He ducked me under the water one last time and shot off to the other end of the pool. I dived down as low as I could go and followed him, cutting great strides through the water. I'd almost made it when a strong pair of hands pulled me upwards. I fought them, and grabbed his waist, trying to pull him down to me instead. His grip on me intensified, and I felt his fingers digging into my arms. What was he playing at?

I broke the surface and began to shout.

"You're hurting me!" I slapped him in the face with my now freed arm.

"Stop it, listen."

It was then that I heard it. The palace sirens were sounding. The last time I'd heard them was the night of the ball.

Xavier took my hand and pulled me to the side of the pool, where he jumped out effortlessly before pulling me out. He grabbed a towel that had been left there and threw it to me, before taking one for himself and wrapping it around his waist.

I remembered the way to the underground safe room, but it didn't matter, two guards had reached us before we'd even left poolside. I felt completely exposed wearing only my swimsuit and a towel as we ran through the palace dripping wet, past frightened staff members who were running to their designated safe place.

Down at the bottom of the stairs, I could hear my mother in deep discussion with my father.

"Is this really necessary? It's only a protest."

"Look how the last protest turned out. People were killed."

"What's happened?" I asked as Xavier and I met them by the safe room door.

"Go inside. I'm just waiting for Elise. Goodness knows where the girl has got to." He ran back up the stairs to the main level, presumably to look for my little sister.

"What's happened?" I repeated my question to my mother, who ushered us down past the shelves of treasures.

"Nothing has happened, really. It's just a precaution. The Magi are outside protesting again, and your father thinks it wise that we stay down here until the police clear it."

"What are they protesting about now?" asked Xavier. I noticed he looked completely at ease in front of my mother, wearing only a towel. In contrast, I was shivering with the cold and felt ridiculous.

"The job cuts at the palace. They aren't happy that we have had to let the Magi go."

"They weren't let go, mother, Father fired them."

"He fired them because they are a danger to us."

"Who says they are a danger?" My conversation with Leo came back to my mind. I'd not told anyone about his theory about the bomb, but I couldn't let the Magi take the blame without the facts. Ignoring my mother shouting, I looked back through the room to the entrance. My father was no longer there, but one of the guards was. I noticed he wore the purple trim on his uniform. He must have been one of the last Magi in our employ. I wondered what he thought of all of this.

"I have to agree with Her Majesty," said Xavier. "The Magi are a scourge on society."

I didn't like this conversation at all. Xavier's voice had taken on an ugly tinge, and the playful side I'd seen of him earlier had gone. I left the pair of them discussing the current situation and ran to the guard.

"Can you tell me where my father has gone?"

"I believe he's gone to look for Her Royal Highness, The Princess Elise," he replied solemnly.

I thanked him and ran back up the stairs before he could stop me. From there, I could hear the protesters. I ran to a room that I knew looked out over the front gardens and peeked out from behind the curtains. At the end of the driveway, beyond the gates, I could see them. They were too far away to make out much detail, but I could see they were harmlessly waving banners. None of them were trying to scale the wall. It was a peaceful protest. As I watched, something flew through the air. It was a smoking canister of some kind. It landed right in the middle of the crowd that began to disperse. Seconds later, another one joined the first. I could hear the screams as the police waded in wearing gas masks and began to hit the Magi as they were attempting to run away.

"Charmaine!" I could hear the anger in my father's voice. "Why are you standing in the window half naked? Do you want a picture of you with no clothes on, on the front page of tomorrow's newspaper?"

"Sorry, Father!" I replied although it was a bit unfair. I was wrapped in a towel and hiding behind a curtain. If anyone had seen me, they'd have only seen my head.

"You are as bad as your sister. Get here now."

I wondered what Elise had done to anger him as I followed him back down to the basement. This time, the doors were closed behind us.

I saw Elise talking to my mother and Xavier at the other end of the vast room. For some reason, Leo was also with them.

"Father," I said, wanting to catch him before we got to the others. "I've been thinking about the night of the ball."

He regarded me with interest. "Do you remember something? Did you see something?"

"No, nothing, but I have a theory." I didn't want to tell him it was Leo's theory in case it angered him.

His interest waned. He didn't want a theory; he wanted cold hard evidence.

"If the Magi wanted to blow us up, they could have done it with wands? Why go to the bother of making a bomb?"

"Who knows how these people think? They are savages."

"How can you say that? I've just watched the police hitting the protesters after throwing tear gas at them."

"They've done what they have to do," he replied which was fast becoming his stock reply to anything to do with the Magi.

"And you knew about this?" I asked incredulously.

"Of course, I knew. Who do you think ordered it? I need to keep you safe. I need to keep all of you safe."

"But those people out there could have been our staff until last week. Some of them have worked here all their lives."

"I don't want to hear any more about it, Charmaine. You don't know what you are talking about."

I watched as he walked in long strides towards the others. The guard at this side of the door stood stock still, staring straight ahead. He didn't look towards me once, but I swore I could see a tear at the corner of his eye.

I stayed down at the opposite end of the room from the others, preferring to examine the years of jewelry and antiques than talk to anyone. I was too upset with them all—with my father for doing this with my mother for making me choose between men I didn't know, and with the other three for being part of it. Technically Elise wasn't part of anything, but she was enjoying the spectacle of it all, and that was enough.

When the doors were opened, and the areas proclaimed safe, I ran right up to my bedroom and put some clothes on.

I was just about to fling myself onto the bed when I saw a small light flickering on my wall.

It was the same light as before. I ran to my window and looked out. Something glinted in the late afternoon sun. Just like all the other times, it came from the top floor of one of the town houses. I watched as it flickered and then went off. Seconds later it was back, and once again it was pointing at me. This was no coincidence. To get me once in the garden was one thing, but to be spying on me in my very own room was something else. I'd not seen any illicit photos of me in the papers, but there was no doubt in my mind that this was a member of the paparazzi, and the light was the glint of the sun bouncing off a camera lens.

I ran downstairs in search of a pair of binoculars. I couldn't find any anywhere, but I did find an old telescope that was used to look at stars. It wasn't ideal as it was so bulky, but it would be powerful enough to see the creep who was watching me.

The light had gone, but as soon as I looked out of the window, it flashed again.

"Gotcha!" I said training the old telescope right at the window. I waited for the light to go off—I didn't want to blind myself and put my eye to the lens.

There, in the top window with a piece of mirror in his hand was Cynder.

The Secret

I'd recognize that curly hair anywhere. He'd been trying to contact me for a week, and I'd shrugged him off as a member of the paparazzi.

I waved and then dropped my hand. If he could see me, it meant other people could too. If they caught me waving at someone, they'd investigate, and Cynder would be caught. I could feel my heart thumping as I gazed through the telescope. He'd seen me wave and that was enough. As I took in his features, I realized just how much I missed him. Our nights together dancing around the kitchen had meant so much to me, and they had ended so abruptly the night of the ball.

The red and blue flashing of a police car's lights lit up the walls of the town house for a second as it passed and Cynder disappeared from view.

I waited for a few moments for him to come back, but he didn't reappear. I could understand why. He'd put himself in great danger trying to contact me.

I fingered the chain around my wrist. I'd not taken it off since the day of the ball. It was my one link to Cynder.

I needed to see him, but how? I wasn't allowed out of the palace grounds and with all the guards stationed around; there was no way I could sneak out. Cynder coming in here was impossible. He'd be caught in no time. He had most of the police in the kingdom searching for him. It was a miracle he'd gone this long without being caught.

By the time Agatha had brought my dinner to my room, I was no closer to figuring out a solution.

Agatha put the silver tray down on the bed next to me. "When you didn't come down for dinner, the queen instructed me to bring food up here for you."

"Thank you, Agatha."

"It's no problem, your highness. I hope you enjoy it."

I looked at her. Despite all her problems and her upcoming firing, she still managed to keep a smile on her face. I don't know how she did it.

"What's going to happen to you, Agatha?" she'd lived in the palace her whole life. Her mother had been a maid here as had her grandmother before her. In all the time I'd known her, I'd never once asked her how she felt about being a Mage. It was just something unspoken between the two of us. Maybe now was the time to change that.

"I've got an aunt and uncle who live a couple of hundred miles away in the south of the country. They'll probably take me in. I'll find something to do when I get there."

"Doesn't it annoy you?"

"I don't like it," she sighed, "but my aunt and uncle are nice people."

"I don't mean that. Doesn't it bother you that you can pick up a wand and do anything you want, and yet, those without wands tell you what to do?"

"Wand use has always been strictly regulated. I'm used to it."

"But why should you be used to it? Don't you want to use your wand and... just fly away sometimes?"

She laughed. "Even if I wanted to, I'm not powerful enough to fly."

"You know what I mean. It's such a waste. All those things at your fingertips, and you use your wand for folding my clothes."

"I enjoy working for you. I do sometimes wish I dared use my wand to conjure up a nice dress like the ones you've been wearing lately, but it's not worth the trouble I'd be in if I did. Besides, where would I wear a nice dress?"

It broke my heart. She had the whole world at her fingertips, and she'd been conditioned not to use her wand for anything but serving others. I stood up and ran to my wardrobe. Most of the beautiful clothes were kept in the dressing room downstairs, but some of the outfits had ended up in here. I picked out a couple of the prettiest dresses and handed them to her.

"These are for you. I want you to have them. We're about the same size. If you don't want them, you can sell them later."

Her eyes went wide as she touched the fabric. "I can't accept these."

"After everything you've done for me, these dresses are the least I can do."

"You know they'll think I've stolen them, right?"

"I'll tell my father I've given them to you. He can hardly complain after what he's doing to you."

She stood up and flung her arms around me. I held on to her tightly. I didn't know if it was the last time I'd see her. Both of us wept in each other's arms. If only I could get my father to see the damage he was causing.

After she had left, I picked at my dinner, thinking of my situation. I felt almost as trapped as Agatha was, neither of us able to do what we wanted to do. I envied her slightly too. At least, she knew what she wanted. All I ever wanted to do was climb trees and read books. It was hardly a career choice.

I brought my mind back to Cynder. The conundrum of how to get to him was in the forefront of my mind, but whichever way I looked at it, I couldn't see a way to manage it. He was so close and yet so far away. Every so often, I'd go to the window and peek through the telescope in the hopes of seeing him, but he was never there. It was only when it had gotten dark that movement in the garden caught my eye. I didn't need the telescope to see who it was. Leo was once again taking food out to feed the homeless. I could see two bags in his hands. I watched him walk down the staff driveway to the back gate, which two guards opened for him. He really was an extraordinary man. I waited for him to return, curious to know how long he spent out in the town when he was giving out food. It also gave me a good excuse to be gazing out of the window. Even though my gaze kept wandering to the town house, if anyone saw me, I could simply say I was watching for Leo. It would make a cute story for the newspapers. Two hours later and he finally returned, his hands empty. In that time, I'd come up with a plan. I was going to see Cynder again! I just had to convince my father. I went to bed fingering the charm he'd given me. At some point in the night, the little gold carriage turned into a pumpkin pulled by mice as dreams took over.

The next morning I was up and dressed early. I needed to see my father before he was too busy to speak to me. I'd gotten halfway down the corridor before Jenny caught up with me.

"Look at you! I normally have to drag you out of bed. What's the occasion?"

I rolled my eyes. "Nothing. I just wanted to have a word with my father."

"There's time for that later. The news team will be here in an hour to interview you about your date with Xavier and Xavi wants to sort your make up out first."

I sighed. As my date had come to an abrupt end, I'd hoped this wasn't something I'd have to do. When Sadie had interviewed me after my date with Daniel, she'd chatted as we rolled bowling balls, this time minus the drinks. The thought of appearing on screen in front of hundreds of thousands of people wearing nothing but a swimsuit was enough to make my blood curdle.

Thankfully, Xavi agreed and asked Alezis to give me a wet look hairstyle while she dressed me, rather inexplicably in a navy blue sailor dress. The interview was to take place in the swimming pool area, with Xavier and I sitting on the edge of the pool with our feet in the water. My mother thought it might show a playful side to the royal family. Personally, I thought we looked stupid as we answered Sadie's insipid questions. Strangely enough, she made no comment on how our date ended, instead, asking lots of questions about our swimming abilities. All the while, all I could think about was talking to my father. I wanted to ask him if I could accompany Leo on his nocturnal aid mission. All my answers to Sadie's questions were in monotone and Xavier didn't say much more. He was elusive when asked about his history, and once again, I wondered exactly what it was he was hiding.

"I think that's all for today," Sadie said to the camera through gritted teeth. Today had not been a success for her, and I almost felt sorry for her. "Tune in on Wednesday for our catch-up with Princess Charmaine and Prince Luca."

I smiled and ran before Xavier could talk to me. I know it was rude, especially as our date had been so short, but I needed to speak to my father. I found him in his study. This time, thankfully, he was alone.

"If you've come to lecture me about the Magi, Charmaine, I don't want to hear it. I've got enough on my plate at the moment."

"No, it's not that, although I should tell you that I've given Agatha a couple of my dresses as a gift."

"Uh huh."

"I was actually here to ask if you would mind if I went out with Leo tonight."

He looked up, surprised. "You want to go out with Leo? I think that's a splendid idea. Where are you planning on going?"

"Is it?" I asked, taken aback by his answer. "He feeds the homeless out in the town. I thought it would be nice if I joined him."

"Splendid. I'll get a couple of guards to go with you. Would you like me to ask your mother to call that Sadie woman? It would make great publicity."

"No!" I shouted abruptly. "I don't think Leo would like the publicity. He's pretty shy." I fabricated wildly. For all I knew, he'd love to be followed around town by a cameraman.

"Ok, just the guards then. What time will you be leaving?"

I thought about it. On the two occasions I'd seen Leo leave; it had been about eight o'clock. If I told my father ten, then we'd miss the guards. I could always come up with some story about how I got the wrong time by mistake. Slipping away from Leo was going to be hard enough; I wouldn't be able to slip away from two guards as well.

"Ten."

"Wonderful, does Leo approve?"

The way he asked the question was strange. Did he know that I'd just made it all up on the spot?

"Of course, daddy!"

"Great! Have fun." He was back to normal, with only that one question making him pause. Although he was awfully keen for me to go out with Leo, strange as he was the one that picked Xavier. Why would he want me to go out with Leo?

I found Leo talking to Elise in the sitting room. They were both so deep in conversation that they jumped when I walked in, making me instantly suspicious.

"You weren't talking about me were you?"

Leo smiled that warm smile of his and crinkled his eyes "Actually we were. We were discussing how much trouble you were having with this whole dating thing. Every time you go on a date, something happens. It's like the public wants you to stay single."

"Our date wasn't cut short," I reminded him. "Actually, that's why I'm here. I was hoping we could go out on another date."

Elise's eyes went wide. "Why? Surely it's Luca's turn?"

It was expected of me to date them each once first without having a second date with any of them, but it wasn't in the rules. Technically, I could ask any of them out on a date whenever and they would have to agree. It was a stupid rule that I'd never follow. I'd never want to go on a date with someone that didn't want to go. What would be the point? Of course, if Leo said no now, I'd have to make an exception.

"Where would you like to go?" asked Leo, not leaving me time to answer.

"I've been watching you go out and feed the homeless. I was hoping that you'd let me join you tonight."

He seemed surprised. "It's not glamorous work I do. The photo opportunities will be thin on the ground."

"I'm not inviting Sadie or her cameraman. I was actually hoping to go incognito. I just want to help." I felt bad for lying, especially as he was doing all this for a good cause, but I could think of no other option. I'd make sure the kitchens gave him some really good food to make up for it.

"Ok, I guess that would be fine. The people I feed know me. I think they would feel overwhelmed by a princess and camera crew turning up."

"Great. I'll sort the food out and meet you by the back door at eight."

I'd done it. Well, I'd planned it. It remained to be seen if I could actually pull it off.

I did as promised and asked Pascal to pack the best food he had to offer. He seemed rather put out when he found out it was to feed the homeless, but he begrudgingly agreed.

In my wardrobe, I picked out the darkest outfit I could find and slipped into it. Xavi would cry if she could see me in the plain black trousers and black sweater, but with any luck, Xavi, nor anyone else would see me.

Eight o'clock couldn't come around fast enough, and I found myself with nothing to do for the first time in weeks. One of the guards told me that Prince Luca was looking for me, but as I didn't want to deal with him, I stayed in my room for the rest of the day, occasionally looking out of the window to see if I could spot Cynder. I didn't see him all day, but I knew he was there and that was enough. At seven forty-five, I picked up the bags of food from the kitchen. From there, it was easy enough to sneak out through the back doors to wait for Leo.

He turned up minutes later and like the true gentleman he was, he took the bags from me. I knew my first hurdle would be the guards at the gates, but they let me through with no problem. The townhouse that Cynder was in was just a short walk down the road, but Leo turned to walk in the opposite direction, and I had no choice but to follow him. He turned down a couple of side streets before coming to a crudely built shelter made from garbage and things scavenged from the streets.

"This is their home," Leo whispered, before knocking on a piece of wood that I suppose could have been a door. A young woman with a baby on her hip opened the door cautiously. When she saw it was Leo, she flung it wide and hugged him. I followed them into the dirty "house" surprised to find eleven people there. Five of them were children, all playing together in the ashes of a burnt out fire. The others ignored us. They all lived together in one room. At one side, was a pile of dirty rags, which I assumed was where they slept. Despite the dirt and the roughness of the place, it smelled wonderfully of fresh flowers. I'd expected a lot worse.

"This is Charmaine. She's a friend of mine. Charmaine, this is Lita and this little one here..."—he tickled the baby in her arms,—"is Juno."

"Pleased to meet you," I said, extending my hand, which she shook.

"Would you like a cup of tea?" the woman asked.

"Yes, please."

Then to my surprise, she pulled out three mugs and filled them using a wand she'd just brought out from her belt.

"You're a Mage?" I exclaimed.

"She doesn't know?" The woman suddenly looked fearful, and the others who had, so far, ignored us, looked up.

"She's fine. She won't tell on you for using your magic." Leo turned to me. "Will you?"

How could anyone live in a state like this when they could change it in an instant with a swish of their wand? It was unimaginable that anyone would choose to live this way.

"No. Of course not. Why would you not want me to tell anyone about you using your magic?"

She looked at me as if I'd just arrived from another planet.

"Because it's illegal, isn't it? Where are you from?"

Illegal? The staff at the palace used magic all the time. At least, they had until they were fired. I picked up the tea and drank it down, so I didn't have to answer her question.

"The police have been around twice this week to check up on us," Lita said to Leo. "Like we are going to do anything with them coming around all the time. Still, I couldn't resist using a flower spell. I can't stand the stink of the diapers otherwise." She kissed her young daughter on her nose. The baby giggled.

So that's why the place smelled so nice despite its obvious decay.

"How's the job hunt going?" Leo asked her

"No luck. No one will hire us. Especially now the palace is firing everyone. I'm sick of looking, but the others still spend all day knocking on doors begging for work."

"Uncle Leo?" one of the children, a scruffy little thing who looked no more than four years old, pulled on Leo's trouser leg. "Did you bring us food?"

183

"Of course, Dylan." He emptied the contents of one of the bags onto the table, and the other kids came running.

"Are you not hungry?" I asked as Lita watched her kids tuck into the food.

"I'll wait for the kids to finish, and then I'll grab a bite." She looked so skinny; I just wanted to give her a sandwich. I was just about to empty another bag out when Leo stopped me.

"Those are for other families."

After we left, I questioned him. "There are more families like that? Magi, I mean." This time I kept my voice down.

"There are hundreds of them all over the city. I try to visit different families every night, but I'm limited to what one person can do. I'm too scared to hire anyone to help because if I get caught I'll end up in jail and they will too."

"You'll end up in jail for feeding the homeless?"

"If they are Magi, yes."

"But why?"

"The non-Magi don't want them around. It's easier to let them starve."

I'd not realized until now, just how sheltered I was living in the palace. I'd lived my whole life among Magi.

"How can using magic be illegal? Most of the staff in the palace use it, or, at least, they used to."

He pulled me to the side of the road and looked both ways to make sure we were out of earshot.

"I shouldn't be telling you this, but I think I can trust you..."

"Go on."

"When I was invited to the palace, I was asked to sign a confidentiality agreement. Most of it was the kind of stuff you'd expect: don't talk to the media about the palace or royal family, don't talk to anyone about the princess without the permission of the family, etc. The last clause was that we should not tell you or Elise about magic being illegal."

"Why?" I had never felt so outraged or confused.

"I think your parents wanted to protect you both."

"In less than five months' time, I'm supposed to be getting married and preparing for a life as the queen and head of the country. How do my parents expect me to fulfill my role if they are keeping things from me?" It was a rhetorical question. I didn't expect him to answer. He answered me anyway by putting his arms around me and giving me a hug. I'd not even known I'd needed protecting, but at that moment, his arms felt like walls around me, keeping the entire world out. I snuggled into him grateful for his presence and warmth.

"Maybe, you will be the queen to change things?" he said.

And maybe he'd be the prince to show me the way.

A noise startled me. It was only a cat, but it brought me back to reality. We'd already been away from the palace twenty minutes, and I was no closer to getting to Cynder.

"Listen, can you do the next one on your own and I'll meet you at the palace gate just before ten?"

"I don't know. I don't like the thought of you out there on your own. I promised Elise I'd look after you."

"I'll be fine. I know someone else that could do with some of this food. It will be quicker if we split up."

"Ok, if you are sure." He passed me one of the remaining bags and kissed me on the cheek.

The townhouse that I'd seen Cynder in had five floors of apartments and a communal entrance. As it was open, I slipped through the front door quietly. The last thing I needed was anyone to spot me.

I ran up all the stairs as quickly as I could until I reached a landing with no doors. It made no sense. Where was the entrance to the top apartment? There was an old writing desk with a wilted bunch of flowers and an empty bookcase. A sliver of moonlight hit the floor from an open window. I looked out, wondering if this is where I'd seen Cynder, but it couldn't have been. It looked out the wrong way.

"Cynder?" I hissed, not wanting to raise my voice.

There was no answer. I was just about to head down a floor to knock on the door there when I heard a creak behind me. I turned to find the book case opening. From behind it appeared a familiar face with a mop of curly hair on top.

Cynder Again

I ran to him. Pulling the bookcase closed behind me he hugged me tightly as though he'd never let me go. I clung to him, fearful that if I let go, he'd inexplicably disappear.

"I didn't think you'd come."

In the half-light, I could barely see him, but his eyes still sparkled as much as they always had.

"I wasn't sure I'd be able to. I've brought you some food." I handed him the bag. He didn't take his eyes off me as he led me into a dimly lit room. He pointed his wand at the curtains which shut immediately and then turned on a light. In the center of the room was a table. A chopping board was out with peppers, onions, and garlic, all chopped neatly on top.

"You have food already!" I exclaimed.

"The police want me for murder. I don't think they'll bat an eyelid at me getting food with my wand. I've got enough for both of us. I hoped you'd come."

I sat down at the table while he resumed chopping.

His last statement, while made in jest was enough to cut me to the bone. He was wanted for murder. Not just any murder, but multiple murders including a member of royalty. If he was caught, he'd not be locked up; he'd be given the death sentence.

"Can't you use your wand to disappear or fly away?"

"I can't literally disappear. Not even the strongest Magi can become invisible or teleport. I can't fly either."

"But you managed to conjure up all this food."

"I didn't conjure it up. It already existed. I just magicked it here. I guess you could say that I stole it. Most of the time, I've been living off bread and scraps, but I wanted to cook something nice for you." He began to add oil to the veggies along with other herbs and spices.

"You thought of me even though you are on the run."

"Charm," he said looking up from his task. "I've thought of nothing but you since the day I left."

He put down the knife and walked over to me, kissing me so lightly on the lips, I barely felt it, and yet my heart nearly sky rocketed out of my chest. He went back to his task of coating the veggies in oil, completely unaware that he'd turned me emotionally upside down.

"Why haven't you run away?" I asked, trying not to cry. "Even without flying, surely your magic will help you escape?"

"Maybe, although there are police officers on every corner now. My photo is everywhere. Where would I go?"

"Anywhere. I want you to be safe."

He wiped his hands on a towel and smiled. "I stayed because of you."

I felt my stomach jump again. My heart was already beating at double time. "Why?"

"You've been here ten minutes, and you've not asked me if I planted that bomb."

"I know you didn't."

"That's just it. You couldn't possibly know for sure. You were in the ballroom with everyone else. Everyone else thinks it was me." He picked up the pan and walked to the stove.

"The way you are talking sounds like you did do it."

"I didn't do it, but you didn't know that. You believed that I didn't do it. You believed in me."

"I do believe in you," I said. I'd never believed in anyone more.

"That's why I'm still here. No one has believed in me before. Pascal never once let me cook, and yet you think I should be the head chef."

"Yeah. Your food is delicious," I grinned, taking a slice of pepper, he'd missed and crunching it between my teeth.

"Hey. They are for dinner!" The tension was broken and all thoughts of the bomb and that terrible night left me. He showed me how to chop the chicken just right and let me help him make the sauce. When he'd finished, the meal was enough to rival anything served at the palace.

Cynder placed the plate in front of me. "I'm just sorry I don't have wine."

"Hang on." I scrambled around in the bag from the palace. There was no wine, but there was a bottle of orange juice. I poured us both a glass.

"To freedom!" said Cynder, raising his glass.

"To freedom," I agreed, clinking his glass against mine.

Were we talking about his freedom or mine, or just the freedom to be together?

"Do you think the Magi will ever be free?" I asked, taking a bite out of the cooked chicken.

"Not with the way things are now. The Non-Magi are afraid of us, and it's only getting worse. The explosion at the palace was a great excuse to run us out of town."

"One of the guests placed you near the scene. Did you see who it was?"

"No. I was walking down the corridor with your shoes. I'd planned to put them somewhere safe for you but somewhere nearby in case you wanted them. I couldn't take them to the kitchen, so I decided to hide them in a huge vase of flowers in the corridor next to the ballroom. I saw that guy walk past as I was pulling the flowers back. What he didn't see was me discovering the bomb. It had one of those countdown timers. I watched it count down from seven to six. There was no time to alert anyone. I only had six seconds to get away, so I ran as fast as I could down the corridor. I'd just managed to run through a door when I heard the explosion. I was knocked to my feet in the blast. The first thing I thought about was if you were alright. I headed to the ballroom door to find you, but I heard one of the king's men in a small room to the side of me. He was talking to your father, I think. He said that a Mage had bombed the Palace. I panicked. The door began to open, and so I

192

ran. I'm sorry. I shouldn't have, but I was scared. I thought that I'd spend the night here in my parents' house and then come back in the morning when everything had calmed down. The next morning, I saw my photo on the cover of the newspaper. Not only did they think it was a Mage that had bombed the palace, but they thought it was me. I ran back upstairs and magicked the bookcase to block the door. Every day I looked through this window, hoping to see you. It was only the next day when I read the paper again that I saw that you had survived and were uninjured. From then on, I spent as much time as I dared looking out to see if I could spot you. I used a mirror to shine it on your room, but you only noticed when you were out in the garden with that bachelor guy. I hoped you'd come to me that night, but you didn't."

"I didn't know it was you. I thought it was a member of the paparazzi."

"I almost gave up hope then," he continued, "but I kept trying. When I saw you leave the palace tonight with the same guy, I was excited, but scared at the same time."

"Scared. Why?"

"Because I knew he was one of your dates. I thought maybe you'd fallen in love with him and were going out to a restaurant or something."

He looked so solemn. Of all the things he could be scared of in his current situation, his biggest fear was that I'd fall in love with someone else.

"Dance with me."

He looked up in surprise. "Here?"

"Yes here."

I stood and walked around the table.

He took my hand and stood with me. Waving his wand, he made a record player turn on. The record was a slow, soulful tune with no words. Perfect for slow dancing to.

He put his hand around my waist and pulled me to him. Dancing with him was effortless. We swayed together as if we knew each other's bodies well. And I did know him. I knew him better than I knew myself. My head rested on his shoulder and my arms wrapped around him. I'd score no points from Stephan with my lack of technical ability, but I didn't care. I'd never felt so safe or so perfectly right as I did in that moment in Cynder's arms.

When the music came to a climax, I lifted my lips to his ear and whispered. "I'm not in love with Leo."

Cynder looked right into my eyes and kissed me. My first real kiss. It felt so natural, so right. I leaned into him and kissed him back, feeling my whole body tingle as he ran his hand up my back to pull me in even closer. All those times I'd thought about kissing had not prepared me for how amazing it was, how completely wrapped up in the moment and how breathless I felt. I knew in that moment, that no matter how good-looking, how perfect, or how nice my suitors were, none of them would ever take the place that Cynder held in my heart. I'd fallen deep, and there was no point denying it. I never wanted it to end, but all too soon it had to.

"You have to go." It was the most heartbreaking thing I'd ever had to say, and yet, I knew that if he stayed in town, he'd be caught eventually. He'd been right earlier when he'd said that there was an officer on every corner. I'd seen them myself. I wanted to be near him so badly, and yet, I wanted him safe more.

"I don't want to leave you."

My heart ached with the impossibility of our situation.

"I don't want you to leave either. When they catch who bombed the palace, you can come back."

"I'll never be welcome here. Even if they catch who did it, I still won't be able to get a job." I hated that he was right. There was nothing keeping him here. Nothing but me.

"One day, I'll be queen, and everything will change." I tried to sound upbeat even though my heart was shattering. We both knew it was a long way off. I felt tears welling up in my eyes.

"You'll be the best queen," he whispered, kissing my tears away.

"If you use your wand, will you be able to get away?"

"I could try. I've heard that Thalia allows Magi. I could attempt to cross the border. If I make it, I'll be safe there."

"Then you should go there," I replied, blinking back the tears. The thought of him being in another kingdom was enough to break my heart even more, but the alternative was much worse.

"I've heard it's beautiful. The flowers will be in bloom at this time of the year. Prince Luca told me that."

"If you marry the Prince, maybe you'll visit?"

I nodded and closed my eyes. I'd not even had my date with Luca yet, and here I was discussing marriage to him with the one who had my heart. In truth, I'd probably never see Cynder again.

I pulled out a gold chain from under my sweater and took it off.

"Take this. It used to belong to my grandmother. It's worth a lot of money."

"I can't. It must mean so much to you."

"Not as much as you do, and besides, I've still got this." I held up my wrist and showed him the charm bracelet he'd given me. "I'll wear it always."

He took my hand and kissed my wrist. I felt goose bumps all up my arm.

The clock on the wall behind him said nine forty-five. It was time for me to go.

I kissed him again one last time.

"I'll see you again one day," he whispered. "You are all I have."

As I left, I didn't bother to wipe away the tears that were falling down my cheeks.

Leo was already waiting for me. He made no mention of my wet eyes. Maybe he didn't even see them in the dark.

The guards let us through without question. When we came to the palace, I could see two other guards by the back door. They were looking around them.

"Let's go around the front," I said to Leo. I didn't want them to see us coming up the driveway.

Leo changed his direction as I asked and began to walk around to the front of the palace. When I was sure we were out of view of the two guards, I kissed his cheek and thanked him, before dashing back into the palace and running through until I got to the back door. Then it was just a matter of opening it and telling the guards I'd changed my mind about going out. To my relief, they accepted it without question. That night, I hopped straight into bed, but sleep was elusive. I spent the whole night listening out for sirens.

In the morning I looked out of the window. The curtains on the window in the apartment were open. Cynder was gone.

Prince Luca

The days following Cynder's departure were a void, a chasm of emptiness, but just because it felt like my heart had ceased to beat, the heart of the palace rattled on, and it became time for my next date. Of all the bachelors, Prince Luca was, on paper, the one I was most suited to. He was only a little older, and, like me, was the second in line to the throne. His elder brother would one day become king of Thalia. Marrying me was the only way he'd be able to rule a kingdom, or, at least, share the rule with me. Like anything on paper, the reality was that I didn't really like the guy. He was good looking enough for me to put him on my maybe pile when I first saw his photo, but after the banquet on the night of the ball, when he'd spent more time talking to a member of the kitchen staff, I'd put his as a firm fourth out of the four. The only reason I was looking forward to my date with him was because after dating all of them, I was allowed to choose one to go home.

I allowed Xavi to do what she wanted with me, something she took advantage of, having me dressed in an extravagant off the shoulder gown more suited to a formal cocktail party than a night at the cinema. When I pointed out that we were only going to watch a movie, she replied "With a prince!" and that was the end of the conversation. I, at least, got out of wearing a tiara for the occasion.

I felt ridiculous as I waited outside the cinema room, but someone must have tipped the prince off because he appeared wearing a tuxedo.

"You look stunning, my dear." He kissed my hand.

"As do you. Did someone tell you I was dressing up for the occasion?"

"No. I like to dress smartly for a date. What are we watching?"

I hadn't even thought to ask for a specific movie. I just hoped that whatever the staff had picked, it wasn't boring.

The cinema room wasn't massive, but it was big enough to house about thirty people. With the whole place to ourselves, we could choose anywhere to sit. Prince Luca pointed to the love seats at the front—huge double-sized sofas covered in red fabric, made for two."

"I can't see when I'm seated so close to the screen," I lied and sat in one of the single seats about halfway back. Immediately, one of the staff came in with two cartons of popcorn on a silver tray, and two large cups of lemonade.

We took one each, and the movie began to roll. To give them credit, the staff had picked out a good movie for us. An action film from the previous year and one of my personal favorites. I'd almost forgotten Luca was with me until I noticed his hand behind my back. I cringed inwardly as his hand came down onto my shoulder. It was such a cheesy move and not one befitting a prince. When the movie was over, and the lights went up, I stood quickly, letting his hand fall. All I wanted to do was go to bed and think of Cynder

"Thank you for a lovely night," I said, making to leave.

"You can't go now. The night is young."

I yawned. The lack of sleep was catching up with me. "I'm sorry, but I'm tired."

"If it is your desire to sleep, then I will not stand in your way. I can't say I'm not disappointed that we have not had more time to talk, but I wouldn't want to keep you here if you didn't want to stay."

He looked crestfallen, and I felt bad. Sure, my date with Xavier had been shorter than this, but then it hadn't been my fault. If I was going to have to pick someone to send home tomorrow, it was only fair I gave him a chance.

"I guess I could stay up a little longer."

His face lit up. "Let's go for a walk in the garden. We can talk there."

My heart lurched. Even though I wanted to see Cynder standing at the window, or a light shining on me from a flashlight telling me he was ok, a bigger part of me wanted to see nothing. That meant he'd escaped.

"Ok," I said, trying not to show any excitement. Even though excitement was the last thing I should be feeling, my heart hadn't gotten the memo, and it was still thumping loudly as we stepped into the cold night. The builders who were fixing the side of the palace had long since gone home for the day, and we only had the sound of the crickets to keep us company. I looked up to the top floor of the townhouse, but it was in complete darkness. I hoped it meant Cynder had gone. I'd been checking the newspaper all week for any news, but after reading them cover to cover, I found nothing, which I took to be a good sign. Once I knew that Cynder had left, I tried to hide my pain and talk to Luca.

"What made you want to come here?" I asked. I'd only asked that question once before, and that was to Daniel. I probably should have asked Leo and Xavier too.

He answered with a question of his own.

"How did you feel being second in line to the throne?"

"I loved it. I loved watching Grace become this wonderful princess who would one day become queen, and I was glad I didn't have to."

"Except now you do."

"Except now I do." I nodded. The grief I was feeling thinking of Cynder had eclipsed my grief over the death of my sister, but now they bubbled together like bile in my stomach. I felt sick with the loss of them both.

"I hated it," Luca said. "Being second to do everything. My brother got everything. I know it sounds as though I'm bitter. I'm not really. I love my brother, and I know he'll make a good king, but I am jealous. I admit it. I would like to be king. He has two sons now, so the likelihood is that I'll never succeed to the throne. When he dies, it will pass to my eldest nephew. That is why I came here. I want to be king."

"You know that even if you marry me and I become queen, your title will become prince consort, not king."

"It's not really the title I care about. King, prince consort. It's just a name. I want to rule a kingdom to make changes. I see the world around me and all the injustices and want to be able to do something about it. Thalia is a wonderful country, with many wonderful attributes, but I can see where things could be changed for the better. My brother likes to keep his head in the sand about such matters. I want to help people."

His answer surprised me. I was pegging him for an empty-headed playboy. "What would you change about Silverwood?"

"I don't want to talk ill of your kingdom or the way it is run It is a fine kingdom. A very fine kingdom."

"And that's a cop-out answer."

He looked me in the eye "You live in fear!"

"I live in fear?"

"Not you, your whole kingdom. You are afraid of change. Take this thing with the Magi. Why can they not live among you peacefully? Thalia is as magnificent as it is because of the Magi. My-own-sister in law is one."

"Is she?" I'd met the daughter-in-law of the king and queen of Thalia once. I'd not known she was a Mage. What must she have thought of us using them to do slave work around the palace?

"What would you do to change things?" I was fascinated now. This was the first conversation I'd had about changing things. It was long overdue.

"Acceptance."

"Acceptance?"

"Yes. As a ruler, I'd lead by example. I'd invite Magi to the palace, not as people to be hidden away to do the menial chores, but as friends. I'd change laws so that everyone was an equal, and no one would have to hide. The Magi would be allowed to go to university and get jobs and wouldn't be treated in the disgusting way that I've seen since being here."

I never thought I'd agree with Luca on anything, but he was right. He mistook my silence for disagreement.

"I'm sorry, Princess Charmaine, if I have offended you, but I would not be able to live in a kingdom that did not respect its subjects. I like you a lot, and I think you and I could be happy together, but if we disagree on such a fundamental topic, then I'm afraid, I will have to step down from this contest."

He turned to leave. Letting him go would make my life so much easier, and yet, I found myself running after him.

"Please, don't go." I hesitated for a moment. "I want you to stay."

And I did. He looked at me curiously. Light flashed in his eyes as he smiled. No wonder a million women wanted him. I felt my knees go weak just looking at him.

"Many people would say that giving Magi the same power as us would be dangerous. What do you think?"

"What do you think Princess?"

"I think that the Magi are just like us. They are just people who happen to know how to use a magic wand. They want the same as us, to be able to feed and clothe their children, to be able to work without fear."

"And what do you think of me?" He was so close to me now. His voice had lowered into a growl. It was intoxicating. Like countless women before me, I was beginning to fall for his charms. It was so annoying. Only a couple of hours before I'd had him at the bottom of the list and here I was being won over by him.

"I like you."

He answered me with a kiss. His rough lips took me by surprise and with a force that almost knocked me off my feet. I wanted to stop him, and yet, I found I couldn't. What was I doing? Somewhere to our right, a camera flashed. I pushed him away, feeling horrified at what had just happened.

"Fucking Paparazzi," Luca growled, pulling away from me and running to the garden wall. At the other side, I heard the sound of a ladder being taken down and someone running away.

I stood there in shock. I'd kissed Luca. I wasn't even sure I liked him. Just an hour ago, I was ready to send him home tomorrow, and now there would be a photo of us kissing on the front cover of the newspapers. My parents would see it. Cynder would see it. Cynder, whom I'd fallen head over heels in love with would read the newspaper and hate me. I wouldn't even blame him.

I turned on my heels and ran back into the house as confused as ever. Ignoring the looks of the staff as I raced past, I ran straight up to my room and threw myself on the bed.

What had I done? The chain around my wrist dug into the flesh, and I let it. I deserved the pain. Cynder had trusted me in a way no one else had, and I'd completely failed him. I felt my heart break in two remembering the last words he said to me. *You're all I have.*

"Whatever is the matter, child?"

I turned to see Jenny in my room. I don't know how long she'd been standing there, but upon seeing her, I launched myself into her arms.

"Elise said she heard you crying and came to get me, but I could hear you all along the corridor."

"I'm sorry."

"Stop being sorry and tell me the problem."

Always the mother hen. I'd never been more grateful for her.

"I kissed Luca."

"Luca? The prince? Well, well. I can't say I'm surprised. He's a very attractive young man. I certainly wouldn't be crying about such a thing."

I couldn't tell her about Cynder. About how it would break him. About how it had already broken me. She wouldn't understand.

"Someone took our photo. They used a ladder to climb up the perimeter wall and took the photo as we kissed."

"Ah. This does pose a bit of a problem unless you plan on picking him out of the four." She regarded me with such intensity; it was almost as if she could see right into my soul.

"I don't know. I hadn't planned on kissing him. Before our date, I was planning on sending him home tomorrow."

"I see. Well, it seems like you have a lot of thinking to do tonight because your father and the public will expect a name. The press has already erected a stage out front for the loser to be interviewed, and they are expecting crowds. About the photograph. I'll speak to your father and see if we can keep it out of the papers."

"Would you?"

"I'm not promising anything, but I'll try."

I wrapped my arms around her. "Thank you!"

"My pleasure, now get some sleep. You'll need to look your best for the TV cameras tomorrow. No one wants to see a soggy princess."

I lay on my bed, grateful for having someone so wonderful as her for my nanny.

My eyes had only just closed when my other door flung open, and Elise came rushing in.

She jumped on the bed with a big grin on her face.

"I was listening in through the keyhole. You kissed Prince Luca!"

She bounced on the bed, full of her usual enthusiasm. Not for the first time, I wished I had the energy she had.

"I did."

"Does that mean you are going to marry him? Who are you sending home? Daniel? Xavier?"

"It was kind of an accidental kiss."

"How do you kiss someone accidentally? What was it like?"

I wanted to tell her that it was horrible, that I hated every second, but it would have been a lie. However much I wanted to dislike the guy, something about tonight had changed my mind. The kiss was only part of it.

"It was nice," I conceded. Yes, there were better words to use, hot, unsettling, delicious, or confusing, to name but four. For now, until I was ready to decide how I felt, 'nice' would have to do.

That night I thought about the four men, one of whom I'd have to send home. There was Daniel who made me laugh, Leo who was the knight in shining armor, and Xavier who was a beautiful enigma, and finally Luca, the boy who kissed me.

Who would I send home? Four beautiful men. Four men who wanted to marry me.

I tried a mental pros and cons list for each, and when that didn't help, I imagined them standing by my side as I repeated age-old vows at our wedding. The only face I could picture as I closed my eyes was Cynder's.

The Choice

Xavi was uncharacteristically flapping around me as I was dressed for the cameras. Jenny had been up to my room and prepped me on the running order of the day. After getting dressed for the public, I was to give the name of the man I'd chosen to formally eliminate to my father. Thankfully, this was to be done in private and not out at the front of the palace like some bad game show. Unfortunately, that's where the dissimilarities to game shows ended. Once the decision had been broadcast, the men would have to go out on stage and be interviewed by Sadie. The loser would get the longest interview, and then I'd have to come out on stage and say lots of nice things about him and how sorry I was to see him go.

I'd already mentally prepared my speech, making it as generic as possible and leaving the most important detail out completely. The name of the guy I was choosing.

I read my speech to myself on the cue cards I'd prepared as a tiara was fitted onto my hair. In ten minutes, I would have to come up with a decision, and I still didn't know who to choose. Everyone else had an opinion, just not me.

Elise favored me marrying Luca because of the kiss, and Jenny wanted Daniel to stay because he was her friend's son. I wished yesterday had never happened because I was quite happy to see the back of Luca until he told me his plans for the future. I tried to pretend to myself that the kiss had nothing to do with it.

The walk down to my father's office seemed to take a thousand years, and yet, it was over in a minute. Elise was waiting for me outside his door, desperate to find out who I was going to pick. How could I tell her I still didn't know?

I knocked on the door and waited for my father to let me in. In my head, the four men fought a battle. As the door opened and my father ushered me in, I could see there was only one choice. It was not the choice I had anticipated.

"Do you have a name?" my father asked, shutting the door behind me. I knew Elise would be trying to listen from the other side.

"Yes, Father. I've been on a date with each of these men, and I think I've chosen the best one to leave."

My father scratched his chin and looked at me warily. "Before you give me a name, I want you to think about the implications for our kingdom."

"I believe I have, Father."

"Have you indeed? I'm not so sure you were thinking about the implications when you allowed yourself to be photographed kissing one of the young men last night."

I squirmed under his glare. "It was an accident."

"Hmm. Can I assume there will be no more accidents?"

It felt like I was three again and getting chastised for breaking something. "Yes, Father."

I knew he wasn't bothered about who I did or didn't kiss; he only cared about who saw me.

"So, do you have a name?"

"Xavier." I said it firmly. Yes, he was exceptionally good-looking, and there was something about him that was magnetic, and yet I'd spent the least amount of time with him, and apart from his glorious, muscular body, I had nothing really to say about him.

"I was hoping you'd pick someone else."

This was news to me. I knew that my father had put Xavier into the mix in the first place, but I had thought that it was because I was dithering over choosing four men.

"I'd like to get to know the others more. I don't really have anything in common with Xavier."

"You both like swimming, don't you?"

I sighed. "It's not enough for a lasting union, Father."

I thought that was the end of it, so I was surprised when he spoke again.

"Xavier stays. Pick another." His tone was forceful.

"Why do you want Xavier to stay?" I asked, and as soon as I had, I wished I hadn't. His face clouded over.

"Don't question me. I've made a decision. Pick one of the other men, or I'll do it for you."

I'd seen my father angry on many occasions, but nothing like this. As far as I was aware, my father barely knew Xavier, so why did he want him to stay? This was supposed to be my choice. I'd only agreed to it because I had the final say in who I picked, and yet, things were changing. I was no longer in control. Arguing with my father was impossible. I'd just have to pick one of the others, but who?

"I don't know," I replied angrily. "This was supposed to be my choice!" I felt tears spring to my eyes. I wasn't crying over the men who would stay or the one that would leave, but the fact that my own future no longer belonged to me.

"There, there now, don't cry." My father's tone changed dramatically to one of concern. "I'll tell the press that you are keeping all of them until after the next date. We should have had five at this point anyway."

I didn't really care anymore, but I nodded my head anyway.

As he left to tell the press and the public the news, I realized I should have just picked someone. The quicker I got rid of the men, the sooner this would all be over and done with.

Xavi stared at me in horror when I got to the backstage area.

"What have you done?" She picked up a mirror and showed me the mess the tears had made of my makeup. Black lines of mascara streaked my face, and my eyes were blotchy.

"For goodness sake, can someone find Louis?" She cried in panic. With only five minutes to go until I was called to the stage, I could understand why she was acting the way she was. Personally, I'd have been happy to show the world the truth about how miserable I felt, but I could only imagine my father's wrath if I tried it.

I listened to the interview of Daniel, the last to speak to Sadie as everyone dashed around me in a panic.

He had the public and Sadie in stitches over some story about his childhood. I felt my heart lifting as I listened to his story of himself as a boy. Of the four men, he was the most real and if I was honest, the one I felt most comfortable with. How easy would it have been if I wasn't a princess, and we'd just met in the village square one day? I allowed myself a small daydream, but then Louis was there, powdering my face with vigor and scrunching his own up in concentration. He'd just reapplied my smudged lipstick when I heard Sadie calling me to the stage. With my head held high, I swallowed my nerves and climbed up to the stage to the most riotous applause I'd ever heard. In front of me, thousands of people filled the palace driveway. The crowd stretched out right to the palace borders and beyond. It was rare for the public to be let in, in such numbers but today was the second time in two months, the last being Grace's funeral. I noticed that metal fences had been erected close to the palace, and the number of guards had trebled in light of the attack at the ball.

Sadie stood to welcome me. The four men were still on stage on a long sofa, and as I approached them to sit at the end, they staged a pretend shoving contest so they could be the one to sit next to me, much to the hilarity of the audience. In the end, I sat right in the middle between Luca and Daniel. Sadie grinned at the horseplay.

"It seems they like you," she began as the noise from the crowd died down.

"I guess so. I'm a very lucky lady."

"You are the princess to be envied right now," agreed Sadie. So tell me, why didn't you make a choice between these four gorgeous men today?"

Because I wasn't allowed! I wanted to say it, but instead, I turned to the audience.

"Would you be able to choose between these four men, ladies?"

A roar came up from the crowd as thousands of women screamed. I looked out and saw banners being held in the air, sporting such phrases as "Do me, Daniel" and "Let me be your princess, Luca." There were about an even number for each man, so I guess the crowd was as split as I was.

"I couldn't either," admitted Sadie, "although I'd like to be in your position to try. How have the dates been going? Any kissing yet?"

I could feel my cheeks redden. Had someone told her or was she just reaching?

"Not yet," I lied. Not only did I not want the public to know, I also didn't want Cynder to either. I had no way of knowing if he was watching this. I fingered the charm bracelet nervously. It was turning into quite a habit.

"Well, I hope you make your mind up soon because your wedding is approaching fast. The queen mentioned a date has been tentatively booked for September the twenty-sixth, which gives you just over four months to whittle these four beautiful men down to one. The next elimination is in a month which means one of these delicious specimens will be free for the rest of us, and I personally can't wait."

There was another roar from the audience. Sadie really knew what she was doing. I could see my mother beaming out in the wings. She gobbled up this talk show vibe.

"Could you give us any hints as to who you might pick next?"

"It has been such a difficult decision, so much so that I haven't made it yet. They are all such wonderful people, and I don't want to make any mistakes. I have to think about my country to which I have a responsibility, as well as to myself. As you have so rightly pointed out, they are all very attractive young men, and beyond that, they are wonderful people, each with his own special attributes. Whoever I choose, it's not going to be an easy decision to make."

"I'd like to see some of those attributes." She winked at the audience, "but unfortunately we are out of time. Tune in next week when we resume the catch-ups for each royal date."

The lights on the cameras went off, and I was led off stage by a member of the crew. My mother hugged me as I passed.

"You did brilliantly," she smiled. I smiled back, but unlike hers, mine did not reach my eyes. It was still only morning, and I was already exhausted. The wedding was five months away. Less, really. In four and a half months, I would be walking down the aisle and pledging my life to one of the men on the couch. Right now, I didn't even want to see any of them. I wanted to be alone. I headed back to my room and stripped off the tiara and expensive dress, throwing them in a pile on the floor. Xavi would be horrified if she knew, but, hopefully, Agatha would pick them up and sort them out for me.

I ran to the shower, knowing it was one of the few places in the palace I could truly be alone, and spent a good hour in there until my fingertips wrinkled.

The only good thing about today was that I had a day off from my duties. Now that the show was over, I could do with my day as I wished. There were no dates and no interviews. I decided to spend it at the library. It had been such a huge part of my life before all the madness, and now I realized, I'd not been in there since the day Grace died.

I dressed in simple cotton pants and a shirt that I found in my wardrobe and headed to the vast room that I once considered home.

The library took up two floors with wooden staircases spiraling up to a balcony.

I loved it in here. The smell of the leather bound volumes never failed to make me feel at peace. I'd not read every book in here—that would be impossible; there were just so many of them, but I'd certainly read a lot. I wandered through the rows of books, fingering the spines as I went, hoping to find a treasure I'd not yet read. I was walking down the extensive fiction section, looking for an escape from my own reality when a thought struck me. I didn't know the history of the Magi. It was not something that had been taught to me in all my years of schooling. If there was a book on them, it would surely be here.

I ran up one of the spiral staircases to the second floor where the nonfiction was kept. I knew exactly where the history books were, I'd had to retrieve one for my tutor on many occasions when he was teaching me the history of royalty in Silverwood which was essentially my own family tree.

I perused the shelves, looking for anything that might have the Magi in it, but all I could find was a thick tome, which covered the whole history of Silverwood. I carried it downstairs and sat in one of the winged chairs designed for reading. I was checking the appendix when I heard a noise behind me.

It was Elise. I don't know who was more surprised, her or me.

"Hey," I waved at her. "It's not like you to be in here." And it wasn't. In all the time I'd spent reading in the library, I'd only ever seen her in here when she was forced to be by our tutor.

"I was just looking for a book."

"Well, you've come to the right place. Do you need help finding one?"

"Actually, I'm not that interested. I think I'll go for a walk instead." And with that, she was gone. Very mysterious!

I found what I was looking for and flipped to the correct page. The Magi were only described briefly as being immigrants to Silverwood, first appearing about two hundred years ago from places such as Thalia and Laidys. No wonder Thalia was ok with them. That's where they originated. Apparently, their magical powers were first brought to light when weird things kept happening in a small mountain village between the kingdoms of Thalia and Laidys. The villagers blamed the spring that erupted near the village. After a while, they realized that they could control their powers, and thus, the Magi were founded. Every Magi has a history that traces from that one village, but non-Magi who travel there and drink the spring water cannot replicate the Magi's powers. It was thought that there were only about a hundred and fifty Magi originally, but these numbers increased over the generations, and the magic was passed down from father to son, from mother to daughter. Eventually, they spread out into the world, and some settled in Silverwood. Right from the start, they were considered outlaws, with the royalty trying to send them back on a number of occasions. Eventually, they were just a part of everyday life, no longer illegal, but considered beneath everyone else and living on the fringes of society. I was surprised to learn that it was only in the time of my grandfather's reign that they were allowed to get jobs. Maybe my father wanted to go back to a time before that.

I closed the book and sighed. The Magi had always had it hard. How could I change a century and a half of mistrust by myself? I thought back to what Luca had said about wanting to change things. Maybe, with him by my side, we could finally change things for the better.

I heard the door open behind me. Thinking Elise had changed her mind about the book, I didn't bother to turn.

A pair of warm hands covered my eyes.

"Is that you, Elise?"

The hands withdrew quickly. "It's me. I came looking for you."

Leo came around the front of my chair and sat opposite me. "I saw that you were upset this morning, and I wanted to see if you were alright."

He'd noticed? "I thought Louis; my make-up artist had covered all that up? Was it really bad?" The thought of being on TV in front of hundreds of thousands of people with a blotchy face left me feeling embarrassed.

"No, you looked perfectly stunning. I'm just more perceptive than most."

"It's nothing, really. Just a little stage fright." He didn't have to know the truth.

"I have to admit I was surprised you didn't pick someone to leave. If I may be so bold, you really don't seem into this whole thing."

"I'm not. I'm sorry. I feel bad for saying it, but how am I supposed to pick from four strangers, knowing that if I make the wrong decision, I have to live with it for the rest of my life?"

He came over and hugged me. What is it with these men? They were all so perfect. How could I complain when any one of them would be a good choice?

"I'm not taking it personally. In your position, I'd hide in my room and lock the door."

"I'm sorely tempted."

"I just want you to know that if you didn't choose one of us to spare our feelings, you shouldn't worry. We are all grown-ups, and we all know what we signed up for. I will not hold it against you if you pick me to leave first."

"Are you hinting that you want to leave?" I smiled through my tears.

"No, not at all. I feel very honored to be here, and I don't want to go. I just don't want you feeling the way you do."

"That's not really it, but thank you."

He really was a nice guy, and I could see he would make a good prince and husband. I thought back to our trip out into Silverwood.

225

He and Prince Luca had a lot in common. I wondered if they talked much or if the men avoided each other? Apart from the occasions that called for them to be together such as today, I'd never seen them in the same room.

"What are you reading?" Leo nodded at the book in my hands.

"I was looking for a book about the Magi, but I could only find this. It doesn't say much."

"I bet it doesn't. You'll not find what you are looking for in here, but I might have something that would interest you. I'll see if I can find it. Just don't let anyone catch you with it, or I might be in trouble."

All afternoon, I considered his words. Why would he be in trouble over a book? I waited for him to bring it to me, but it was only as Agatha was helping me dress for bed that Elise came in with it tied in brown paper and string.

"Leo asked me to give this to you. What is it?" Her usual curiosity shone through, but I couldn't tell her the truth. I'd made a promise to Leo.

"I asked Leo for a book about gardening. Apparently, he is a keen gardener," I improvised. "It must be that."

"Is he?" she asked in surprise. "I wonder why he's never told me that."

When both she and Agatha had left for the night, I unwrapped the book and began to read.

The Wedding Plans

and the Newspaper

I decided to give myself a few days off from the madness. I wanted to read the book that Leo had given me in peace and just clear my brain from everything that had been happening to me. The last few weeks had been a whirlwind, and I needed a breather. I spent the first couple of days out in the garden, ignoring the world and trying to ignore the builders that were still working on the palace wall.

I'd just gotten to the point where I'd all but blocked out my situation when a white peacock walked past me on the lawn. I turned and saw three more, just strolling about as if it was the most natural thing in the world. It wasn't so much the peacocks that bothered me, although I did find it strange that they were there. It was the truck full of boxes that were being delivered up to the house that had me on edge.

"Mother?" I shouted, knowing that she had something to do with it. I found her signing a document for one of the deliverymen. Next to the boxes were reams of white satin and silk. They filled the entrance hall. As if by magic, a dozen or so members of the palace staff appeared and started to carry the boxes away. One picked up the top ream of satin.

"That needs to go to Xavi in the dressing room," mother said when she noticed what he was holding.

"What's going on?"

"I'm getting ready for the wedding. I know it's a few months away, but these things take a lot of preparation."

"The wedding?" Ok, I'd known it was happening, but I'd managed to file it into a vague time in the future in my mind. Seeing all the white in front of me turned it into reality. A reality I wasn't ready for.

"Yes. I've chosen white as the main color for your dress, but Xavi tells me that you can add some color to it if you want. Just let's keep it pretty neutral. I've ordered some cakes so we can do a cake tasting next week although I'm thinking at least ten tiers so we can mix and match the flavors. What do you think?"

"Ok," I answered bleakly. How could I choose a wedding cake flavor when I couldn't even choose a groom?

***

There wasn't a day that went by without me thinking of Cynder, but without any means of communication with him, I had no way of finding out if he was ok. I checked the papers meticulously every day for news of the palace bomber, but it seemed the only thing anyone wanted to know about was who I'd choose to marry. Three weeks passed in a blur as I went on date after date and was subjected to interview after interview. Sadie was beginning to get impatient with the lack of gossip, and as I'd not kissed anyone since Luca, I really didn't have much to say to her.

It was the third week since the last elimination and one week until the next when something in the paper caught my eye. As usual, the paper was full of the same speculation as every day. Old school friends and past acquaintances of the four men were coming out of the woodwork to give interviews and, as always, there was the obligatory poll with the public deciding on a daily basis who they liked best. I noted that Leo had taken the lead with Prince Luca slipping into a close second. Xavier was next and then with a long drop between them, Daniel. I couldn't understand it. Daniel was probably my favorite, and he always did well in the interviews. But although he was gorgeous, he didn't have the dangerously good looks of Xavier, the Royal title of Luca nor the philanthropic history of Leo. In short, he was just a regular boy next door, and according to the paper, that made him boring. In reality, he was probably the least boring of the four, but since when had the newspapers dealt in reality? I was just about to throw the paper to one side in disgust when I noticed something I'd not seen before. It was a small advertisement, hidden between all the other adverts in the middle of the paper. It would have been so easy to miss, and I had almost missed it. It was a photo of a charm bracelet identical to the one Cynder had given me. Above it were the words A CHARM FOR ALL OCCASIONS. I read the copy beneath.

Tell her you love her with this beautiful charm bracelet. A lucky charm for your Lucky Charm.

There was no number or address listed as a contact, but I knew it was him. He'd said those exact words to me. It was no coincidence that the last words were capitalized. He was talking about me. This was his way of telling me he'd escaped and he was alright. I pulled out all the old copies of the newspapers that I'd stashed under my bed and flicked through them all. This advert had run every day since I'd last seen Cynder. He'd been trying to talk to me this whole time, and I'd not noticed.

I scrabbled around in a drawer for a pen and piece of paper. I was going to reply.

SAY I LOVE YOU WITH PRINCESS CHARMS

When he gives you a charm, tell him you love him.

Ok, it was feeble, but it could pass as an advert. If anyone saw it, they'd think it was a rival company to Cynder's ad. Maybe even the same company. To Cynder, it would tell him that I love him and that I knew he was alright. There was so much more I wanted to say, but those were the only words I had. I put the paper in an envelope, being careful to pick one without the royal crest, and handed it to Agatha along with some money to cover it.

I made her promise not to tell anyone she was putting the advert in the paper on my behalf.

The next morning she was gone. As were the rest of the Magi. There was no point crying over it. We both had known it was coming and had already said our goodbyes. I'd given her enough clothes to sell to make a bit of money to travel to her family, and, from there, I prayed she'd be ok.

The day she left was miserable. I didn't know if I'd ever see her again. I vowed to myself that when I became queen, things would change. Agatha would come back to the palace, as would the others. That night, when I opened the paper, I saw my advert. The small ad, comprised of just a few words was completely drowned by the snazzy ads with photos, but it was there. I only hoped Cynder would see it.

***

Between the dates and interviews, I read Leo's book. It was short, only about fifty pages, but I scoured it time and time again. It contained the true history of Magi in Silverwood, and how they had been persecuted through the ages.

They were still being used as slaves as late as during my grandfather's reign. Apparently, my grandfather owned over a thousand, all of whom worked in the palace. Things changed drastically when he was in his fifties when he had a drastic change of heart and started to pay the staff. They went from living in dormitories with no running water to having their own quarters within the palace for those who wanted them. Life improved on the outside of the palace too with the abolition of slavery of Magi happening around this time. This had continued until my grandfather's death the year before I was born. Apparently, upon the death of my grandfather, things immediately began to get worse for the Magi again although it never deteriorated into how terrible it was before slavery had been abolished.

In all my years of learning the history of Silverwood, I'd never known anything about any of this. How could I not have been taught such a large part of my own history?

I wanted to speak to Cynder so badly to see if he knew about this, but I couldn't. I couldn't ask anyone else as I'd have to tell them how I knew. The only person I could think to ask was Leo, but I couldn't find him anywhere. None of the staff had seen him. I decided to walk out to the bungalows where he was staying. There were four bungalows reserved for guests in the grounds. Leo, Luca, and Xavier had one each. The third one had been reserved for Alexander, but as he'd not stayed, it was currently standing empty. Daniel still lived in town with his father.

I'd not been to visit any of the men here. For some reason, it felt intrusive. Also, I didn't want the paparazzi getting any shots of me going into the men's private quarters. I scoured the garden wall, looking for paparazzi but apart from the guards at the bottom of the wall, there was no one to see. Feeling confident that I wasn't being watched, I knocked on the second bungalow's door. Luca was in the first bungalow and Xavier in the third.

I waited for a minute before knocking again, but there was no answer. As I'd scoured the whole palace and garden, I concluded that he must have left the grounds for the day, although the doorman had not seen him leave. It was feasible that he'd decided to go out the back door, and I'd just decided to go and ask the guards at the back gate if they'd seen him when I noticed movement in the window of the supposedly empty bungalow.

Cynder!

It was my first thought. What if he'd managed to sneak in, and he'd been hiding here all this time? Maybe he just couldn't find a way to get into the main part of the palace to see me.

I ran over, once again checking that no one could see me. The way this bungalow was positioned meant that not even the guards were in sight. It was the perfect hiding place for Cynder, and I don't know why I'd not thought of it before. There was no point in knocking on the door. He wasn't going to answer, so instead, I tiptoed round to the front window.

There was someone in there! I was about to knock on the window before realizing he wasn't alone. There was someone with him, and he was kissing her. My heart caught in my throat as I ducked out of view. What was going on? Why would Cynder come all the way back here and chance being caught, only to kiss someone else?

I peeked back in which is when I got my next shock. Actually two shocks. The girl was Elise, and the guy I thought was Cynder wasn't him at all. It was Leo!

The Betrayal

"I'm sorry, I'm sorry, I'm sorry," Elise repeated over and over again. They'd seen me loitering outside and had pulled me in. Elise was in tears. I could see that Leo wanted to comfort her, but in the current situation, he couldn't. Remorse filled both their faces as they both realized the enormity of what they had done.

I sat on an old-fashioned armchair, while they sat back on the sofa I'd seen them making out on, only this time, they sat at opposite sides, putting as much distance between them as possible.

I looked around the small guest house, not quite knowing how to react. A spot of wallpaper was coming off in the corner of the room, and it needed a new coat of paint. It's funny what my mind went to in the situation. I didn't know how to think, how to react.

No one spoke although I could hear Elise quietly sobbing and whispering "I'm sorry" under her breath.

I wanted to go over to her and hug her and tell her everything would be ok like I always had when she was upset, but I couldn't—not this time. I wasn't sure everything was ok. I took a deep breath and followed it up with a few more.

My sister had betrayed me in the worst possible way, and yet, when I searched my soul, I found I didn't mind. There was no sting in my heart when I saw them kissing. My heart was filled with too much pain at losing Cynder to fit any more in there. As I took emotion out of the equation, I realized, she'd not really betrayed me at all. Ok, she'd not been honest with me which hurt; but I was not betrothed to Leo, nor had I told her I had any interest in him romantically. In fact, on the few occasions we had spoken about my four suitors, I'd been nothing but ambivalent about them. I didn't love Leo, and he didn't love me, and Elise knew that. Sure, I enjoyed his company, but romance wasn't in the cards for us. I wasn't even sure it was in the cards for me at all.

"When were you going to tell me?" I was addressing the question to Elise, but Leo answered.

"We weren't deliberately keeping anything from you; it's just that we weren't..."

"Telling me?"

"How could we?" whispered Elise through her tears. "I didn't do it on purpose. I just fell in love with him."

And there it was. "You're in love?"

Leo stood up and came over to me.

"I'm in love with your sister. I have been since the first moment I saw her. Neither of us planned it. How can you plan a thing as perfect as love between two people?"

I wanted to hate him, to hate both of them, but I couldn't. I felt the same way about Cynder. I loved him in a way I couldn't even have imagined was possible just a few months ago. Just thinking about him left me breathless. If Leo and Elise felt the same way about each other—if they felt only a fraction of the sweet pain I did when being away from Cynder, then what right did I have to stand in their way? Or to make them feel bad about it. I'd not chosen to fall in love with Cynder, it happened so suddenly. Any anger I felt melted away.

"Please stop. You are going to make me barf. I don't mind that you two are in love." And I found that it was true. I'd been shocked at seeing them together, but beyond that, I hadn't felt any particular emotion. My heart didn't lurch every time I saw Leo the way it did with Cynder. In fact, when I thought about it, there was only relief. Relief that I had one less man to choose from, one less man to have to worry about eliminating.

"I'm happy for you," I conceded, and I was.

"You are?" Elise looked up at me through those perfect green eyes of hers. How could I be mad at her? Hadn't I done exactly the same thing? Fallen in love with someone I shouldn't have. I thought of Cynder again. He was never far from my thoughts. Wouldn't I sneak around the palace to see him? Of course, I would. I'd already proved I would by sneaking outside the palace grounds to see him.

"I don't love Leo, and I never have. I don't love any of the men. I was hoping to fall in love with one of them, but it's not happening for me. I'll tell my father that I want him eliminated in the next round. You'll have to lay low for a bit, but when this all blows over, you can announce yourself as a couple. I expect people will think it's romantic. Sadie will love it. More gossip for her TV show."

"I love you!" Elise sprang up and threw her arms around me. I hugged her tightly, glad that at least one of us was happy.

"There's just one thing," she began after untangling herself from me. "I don't want Leo eliminated. If he left the palace, I'd never see him."

It was true. There was only one way I knew to sneak out of the palace, and that was with Leo's help from the inside. If he was on the outside, there was no chance.

"If you wait until after the wedding, people will be so happy, they won't care who you date."

"That's four months away!"

"It's fine, Elise," said Leo finally going over to her. "We still have until the next elimination together. After that, the time will fly by until we can next be together."

I watched how relaxed she was in his arms. My flighty joyful sister had almost melted into him. I didn't think I'd ever seen her so still. It occurred to me how good they looked together. The love in their eyes was unmistakable, and just being in the same room as them made me feel like a gooseberry. My list of four men had now gone down to three.

"Fine. I'll keep him in this round." What with my father keeping in Xavier and now Elise making me keep in Leo, this competition was looking like I had no say in it at all.

Leo came over to me and hugged me too. Damnit. Why did he smell so good? I could totally see why Elise was in love with him.

"You know, I should have guessed. Every time I came looking for you Leo, you were with Elise. That time in the library?"

Elise looked uncomfortable. "We used to meet in the library, but when we saw you there, we knew we had to find somewhere else."

"So you weren't coming to see if I was ok after all?" I teased Leo.

"I'm sorry, no. I was looking for Elise, but I knew something was wrong. You looked so distant."

"Everything *is* wrong." I thought back to the book about the Magi and how Leo had trusted me in the past. "Listen, you are asking me to keep a big secret. Can I ask that you do something to help me?"

"Sure! Anything!" Elise was back to her exuberant self. In fact, she looked lovelier than ever despite her red eyes from crying. No wonder Leo fell in love with her.

"Actually, it's Leo I need help from. I've read your book. In fact, I was looking for you to return it." I handed the well-read book back to Leo.

"Did you see anything of interest?"

"I did, and that's what I want your help with. What happened to make my grandfather change his mind about the Magi?"

"No one really knows. As you have seen yourself, there is little documentation about the Magi. You won't find anything about them in any library in Silverwood. History books barely mention them, and books of spells and anything associated with them were banned long ago."

"But you know, don't you?"

Leo looked at me intently. He was searching my eyes to see if he could trust me further. He must have decided he could. He took a deep breath and began to talk. "I only know the rumors. Everything I'm about to tell you is hearsay."

"Go on."

"There are rumors that your grandfather had an affair with one of the Magi. He brought the Magi into the palace and put them in private rooms as a way to carry on the affair. After that, he had to tell people that he'd started paying them. Maybe his lover had talked him into it?"

It amazed me how little knowledge of my own past I had. "What happened to her?"

"None of the Magi were ever really documented. Even when they became legal, they had no real proof of who they were. It has been assumed that the Magi was your grandmother's maid, Molly. She died a few years after your grandfather and kept the secret to her grave. As I said, no one knows if it's really true or not, but it does explain the change of heart."

"How do you know all this?" asked Elise, open-mouthed.

"I don't for sure. I've only heard what people tell me when I go out and feed them."

I suddenly had an idea. I'd seen for myself what it was like for the Magi; Elise hadn't. Maybe it was about time she got an education. It would mean she could spend more time with Leo too. "Why don't you go out with him?"

"I couldn't do that. Father let you, but he wouldn't let me."

"I'll tell him I'm going. Make sure to wear something with a hood. No one will know it's you and not me."

"You'd do that for me?"

"I'd do anything for you, Elise, just do me a favor."

"What?"

"Don't get caught!"

That night Elise came to my room to thank me again. I hugged her tightly as she lay down next to me on the bed.

"I meant it when I said I was happy for you."

"I know you did. I couldn't wish for a better big sister." She sighed. "I really didn't mean to hurt you. I didn't even know I was falling for him until it was too late. Every day I've been worried about you. You've looked so sad throughout this competition, and I was worried that I might be taking your one chance at happiness. I was scared that, despite everything you said, you might be in love with Leo too. Especially when you went out with him that night. Part of me hoped you'd come back and tell me you were choosing to marry him and then I could try and forget about him, but a much bigger part died at the thought of it. I cried all night until Leo came back and told me you'd barely spent any time together. That you'd gone off on your own. It was like a huge weight lifted from my heart. I thought if you loved him, you'd want to be with him."

"I never loved Leo. I didn't lie about that."

"You don't love any of them, do you?"

I thought of the three remaining men. "No, I don't."

"Do you think you could learn to love one of them given time?"

I wanted to tell her about Cynder. About how I didn't think it was possible I'd ever love anyone else as much, but I didn't.

"I don't know."

When she'd gone, I pondered the question. The truth was, I'd probably never see Cynder again. He'd escaped, and even if they found out who did plant the bomb, there was still no life for him here now. My mother had invited no Magi to the party for a reason. No member of royalty could ever marry a Mage. It just couldn't happen. I had to pick one of the three remaining men and hope that one day I'd fall in love with him. I had a feeling it would be a long time coming.

Xavier

Since we had passed the first elimination, even though there really hadn't been one, scheduling dates had been slightly more relaxed. This was partly due to my mother taking up all my time on wedding preparations. It didn't seem to matter to her that I was no closer to finding a groom, as long as the table centers were just so. We spent one morning, along with Elise and the four men, tasting cakes. As mother wanted ten tiers, we had a lot to go through. Hundreds of cakes had been laid out in the breakfast room, each delicately labeled with its flavor. I saw everything from passion fruit to red velvet, each decorated in a different style. I watched the men as they tasted cake after cake. Leo looked completely at ease, comparing notes with my mother. Elise kept apart from him, instead choosing to chat to Prince Luca and Xavier while Daniel and I squabbled playfully over the best chocolate flavor. Sadie and her cameraman, Martin, captured the whole thing.

From the outside, it looked like we were all having fun. Inside, the reality was different. I'd enjoyed the cake tasting, but the hours of going through different fabrics and color schemes and songs for the wedding left me drained. It was going to be the biggest occasion that Silverwood had ever seen, and yet, there was only a reluctant bride and still no groom with less than three months to go.

In between cake tastings and bridesmaid fashion shows, I had a bit of time to myself. I spent most of it pouring over past newspapers to find out any more information, but I saw nothing else. The case of the bomber had almost disappeared, with only the occasional snippet that the perpetrator still hadn't been found. As the police thought it was Cynder, no one was looking for the real bomber, and as he hadn't been caught, there was nothing much to say. It gave me a little relief, and yet, the propaganda against the Magi grew every day. Each time I opened the current paper, my heart would sink after finding some news article about how some Mage or other had committed a crime. One had a whole page devoted to all the crimes that had been committed in the capital in the last month by Magi. It sounded bad until I read the list of crimes. Stealing bread, breaking into a deli, wand usage. They were starving. Stealing or magic was the only means they had left to get food. These so-called "horrific crimes" gave the police more excuse to make them leave the city. I thought of all the cake we had wasted and hoped that Leo had been able to take some of it out on one of his trips into the city. It was madness that people were starving when Silverwood had an abundance of food. The only good thing to come from looking at the papers was knowing Cynder was free. I knew I should have been happy, but it just meant he was further away. My heart felt a little heavier every day.

After a few weeks of doing very little and with the wedding-without-a-groom looming, even my mother was beginning to panic. She wanted to sort out the groom's attire, but with four men still in the game, it was she that decided I had to schedule final dates with the men to come to a decision. The wedding was now less than three months away, and my mother's panic was catching.

With Leo out of the equation, my first thought was Daniel. If nothing else, he was guaranteed to make me laugh, something I sorely needed, but my curiosity about Xavier and the link to my father overcame me.

I sent one of the guards down to his bungalow with a note to meet me in the garden.

Just ten minutes later he showed up wearing only a pair of jeans. Why was it that every time I saw him, he was practically naked? The guy had chiseled abs and liked to show them off.

"Did I catch you coming out of the shower?" I inquired irritably. He was too good looking for his own good, but if any photographer was to catch me with him dressed like this, it would make front-page news. I'd have to explain to my father how I had been caught in a delicate position for a second time. I wondered if that would be enough to have my father let me eliminate him. I scoured the wall, but this time there were no paparazzi to be seen.

"No. Why?"

What was it my father saw in this guy? I knew why half the women in Silverwood drooled over him, but I couldn't see my father drooling over men's body type.

"Never mind," I answered dryly. I sat on the scorched-by-the-sun grass and patted the ground beside me. Trying to ignore his chest, I deliberately kept my eyes on his. I was interested to see that he couldn't hold my gaze. "Did you know my father before you came here?"

"Yes, of course. He is the king. Everyone knows him."

Why did I get the feeling he was evading my question? I tried again.

"I don't mean know of him. I mean had you actually met him?"

His eyes went to mine for a brief second before looking back to the grass. A sure sign a lie was imminent. "No, I had not had the pleasure. Of course, I have met him since. He is a very good man and a great ruler."

His answer was generic and bland. Now I knew why he kept his body so beautiful. It was all he had. I tried to remember a decent conversation I'd had with him and found I couldn't recall one. I'd thought him mysterious, when in reality, he was dull. Still, he was hiding something. I just needed to find out what

"What made you decide to enter this competition?"

He moved forward and gazed into my eyes. A month ago, it would have made me melt, but now all I saw were my own suspicions.

"I entered because I thought you were the most beautiful woman I'd ever laid eyes on. I thought that maybe I could be the one to stand by your side forever if you let me love you." He took my hand in his. His palms were clammy and cold. "I wanted to kiss you."

He moved even closer. Many girls might have thought it romantic, but it felt like a diversion tactic. Besides, I'd fallen for the romantic kiss routine once with Luca, and I'd been caught by a photographer. I wasn't about to do it again. I backed away, leaving him dangling there with his lips pursed.

I'd caught him in the lie I knew he was going to tell. When the men had applied for this competition, it was Grace they were competing for. It was only at the last minute that I was roped into it.

"Do you not like me?" His accent seemed stronger than ever, and even though the question was pretty harmless, there was a tinge of anger to it.

"I'm not attracted to you in that way." Ok, it was an out and out lie. The man was probably the most attractive man I'd ever laid eyes on. There couldn't be many women in the kingdom that would have resisted a kiss from him, but I didn't trust him as far as I could throw him.

"I see," he said, his eyes narrowing. "I cannot say I am not upset by this."

His voice deepened. Yet another sexy thing about him, but I wasn't going to be swayed. I didn't trust the guy. Why did my father want me to marry him? There was a reason; I just didn't know what it was.

"I'm sorry. I've got to go." It wasn't working between Xavier and me, and I had to tell my father. It was pointless keeping him in the competition, as I had no intention of marrying him.

I marched straight to my father's office and knocked on the door. Surprisingly, he was alone.

"Father," I began, trying to sound as defiant as possible. "I cannot keep Xavier in this competition. Not only do I not love him, I don't think I ever could. There is no way I could marry him."

"I see." he tapped his pen on the table.

I waited for him to finish, but it seemed that was it.

"So can I eliminate him at the next round?"

"I would have thought you'd want to eliminate that Leo chap after catching him with your sister." His mouth turned up slightly at the sides as though he was happy to impart this information.

I stared open-mouthed in shock. How did he know about that? I'd not told him, and I was pretty sure neither Elise nor Leo would have wanted him to know. They'd been very low-key since I caught them. Not for the first time, I wondered if one of the palace staff was spying on us.

"I want to eliminate Xavier," I repeated.

His jaw set and his voice firm, he replied. "No."

"No? Didn't you hear me? I'm not going to marry him, so what's the point of keeping him in the competition?" I was aware that I was shouting, but I didn't care.

He regarded me calmly, and yet, I could see it was just an illusion. The pen began to tap on the table again, and his mouth twitched. He was really angry, but then so was I. I held my own, not dropping my gaze for a second. After what felt like an eternity, he spoke.

"Fine," he replied with a sigh "I'll see."

"Fine!" I repeated back at him.

I stormed out of the room. "I'll see" was not what I wanted to hear, but it was better than the outright "no" he'd started with. I wasn't sure what he meant by it, but I'd just come up with the most brilliant plan. One that meant that not only would I not marry Xavier, but there would be nothing my father could do about it.

I was going to propose to Daniel.

The Proposal

I marched down to the front gate of the palace and handed the hastily written note to one of the guards. I had no official date planned with Daniel for the day, so he would either be at his home or at his place of work with his father.

The note was simple. I'd asked him to come to the palace urgently. If anyone intercepted it, they'd assume I wanted another date with him. As the guard left to deliver the note, I realized it had been a while since I had been on a date with Daniel. As I was about to propose to the guy, I should, at least, make some effort.

I ran to the kitchen and asked Pascal to pack up a picnic for us. For a second I thought I saw Cynder washing up where he always used to stand, but it was just his replacement. I tried to get the thought of Cynder out of my mind, but it was difficult, especially as this room reminded me of the hours I'd spent down here with him.

I especially couldn't think of him now in light of what I was about to do. I didn't love Daniel, but I liked him a lot, and that's as much as I could hope for. I'd not heard anything new from Cynder for weeks, and although he filled my thoughts and dreams constantly, I'd come to realize that he was gone, probably for good. No matter how much I loved him, it didn't mean we could be together. The likelihood was he'd managed to skip over the border to Thalia. I hoped he had. It meant he could live a life of freedom. Staying in Silverwood would amount to him looking over his shoulder all the time and never being able to get a job or find food. Neither choice meant we could be together, but, at least in Thalia, he'd have the chance at a happy life.

Daniel was a good choice for me, and maybe one day, I could hope to love him.

Maybe.

My heart was breaking as I ran back upstairs to my room and threw on the prettiest dress I could find in my wardrobe. Nothing in there was as fancy as the clothes that were kept in the dressing room, but the whole point was I didn't want anyone knowing what I was about to do.

I wiped the tears from my eyes. I was not the type of girl to daydream about my future husband or wedding, but even so, I couldn't have imagined it being this way. I was proposing to a man I didn't love to save me from marrying a man I definitely didn't love, while the man I did love was lost to me forever. It was horrific, and yet I couldn't see a way out of the situation.

After doing my best to make myself look presentable, I ran to the kitchen to pick up the picnic and headed out into the garden.

I could see Daniel's blond hair from this distance as he came through the gate. I waved and watched him stroll over to me. For a second, I was filled with dread with the enormity of the thing I was about to do. I wondered if I should have chosen Luca instead. Together, Luca and I could have changed Silverwood for the better, but that would only be when we came into power. I'd only become the queen on my father's death, and how long would that be? Could I live with Luca for all that time in between? I wasn't sure.

"He's the right choice!" I whispered to myself as Daniel bounded over. At least, I felt comfortable with him, and he made me laugh. I was sure I'd read somewhere that laughter was the solid foundation for any marriage. I sure hoped so.

"Hi. I wasn't expecting to see you today. Is everything ok?" He had a look of concern as he kissed my cheek.

"Yes,"

"Ok, it's just that you interrupted me in the middle of my unicycle competition. I was winning!"

I burst out laughing. Yes, he was the right guy. I didn't need to pick someone to leave; I only needed to choose this man to stay.

"I wanted to speak to you about something important."

"Shoot!"

"Not here." If my father knew about Elise and Leo, I could only assume he had spies watching everywhere. I needed to get Daniel as far away from prying eyes as possible. We walked to the furthest end of the large garden. There was a small gazebo covered in blooming pink clematis, which would be the perfect place to sit, but because I was paranoid, I took him to the center of the garden lawn instead.

I slowly unpacked the food, trying to figure out how to word what I was going to say. I didn't want to whisper words of love I didn't feel, but at the same time, I wanted to be sincere. I handed him a glass and filled it with juice, wishing I'd thought to ask for champagne instead.

"Whatever is the matter? You are shaking." He was right, I was. It was either from nerves or from fear. Nerves because I wasn't sure I was making the right decision and fear because of the consequences for both of us if it wasn't.

He took hold of my hand which instantly calmed me. I hadn't noticed I was hyperventilating until then. I took a deep breath and continued.

"I've been thinking a lot recently about us, and about the competition. I like you a lot and..."

"I get it. I'm the one you've picked for elimination in a few days, right? It's fine. I knew right from the start I couldn't compete with those other guys. I'm just a regular guy from town, and you need someone more suited. I want to say with sincere honesty, that I've enjoyed every second of my time with you, and I wouldn't take back a second of it."

"Willyoumarryme?" It came out all in one word.

His face contorted into an expression of confusion. "Sorry?"

"Will you marry me?"

He sat there for so long staring at me, that I thought that he was going to turn me down.

Then he began to laugh. Great big guffaws. It was only a few minutes later when the laughter died down that he looked at me and realized I was being serious.

"I was expecting you to tell me..." He was lost for words. It would have been cute if it wasn't for the fact my own heart was pounding at a million beats per minute.

"I feel the most comfortable with you. You make me laugh when I don't feel like laughing. I think you'll make a great leader one day and in the meantime, you can live in the palace with me. It will show your father what a great son he has."

I saw tears in his eyes which he quickly tried to hide by wiping them with the back of his sleeve. It was a side of him I'd never seen before, but it was nice to see he had a serious side too.

"Do you love me?"

It's funny, but this wasn't a question that I'd expected to come up in this conversation. I didn't want to lie to him.

"I like you a great deal, and I'm hoping that love is something that will grow between us. That is if you'll have me."

"Yes!"

He picked me up from the grass and spun me around, making me squeal with delight. If every day of my future with Daniel was going to be like this, it was a future I could live with.

"Sadie is going to love this!" he said as he finally put me down.

I could see her face now. Yes, she'd love the ratings boost it would give her. I was about to skyrocket Sadie's career into the stratosphere.

"And I'll look darling in a long white gown," he grinned. I playfully punched him in the shoulder.

Looking at how happy he was, I could almost forget that I was essentially being forced to do this. I could almost forget how my heart beat only for Cynder.

Almost.

"I want to put off telling everyone until the elimination show on Saturday." The last thing I needed was my father finding out and putting a stop to it.

"But, don't I have to ask for your father's permission to ask for your hand in marriage? I've never proposed to a princess before."

The excitement emanating from him was enough for me to know I'd made the right decision.

"That won't be necessary. The choice is mine and mine alone. Besides, I proposed to you, remember?"

"But why does it have to be a secret? Surely, we should at least tell the king and queen?"

"No!" I replied a little too forcefully. "I want to surprise everyone at once. It's only a few days away. I'd like it to be our secret until then."

"Ok. I love it!" He picked me up and spun me again. For a little while, I could pretend that this was exactly what I wanted.

For the next few days, I saw a lot more of Daniel. I still had my set date with Leo to keep up appearances, but my heart wasn't in it. I'd made my decision, and by Saturday, this whole charade could end. My mother could plan the wedding of her dreams for me, and I could pretend that my heart wasn't completely broken.

Luca, on the other hand, was a different matter entirely. I'd been reluctant to see him as every time I did, the memory of our kiss stuck in my mind. He'd not attempted to kiss me again which I was grateful for, but I was beginning to enjoy his company much more than I thought I would at the beginning. He was worldly and knowledgeable although when I'd asked him about my grandfather, he knew nothing. I almost felt sad at our last date that I'd not picked him, but my mind was made up. I was going to marry Daniel!

I kept my time with Daniel as secret as I could, so we hid in places that were very rarely used. Most of the time we spent at the bowling alley where I was yet to beat him. For a while, he seemed utterly excited about marrying me, enthusing about the wedding almost as much as my mother was, and I found myself having the same conversations as I had with her about the best china to use for the wedding breakfast and what color the floral arrangements should be. As soon as Saturday came, the pair of them would be able to chat about it to their heart's content. It would save me from doing any planning. By Friday, though, his enthusiasm had waned, and he seemed preoccupied.

When he missed the pins for the third consecutive time, I knew something was wrong.

"Are you ok?" I asked, putting my bowling ball back down. "What is it? Cold feet?"

"Are you sure you want to marry me?" he asked me for the tenth time that day.

"Shhh." I'd asked him to keep his voice down about the whole thing in case anyone overheard. No wonder he was getting paranoid.

"Yes. I've told you I do. I'm only asking you to keep it quiet until Saturday. After that, we can shout it from the hilltops if you like."

"Hmmm."

"I don't want you thinking I'm trying to hide you or that I'm ashamed of you. I just want the news to have a big impact."

And it would. My father was going to be livid with me, but once I'd spoken on national television, there was nothing he could do. I'd get him off my back and Xavier out of my hair for good.

"I know. Come on let's bowl!" He seemed a little cheered up after that, but he wasn't his usual effervescent self. I went to bed that night with a heavy heart.

I couldn't sleep. I tossed and turned until the early hours, but it was no use. Sleep was evading me. It wasn't Daniel's sudden change that had me worried, but the thought of Cynder. I'd been so worried when I thought he'd see me kissing Luca all those weeks ago, and here I was just about to announce I was engaged to be married. I fingered the charm bracelet and eventually took it off. Cynder was someone in my past. I'd never forget him, but I needed to concentrate on my future. I eventually fell asleep in the early hours, but it only felt like seconds later that Jenny came to wake me up. As we were leaving, I picked up the bracelet and put it back on. My middle of the night reasoning made no sense to me in the cold light of day. I might be forced to have a future without Cynder, but that didn't mean I had to forget my past with him.

I felt my nerves heighten as Xavi and her team worked on me. I was as compliant as possible, letting them do what they wanted with me because I had to get out of there quickly to speak to Sadie before the big show.

I needed her to forgo the interviews with the men first. It was imperative that I get on stage before seeing my father and that meant changing the schedule slightly. Until then, I planned to keep out of my father's way.

Sadie was surprisingly okay with me changing things around. I think she had an inkling that something big was going to happen, so she agreed to introduce me to the stage first.

About an hour before the big show, Daniel finally turned up. Xavier, Luca, and Leo were all ready and waiting in the room set aside for them before these events. Elise was also there although she sat a respectable distance from Leo to not arouse suspicion.

When he walked through the door, I knew something was wrong. He looked like a man condemned to death, not a man who was just about to tell the world he was getting married.

"Daniel, can I have a word please?" I tried to pass it off as nothing, but I caught Luca raising an eyebrow as we left the room.

"What is it?"

"I don't know if I can be a king. I'm a carpenter. It's all I know."

"And you can continue to be a carpenter," I whispered. "I'll only come to power when my father dies, and that could be years and years. Even then, you won't be the king; you'll be the queen's husband."

"Hmm."

He seemed so utterly conflicted, but I didn't know why. Either he had a bad case of nerves, or he truly didn't want to marry me. I wasn't sure I wanted to know which one the problem was.

"I already told you that I know I've made the right decision. I pick you. Out of the three others, and out of the hundred men that came to the ball. You are the one I want by my side." I took his hand and laced my fingers through his. For the first time, we felt like a real couple. "This is what I want. Is it what you want?"

"Yes," he replied, a small smile on his face.

"Well, let's do this then!"

I stood on the side of the stage waiting to go on while Sadie did her introduction. I couldn't see the crowds out front from where I was standing, but I knew they were there in force. I could hear them screaming and cheering. They were so loud; I could barely hear Sadie speaking over the sound of them.

My mother and father were nowhere in sight, but they must have been looking for me. They must be wondering why I hadn't turned up to tell them which man I was eliminating. Because of this, I was hiding behind a piece of the stage and hoping they wouldn't see me before I was due to go on.

I listened as Sadie worked the crowd up into a frenzy. I had to give it to her; the woman sure knew how to do her job well.

I could feel my heart pounding with nerves. I'd never done something like this before. I'd always stuck to the rules. This was the first time in my life I was going to disobey my father, and I was going to do it in front of thousands of people. Hundreds of thousands if you count the people watching at home on the TV.

I'd already prepped Daniel to be nearby when I went on stage. In my mind, I told the audience I was engaged to a rapturous applause, and then Daniel would come on stage, and we would share our first kiss.

Our first kiss in front of all those people. I felt sick.

I needed Daniel! I needed to kiss him first. I needed to know I wasn't making a terrible mistake.

I saw him on the steps waiting to come up to the wings of the stage and beckoned him over. He looked almost green with nerves, which was pretty much how I felt too.

"Charmaine, there is something I have to..."

I cut him off by placing my lips to his. In the background, I could hear Sadie begin to announce me on the stage. I kept on kissing Daniel, hoping for a spark, but it never came. It felt like I was kissing my brother.

He pulled back and looked right at me.

"Ladies and gentlemen," said Sadie "Her Royal Highness, The Princess Charmaine."

"Charmaine," Daniel whispered.

"What?"

"I'm gay."

The Elimination

How I walked on to that stage, I'll never know. A thousand light bulbs flashed as people took photos waiting to find out whose name I would call. At one side of the stage, I could see Daniel looking stricken. To my other side, my parents stood watching. They had finally found me. I could see the thunderous look in my father's eyes. He thought I was going to eliminate Xavier.

"So you wanted to come on stage by yourself. Do you have a name for us?"

"Yes. Sadie I do." I looked over to Daniel. Even from here I could see the pain in his eyes. I looked back at the crowd and stood tall. "I'm eliminating Daniel."

I hated myself. It seemed some of the crowd did too. I could hear their boos although many were cheering too.

Sadie took it in her stride. "Daniel. I'm surprised. It's been noticed that you've spent more time with him than the others this week. What made you choose him?" She thrust the microphone back towards me.

"Daniel is the most wonderful, funniest, and kindest guy I've ever met. Right from the start, I've known what a compassionate man he is. He would make any person an excellent husband, and it saddens me deeply to have to let him go. Nothing he did made me come to this decision. He is the most amazing artisan, and his father should be extremely proud of him. He felt that he had more to give by helping his family than becoming a member of royalty. I disagree. I think he would make the most excellent ruler one day, but his heart is at home, and I couldn't take that away from him. One of the things I found most special about Daniel is how important his family is to him. Unfortunately, at the end of the day, it is that love and loyalty, that is keeping us apart."

"Wow," said Sadie. "I wasn't expecting that. Would you say it's a case of love that could never be?"

"Something like that."

I looked to my right with tears in my eyes. Daniel stood there. He too was crying.

"Thank you," he mouthed, and I beckoned him onto the stage. He came out and hugged me tightly much to the enjoyment of the crowd. It wasn't a staged hug for either of us. I loved him then, I truly did, but I'd been right before. I loved him like a brother. He pulled back and gave me a quick kiss on the lips. Strangely enough, it felt much nicer than the kiss we'd shared just moments before. He held my hand, and I raised it to the sky.

The crowd went wild.

Afterwards, when Sadie had finished grilling us about our relationship and pegging us as star-crossed lovers, we exited the stage hand in hand. My father smiled and patted me on the shoulder as we passed him. He'd gotten his way. Xavier was still in the competition.

Behind me, I heard Sadie introduce the three others to the stage for their interviews, but I didn't hang around to hear them. I wanted to spend the rest of the afternoon with Daniel.

I finally got the truth out of him. His father had caught him kissing another man and had disowned him right around the time that the ball was first mentioned to the public. He'd put his name down so that his father would speak to him again.

"I would have married you, you know," he said as we walked hand in hand at the far side of the palace away from the stage and the people.

"I'm sure you would, and I'm sure we would have both been happy, but there would have been something missing for both of us. I wouldn't have wanted to wake up every morning, seeing you with that sick look on your face like you did when I was about to kiss you."

"Yeah, sorry about that. You should have warned me."

"What will you do now?"

"I don't know. My father will probably still never speak to me."

"What about the boy he caught you kissing?"

Daniel looked down at his shoes and was uncharacteristically pensive. "I loved him. I think I broke his heart when I broke it off. I broke mine too."

"You should go find him. Nothing is more important than love, and I know what it's like to be apart from the one you love. It eats at your soul."

He was the first person I'd hinted to that I was in love with someone. He had the decency not to push me on it.

"But what about my father?"

"Your father is an idiot if he can't see what a wonderful son he has. Besides, I think he'll come around when he gets a huge order to replace all the chairs that were lost in the explosion. I'll tell my father that I've given the contract to you. Of course, it's up to you if you decide to work on it with your father or go solo."

"I really could have loved you," Daniel said forlornly.

"And I really could have believed it," I replied.

Daniel left to pack his things. He'd not be leaving empty-handed. As well as the chair contract, he'd get a nice monetary prize for being one of the runners up. I'd hated that clause when it was put in. It made me feel like a prize at a circus, but now, it made sense. Daniel had given up a lot of his time for this. He deserved to be compensated for it.

I went back to my room feeling empty. Losing Daniel was somehow worse than losing Leo. At least, Leo had found someone, and Elise was deliriously happy. Now I was down to two men.

Two gorgeous men. I wasn't sure I wanted either of them.

I sighed as I kicked off my shoes and picked up today's copy of the newspaper that had been left on my bed.

Ever since I'd put the advert in, I'd been checking it religiously. I'd only thought to have it run for one day so there was a good chance he'd not seen it. His original advert was still running. It was always in the same place. It never changed.

I opened the paper, and sure enough, there it was. The advert. I read it again.

A CHARM FOR ALL OCCASIONS.

Find your new love with this. A lucky charm for your Lucky Charm.

It had the same picture. I threw it aside feeling hopeless. He was gone.

I lay back on the bed and thought about everything. It all seemed like such a mess. Elise was happy; Leo was happy; hopefully, Daniel would be happy. Hell, even my father was happy now.

Why couldn't I be?

I kicked the paper off the bed where it spread out all over the floor. Bending down to pick it up, I saw the ad again.

It was different! I'd not noticed before because it looked so much like the old one.

I scrabbled around under the bed for one of the old papers and compared the two ads. They were in the same size in the same place with the same picture. Even the headline was the same, but where it had said, "Tell her you love her with this beautiful charm bracelet,' it now said, "Find your new love with this." What did that mean? He'd found someone new? He was happy. My heart could barely take it.

I sat there for ten minutes trying to find meaning in his change of words. If he'd found a new love, why was he still calling me his lucky charm? Why even tell me at all. It didn't make sense.

Maybe he was telling me to find a new love. Well, that wasn't going so well. One of the men I'd been dating preferred my sister and another one preferred men. I guess he'd been watching all the coverage of it on TV. He wouldn't even have to do that. There was plenty of it in the newspapers too. The front cover of this particular issue had a photo of me and Daniel. It was one of the official ones we'd had taken at the ball.

They were speculating why we had been spending so much time together this week. There was definitely a spy somewhere. If they weren't tipping off my father, they were tipping off the press. I guess tomorrow's edition would be all about how he was eliminated. I was irked to see that Xavier was riding high in the polls.

I still hadn't found out why my father wanted him to stay. As I had another month until the next elimination, I was determined to find out the truth. I just didn't know who to ask. I didn't know anyone on the outside. Not unless I counted Cynder, but I could hardly speak to him. I couldn't even decipher his message in the paper.

A new love. Where would I find a new love? Apart from at a ball, I didn't know. I'd found Cynder in the kitchen. Did he want me to go down to the kitchen?

No. He wasn't down there. Someone else had taken his place. Someone else who didn't make music and dance as he washed up. Where else? The personal column?

I turned to the personals section and searched down the list of men and women looking for mates. It seemed such an easy way to do things. About half way down I found what I was looking for.

There was an advert mentioning a lucky charm.

Looking for a lady to be my lucky charm.

She must like my parents.

It was for me! Once again, there was no contact number or address, but I knew what it meant. He'd only mentioned his parents to me once. The apartment belonged to them. He was right here!

I jumped out of bed and put on my shoes. There was only one person I needed to see now. Actually, two because I couldn't enlist Leo's help without getting Elise involved.

I found them both in the parlor, sitting and laughing at some shared joke. They looked so natural together, so at ease in each other's company. They also looked like they were dating which would be a problem if my parents were to walk in on them.

"Maybe you guys should sit a little apart. You know, at least, pretend you aren't mad for each other."

"Father knows."

I arched my brow at hearing this from Elise. "He knows?"

Ok, I knew he knew, but I didn't know Elise knew it too.

"Yeah. I don't know how he found out. I guess one of the staff saw us sneaking around together, but he called us into his study a couple of days ago and gave us his blessing."

I stared open-mouthed while Elise carried on.

"He said it was fine as long as we kept our relationship discreet and told no one else about it."

I don't know why it irked me, but it did. I couldn't help but feel the injustice of Elise being able to date who she wanted while I was being forced to pick a man I wasn't even sure I liked, let alone loved.

"So Father is fine with you dating one of the men I'm supposed to choose from, but not about me choosing whom I want." I huffed and sat down on the opposite sofa with my arms crossed.

"Cheer up, you've still got Xavier and Luca to choose between and let's face it, the pair of them are gorgeous. Most girls in the kingdom would pull their right arm off to be in your position right now."

"I don't want to choose between them."

"Well you can't have them both," she said, coming to sit beside me. "That really would be unfair to the other girls in the kingdom."

I pushed her playfully and tried to hide the smirk. I was too depressed for smirking. She wrapped her arms around me and hugged me.

"Seriously, though. I'm sorry we did this to you."

"Oh, this isn't about you and Leo. I'm happy for you. I actually came for your help."

"Sure, what do you need?"

"Let's go somewhere else to talk. It's a lovely day outside. Let's go out there."

The fact my father knew about Elise and Leo disturbed me. I wasn't so sure that Elise was right about a member of staff seeing them. The more I thought about it, the more convinced I was that my father had the rooms in the palace bugged. I was glad that the weather was holding up so I could use it as an excuse to go out in the garden. It was the only place I could think of that I wouldn't be overheard.

"What is it?" asked Leo when we were safely in the garden. "What can we do to help you? I'm assuming it's something you don't want the palace to know about, and that's why we are out here?"

"You think the palace is bugged too?"

"I have my suspicions."

It calmed me, knowing that Leo thought along the same lines as I did. It also made it easier to tell him the truth.

"I want to speak to you about the Magi. You know how they are being treated and how unfair it is. You go out to help them every night, but what have you done to really help them?"

"What do you mean?"

"You bring them food which helps for one day. All the while, their opportunities to be able to get it for themselves are getting smaller and smaller. They can't rely on you to feed them forever. Then what?"

Leo massaged his temples and sighed. "I've thought about what I can do, but I'm limited to the law. I tried organizing a benefit a few months ago, but the palace shut it down as soon as they got wind of it."

"They did? Why does my father hate the Magi so much and why now? They have lived and worked at the palace with no problems since my grandfather's time."

"I cannot say. You asked me before why your grandfather had such a change of heart about the Magi, and now you are asking me the same question about your father. I'm afraid I have the same answer now as I did then. I simply don't know."

"I want you to help me find out. Something happened in my grandfather's time, and something is happening now. My father won't let me pick Xavier to leave, and he won't tell me why."

"Xavier?" replied Elise. "You'd have thought he'd want you to keep Luca in. After all, this whole competition is really about making our ties to other countries stronger and who better for you to marry than the son of the king and queen of Thalia?"

"Exactly. If he wanted Luca, it would make sense, or even if he wanted me to marry you, Leo. After all, you are a well-respected member of our local community, so why Xavier?"

"Who is he?" asked Elise, sitting closer and lowering her voice as if to hear some amazing secret. Even she was beginning to get paranoid that we were being overheard. "You've been on dates with him, right? I barely know the guy."

"That's just it. I barely know the guy either. Our dates have either been cut short, or he's lied to me throughout. He says his mother died when he was young, and he spent his childhood traveling around, but I don't think so. He has an accent which isn't from around here although he told me he's never left the kingdom."

"So you want us to find out why the king has turned against the Magi and look into Xavier's past? Is that it?"

"Not quite...There's something I've not told you."

I leaned in now and quickly checked around the garden to see if there was anyone in earshot.

"I'm in love with a Mage..."

The Truth

The squeal Elise made was loud enough to be heard in the next city. She realized what she had done and apologized with an excited whisper.

"...and he's the one they think planted the bomb at the palace."

"What?" Elise's voice rose considerably again, causing the three of us to check around us to see if we were being overheard. The closest guard didn't even look in our direction. She lowered her voice back to a whisper. "You know who did that?"

"No. He didn't do it. My father is using him as a scapegoat because he was nearby at the time, but he didn't do it."

"Who is he?"

"His name is Cynder, and up until the night of the ball, he washed the dishes in the kitchen at the palace."

"You are in love with a guy who cleans dishes?"

"He's so much more than that," I replied defensively.

"No. I love it! You are in love. I am in love. It's utterly wonderful. I can't believe my big sister has found someone too. I bet he's amazing."

I always admired her innocent optimism and joy of all things, not to mention, only seeing the good in the situation and being able to block out the bad stuff.

"He's on the run, Elise. He's being hunted for a crime he didn't commit, and when the police find him, they'll kill him without a trial. In the meantime, I publically have to choose between three men, one of which is your boyfriend, and privately, I'm being forced to pick the one I like the least."

"Oh," her face dropped when she thought of the implications of it all. Her fairytale happiness was not shared by me.

"Can't we speak to Father and tell him? I'm sure he'd listen. He was great when he found out about Leo and I."

"No!" cried out Leo and I at the same time.

"The king was fine with us because it fit in with his plans," he explained. "If he wants Charmaine to marry Xavier, having me out of the running helped his cause, and as long as we are discreet and don't let it slip to the press, our being together won't be a problem. You are right, Charmaine. Something is going on, and we need to find out what. Maybe then, we can begin to help the Magi fight back against oppression, and maybe we can help your boyfriend too."

It's funny how my heart soared at hearing someone calling Cynder my boyfriend. In a way, I guess he was the closest thing I'd ever had to one.

"If I tell you something, I need to be able to trust you."

Leo smiled. "I think we are a little past that point, don't you? Don't worry. Whatever it is, we will keep your secret."

"Cynder is in town. I need to see him. I was hoping you'd let me come with you tonight when you go out to feed the Magi."

I could see a light bulb go on in Leo's mind "So that's where you went last time. I did wonder."

"Yeah. I'm sorry. It was the only way I could think to get out of the palace."

"Elise has been going with me over the past couple of nights, but the more, the merrier."

"Actually, I think it would be better if just the two of us go."

"I can do this!" said Elise indignantly.

"I know you can, but we are being watched. If father thought it was you going out with Leo, he'd not ask any questions. I was hoping to wear your clothes and pretend to be you. That way if he sees me, he won't question it."

"Why would he question it? You've been out with Leo before."

"Things have changed."

"I agree," said Leo. "Besides. I was beginning to think it's unsafe myself. When I started going out to feed the Magi, I held back that it was the Magi I was feeding. I told people it was the homeless. In the last month or so, I've seen an increased police presence. They've let me go about my business for now, but I'm sure that won't be the case forever."

"So you'll take me with you tonight?"

"Yes."

That night, Elise gave me some of her clothes. She dressed much more girly than me, so with a hoodie on over the top of a cute dress, I could easily pass for her. She gave me a quick hug before I left and promised to lock my bedroom door behind me. That way, if anyone came to find me, they'd assume I was in bed.

The journey out of the palace was unhindered, and as before, the guards at the end of the staff driveway let us out without question. Leo agreed to help me get to Cynder before going out into the community with the food, but when we got to the street with Cynder's house on it, there was a policeman there, just a few feet away from Cynder's door.

"What now?" I whispered in a panic.

"He is just on duty. It's a coincidence that he's by Cynder's house. If he thought Cynder was there, he wouldn't be looking so casual. I'll go and distract him so you can get into the house."

"Thanks."

I stayed in the shadows as Leo approached the policeman. I couldn't hear what he was saying, but it was enough to make the policeman follow him, leaving the coast clear for me. I ran to the house and bounded up the stairs to the top floor where Cynder was waiting for me with open arms.

"Quick. Come through."

I followed him through the hidden doorway and up to his apartment. When he stepped out of the shadows, I gasped. His face was covered in bruises. Some were old and had yellowed, but a bruise and cut around his right eye were fresh.

"What happened?"

"The police found me up north. I was put in a cell and beaten. I thought they'd kill me, but they starved me and beat me instead. I've been there for weeks. Last week, one of the guards didn't lock the door properly, and I escaped. I came straight here. A friend of mine put that ad in the paper. I had to see you."

I kissed him then, but he winced. His face was so swollen that I'd hurt him.

"I don't have any ice for the swelling. I have food. Here."

I passed him all I'd managed to take from the kitchens. He took it gratefully and began to rip chunks out of the bread. It was such a contrast to the last time I saw him where he cooked me dinner. He looked so thin.

"When was the last time you ate?"

"I don't know," he replied between mouthfuls. "Two, three days ago."

I sat beside him and waited for him to eat his fill. In my mind, I'd imagined a romantic night filled with a delicious meal and candles. I'd skipped dinner especially, but seeing him so hungry made me realize that things had changed for him too. He needed the food more than I did. I took a couple of the raw eggs from the bag, and for the first time in my life, I cooked a meal. I chopped some peppers and tomatoes the way I'd seen him do and added some salt and pepper I found in a cupboard. Then I added the whole lot to a frying pan and along with some eggs, made an omelet. It ended up more like fried, mushed eggs, but it smelled nice. I placed it on a plate and handed it to him along with a knife and fork.

He put down the loaf of bread he was chomping on and tucked in.

"I'm sorry, it's not very good."

"It's the most delicious thing I've ever tasted in my life," he replied, his mouth full.

Seeing him in the state he was in was breaking my heart, and yet, just being near him filled me in a way nothing else could. It was the strangest feeling, a feeling of happiness and sadness rolled together. I also felt inadequate. I'd given him a plate of runny eggs, and in doing that, in just being here, I was probably risking his life.

It reminded me why he'd left in the first place.

"Why did you come back? There is a policeman outside your door."

"I needed to see you."

"But you could get caught. You could get killed. It's not safe here, so close to the palace."

"It's not safe anywhere anymore. Anti-magic feeling has pervaded throughout the kingdom. I saw them forcing Magi out of their homes in the north. They were burning their houses down and forcing them to take the dangerous trek through the mountains to the next kingdom. I've heard from a few sources that it's the same in the south. We are effectively being driven from the land."

"That can't be true. The south has loads of communities of Magi. My maid went to live with her aunt and uncle there."

"Your maid is probably in another kingdom by now. Those that are trying to stay are the ones that are going into hiding, but I don't think it will be long before they get caught either. I found out that a couple of months ago; there was a massive wand cull in the south. Those that didn't give up their wands were sentenced to death. The Magi have nothing left to fight with."

"Can't you do magic without your wand?"

"No. We have the magic in us, but it's channeled through our wands. The wands come from an elder tree in Thalia. It's the only tree that produces them. I lost mine in the cell."

"What are we going to do?"

"We are going to dance." I looked up into his eyes. The right was slightly bloodshot and yet he was still the most beautiful person I'd ever laid eyes on. He turned on a record player, and we danced. It was not the quick dances he'd shown me, nor was it the slow dance he'd taught me for the last dance at the ball. We just held on to each other, our bodies entwined and swaying to the somber record. When it came to a stop, we carried on dancing to our own music.

An hour or so later, I knew I had to go. I'd agreed with Leo to meet him down at the front door, but I couldn't go. If it was a choice between being caught out of the palace or leaving Cynder, I'd take all the punishment I had to. I couldn't leave him. Not now. Not tonight. Maybe not ever.

We fell asleep together on his couch. It was lumpy with years of people sitting on it, but I didn't care. I rested my head on his shoulder while he twirled a lock of my hair around his fingers and sang me a sweet lullaby. His voice took me off to a world in which we could live side by side and no one ever had to pick a husband they didn't want or go into hiding because of who they were.

A sliver of light shone through the threadbare curtains signaling it was time to wake up. Cynder still slept peacefully, his chest moving up and down with each breath.

I could have stayed watching him all day. I loved to see him looking so peaceful after everything he'd been through, but it couldn't last. He was a fugitive on the run for blowing up a palace, and I was a princess set to marry a stranger in little over three months. In the entire history of impossible relationships, ours had to rank way up there. I kissed him lightly on his lips, trying to stay away from the bruising there. He opened his eyes and smiled up at me.

"I dreamed you were here and you are."

"I wouldn't be anywhere else."

"I love you my lucky charm." He reached forward and kissed me again. This was so much more than the small kiss I'd given him. His bruised lips must have been hurting so much, and yet I couldn't stop. When I was kissing him, the rest of the world didn't exist. I would have probably stayed there forever if it hadn't been for the sound of a bird calling. It sounded like the hoot of an owl. Cynder sat up immediately.

"What was that? An owl?"

"It's my neighbor downstairs. He knows I'm here. The owl hoot is his way of telling me to open the bookcase. There might be trouble. Stay here."

My heart rate increased as he headed down the stairs to the lower landing. Trouble?

I knew it was because of me. I shouldn't have stayed the night. I'd put Cynder in real danger because of my own need to be with him.

A second later he was back with another man. He was tall and slim and dressed impeccably in a gray suit. When he saw me, his eyes widened.

"This is Mr. Frost. He was a friend of my parents."

Mr. Frost held his hand out to shake mine. "Call me Sam, please Your Highness."

I took the older gentleman's hand and shook it. He turned to Cynder.

"My, my. Of all the trouble you could get yourself in, I must say, you've far surpassed my expectations."

"What's happened?" I asked. "Have the police been looking for Cynder?"

"The police are looking for you, Your Highness. I came up to warn Cynder not to make any noise or look through the curtains because there is a citywide search for you. I can't quite believe you have been in the apartment above me all this time."

So they already knew. I'd not only put Cynder in danger, but I'd put both Elise and Leo in jeopardy too.

"Can she go down to your apartment?" asked Cynder. "You can say that you found her unconscious on the street last night and took her in. It was only this morning when you turned on your TV that you realized she was the princess. If you call the police straight away, there will be no reason not to believe you."

"Can't I just stay here with you? I don't want to go back. We could live here forever. No one will find us behind that bookcase."

Cynder came to me and stroked my face. "It's not like before. I have no wand. The food you brought will only last us a couple of days. Three at most. If you go home, you'll be safe. You might be in trouble for a bit, but if they think you were unconscious, they'll take pity on you. After all, you are the heir to the throne."

"I can't leave you."

He kissed me again, neither of us knowing if it would be our final kiss.

"I'll never forget you, but I have to go. Being near me is putting you in danger."

I wanted to tell him to go to Thalia, but I'd told him that the last time I'd seen him. That's probably where he'd been heading when he got caught. I had no other advice and no other choice but to tell him goodbye.

I felt something cold pressed into my hand. When I looked down, it was another silver charm for my bracelet, this time a tiny silver shoe. I kissed him lightly on the lips and on the inside I died.

I followed Sam down to his apartment and lay on the sofa while he called the authorities. I closed my eyes and waited for the inevitable fallout of my actions.

The Royal Visit

The next week passed in a blur. Mainly because the doctor had prescribed me drugs for anxiety and sleeping pills, and between them both, I spent most of the week sleeping.

Sam had called the police, who had duly taken me back to the palace. As my story and Leo's had not matched in any way, my father wanted to put him into police custody for kidnapping. As soon as I found out, I told them that he was telling the truth and that I was just confused because someone had banged me over the head. I took full responsibility for going out with Leo, telling my father that I just wanted to help the homeless, and after a bit of begging, Leo was released, and I was prescribed a week's bed rest and a great number of pills that Jenny forced me to take twice a day.

In my more lucid moments, the guilt and fear washed over me, almost paralyzing me. I worried about Cynder, about Leo, about the Magi, and about my upcoming dates. No one had mentioned any more dates to me, but I knew they'd have to resume sometime. Just the thought of spending time with Xavier now had me in a full-scale panic. When Jenny came to my room and saw me, she'd just give me another pill, and I'd drift off for a few hours. After a week of this, Elise came to visit me.

"I'm so sorry, Elise. How's Leo? I feel so terrible."

"It's fine. Leo isn't mad at you. In fact, he's been doing a bit of digging. He's found out the name of someone who used to work in the palace at the time of our grandfather. Apparently, she was a good friend of Molly. They worked together here at the palace."

After a week of nightmares about Cynder, it felt refreshing to think of something else instead.

"Will he go and speak to her?"

"He set off two days ago. I wanted to tell you sooner, but Jenny told me you were too ill to have visitors. She's been turning Luca away all week."

"She has?"

"Yeah. He keeps asking me if you are ok like a lovesick puppy. I really think he likes you. It's such a shame that you are ill."

"I'm not ill. I'm ashamed and terrified and sad. I'm also drugged up to the eyeballs and finding it difficult to keep awake. Will you tell Jenny that I don't want any more pills, and that I'll take dinner in my room? If you don't mind bringing it up, I'll tell you everything."

"Sure!"

She left and reappeared twenty minutes later with a silver tray with two plates on it. One for her, and one for me. She locked the door behind her and sat next to me on the bed.

I quietly told her everything I knew, including everything Cynder had told me about the Magi being deported across the kingdom. She, in turn, told me what had happened to Leo the night I'd spent with Cynder. Apparently, he'd been caught giving food to a family of Magi. They'd been taken away, and he had been taken in for questioning. They'd questioned him about where Elise was, and when he refused to answer, they came looking for her. She was in her room, but they soon found out that I wasn't. The guards on the staff driveway couldn't remember if it was me or Elise that had left with Leo, so they were both fired, and Leo was kept in his cell until they got the call that I was at Sam Frost's house. They wanted to keep him in the cell for good, but between Elise and I, he was let out. Apparently, my father didn't want the negative publicity. He had been told to never go near the Magi again.

"What are we going to do?" asked Elise fearfully. For the first time, this whole nightmare was becoming as real to her as it was to me.

"We are going to find out the truth, and then we are going to do something about it."

"What can we do?"

"I don't know. That's what we are going to have to figure out."

Elise told me she was on board, but I could see the apprehension in her face. She must have seen how the Magi were living when she went out with Leo, but in her world, nothing was ever wrong. I guess it was a wake-up call for both of us.

Once the palace doctor declared me fit enough to get out of bed, on my parent's orders, the dates started again. As Leo was away from the palace, I had Luca and Xavier to choose from. Part of me knew that I should have chosen Xavier and tried to get more information from him, but I couldn't face it, so on the day of the next date, I picked Luca. On the morning of our date, Jenny came to see me.

"You are going out for your date," she began without even her usual "Good morning."

"Going out?" I opened my eyes. It was still dark outside. "What time is it?"

"The king and queen of Thalia have announced that they are coming over for a royal visit, and as you are dating their son, they have decided to fly over today to spend the day with you. Your mother has asked that you dress in your best clothes for the occasion which means you aren't going to get away with throwing on the first thing you find in your closet. Your mother and father will be joining you all this evening for a meal in honor of the occasion."

That spoiled my plans. I was hoping to talk to Luca a bit more about the Magi.

"Where exactly are we going today?" I asked, heaving myself out of bed and rubbing my eyes.

"You are going to give them a guided tour of the city. Your father has ordered a carriage for you all, and the press have been informed, so you have to look nice. They are expecting a lot of crowds."

As we walked down to the dressing room, I thought about Luca and his parents. He'd told me that Thalia was accepting of Magi which meant his parents would be too. I wondered what they'd make of my parents and the state of our kingdom.

Xavi was in her element today and had already picked out an extremely pale pink gown for the occasion. Alezis did my hair and finished up by putting a pink diamond tiara on top. Louis was noticeably absent and one of the other make-up artists, a girl called Agneta, had taken his place. I was about to inquire where he was when I realized he must have gone in the cull of the Magi.

Agneta, whilst not doing quite as good a job as Louis would, certainly did better than I could ever do, and as I pulled the flowing gown over my head, I had to admit I looked like the princess I was.

I had met King Theron and Queen Sarina of Thalia on one occasion, but it was so many years ago that I barely remembered. I'd have been a young girl at the time. This time, I felt nervous as they were brought into the giant hallway and introduced to me formally.

Luca's father was a much shorter man than I remembered and much stouter than his lean son. Luca didn't get his looks from him. His mother, on the other hand, was tall and willowy with a divine beauty. They made quite the odd couple. I curtsied as I shook their hands. Behind me, I could feel Luca's hand on my back. It felt comforting on a day I needed all the comfort I could get.

After a few formalities, we were ushered into the royal carriage. It was a white carriage, pulled by six stunning white horses. Each had a plume of feathers in its mane. I was seated facing forward with Luca to my right and the queen opposite me upon pink velvet seats. The king sat opposite Luca.

"How are you finding dating my son?" asked the queen as we set off down the driveway. I could already hear the noise of the crowds that had gathered there. I'd never known the royal family to be so popular as it was now and all because of a stupid competition.

"He's a gentleman."

"Doesn't sound like my son," laughed the king who got a nasty look from his wife.

I could feel Luca tense up beside me. I held my hand out to him. He was finding this weird date with his parents as hard as I was. He took my hand and gave me a grateful smile.

I wanted to ask the queen about the situation with the Magi, but couldn't think of an opportunity without appearing rude. Luckily, one presented itself as we were leaving the palace grounds.

Among all the people who had come out to wave at us, was a small group with banners. I recognized a couple of them from the house Leo had taken me to the first time we went out.

They had banners that had slogans such as "Equal rights for Magi," and "Magi - not slaves." As we passed, a group of police closed in on them and began to drag them back through the crowd. I watched the queen's face to see what she made of it. Luca and the king were looking the other way, but the queen saw everything. I watched her expression change from one of polite interest to mild disgust. However, she kept her plastered-on smile and carried on waving as any good queen should.

"What do you think of the Magi situation Your Majesty?" I asked as sweetly as I could.

"You are free to run your country as you see fit. I have a high regard for your parents."

Now that was interesting. She didn't directly answer my question, which in itself did answer my question. She didn't like what we were doing; she just didn't want to appear rude.

"That's very kind of you. Personally, I'd prefer more leniency for the Magi. I believe in equal rights for all. You son tells me you are a much more tolerant nation and indeed, have a Mage in your own family."

She regarded me with curiosity and a little apprehension.

"We do. My darling daughter-in-law is a Mage, and we couldn't be without her. We do have troubles in our kingdom; I mean, show me a

302

kingdom that doesn't, but we do have equal rights. We try to treat all our subjects the same regardless of their magical ability. My daughter-in-law has been a leader in the advancement of Magi. She does some wonderful work. It's a shame she couldn't come here today."

Her voice got quiet then as if she was saying something she shouldn't. With all the cheering outside the carriage, I could barely hear her.

"Why couldn't she come?" I asked.

"Because your borders have been closed to all Magi. One way, of course. Many of your Magi are coming into Thalia."

Our borders were closed and not even royalty could get in? It was worse than I thought.

"I wasn't aware of that." My own voice had lowered to match hers. "I hope to change things when I am queen."

"That is a long way off, and much damage has already been done. I fear it will be too late by then. There have been too many generations of hate against Magi in Silverwood."

"That's not true. My grandfather was an advocate for them."

"In his older years, yes. But that's only because of the baby. He had to, don't you think?"

"Baby?"

She finally looked like she had said too much. Her hand rushed to her mouth. "Silverwood is beautiful. Your people look so happy."

She turned back to the open window where she began waving again in earnest.

"Your highness. What baby?"

"Forget I said anything. It is unlike me to speak out of turn, and I believe I have done so. I hope you'll forgive me. Pray, tell me what that building is over there in the distance. It looks so pretty."

It was her way of ending the conversation and no matter what I said; I couldn't get her back on the topic. In the end, I gave her the tour that I was supposed to give, telling her and the king about all the buildings before we had done a full circuit of the city and ended up back at the palace.

Sadie was there with her photographer, and we were all lined up to take some official portraits before heading inside to eat.

Elise was already at the dinner table, but Leo wasn't by her side. I had so wanted to speak to him, to ask him if he knew about my grandfather fathering a baby other than my own father, but the other bachelors were not invited. Of the three, only Luca was there with his parents. I was seated next to him on one side with my mother at the other side. Elise was two seats away, and so I was unable to ask her if Leo had gotten back yet.

At the end of the meal, King Theron stood and announced a toast.

"To The Princess Charmaine and Prince Luca, and may they have many happy years ahead of them."

I raised my glass out of politeness. Luca winked at me and clinked his glass against mine.

"Either together or apart," my father added. "Remember, Charmaine has to pick fairly."

How he could in good conscience say that was beyond me with what he was doing, but I remained silent. Now was not the time for an argument. King Theron, obviously, didn't agree.

"Nothing against the other young men," he replied, "but my son really outshines them all. He is a prince, the only prince your daughter chose."

"But you can't always choose who you fall in love with," my father retaliated.

I seemed to be right in the middle of a battle of toasts. I stood up and raised my glass high.

"To Prince Luca. A wonderful man whom I've become very close to and who I know will do amazing things."

It dispersed the tension that was building up between the two kings. Everyone held their glasses up.

"To Prince Luca!"

Luca beamed. This was probably the first time he'd been the center of attention at a royal occasion.

The Last Date

W hen the meal was over, I managed to get a minute with Elise. She whispered that Leo had returned and wanted to speak to me.

There was no chance of me escaping while the King and Queen of Thalia were still here, so I told her to set up a time to meet him in the library after dark.

Luca and I were not only expected to leave the party, we were practically ushered from it by King Theron who said something along the lines of "You lovebirds need some quality time alone."

As with most of my other dates, we ended up in the garden.

"Let's hope that when we kiss again, there will be no one to photograph us." Luca winked.

I nudged him and pointed at the stage where Sadie and her photographer were still packing up from earlier. As we'd taken a good hour to eat, they must have been hanging around to see if they could get more candid shots. I took Luca's hand and pulled him away from them to the back of the palace where we wouldn't be seen.

"I heard that you came to see me when I was ill," I began. "That was nice of you."

"You are all about the nice aren't you?"

"Pardon?"

"I wasn't being nice; I was worried. I wasn't doing anything to be nice. I don't want to be thought of as nice, especially by you. Nice is boring. I want to be..."

"What do you want to be?"

"I don't know. This whole competition has me messed up. One day I think we are getting on really well, the next I see you in the papers with Leo."

"You know as well as I do, those photos are for show."

"I know that, but deep down, I wonder. Do you know how hard it is dating someone who is also dating three other men? I'm not going to lie to you. I've never had to compete for another girl's affections before, and it's driving me crazy. I don't know what to do or what to say to make you like me. I feel like I'm going out of my mind, and when you are with those other men, I'm consumed with such jealousy that I don't know what to do with myself. I miss you when you are not with me. That's why I came to see you when you were ill. I wasn't being nice; I was desperate to know if you were ok."

The August sun beat down on us, and the once green grass was almost completely brown despite the daily use of sprinklers. It was all I could think about as Luca poured his heart out to me.

In two months, I was going to have to walk up an aisle and pledge my love to someone. Would it be so bad if it was Luca? He loved me enough for the both of us.

Luca picked a few daisies that had managed to survive and passed them to me.

It was a sweet gesture. As a princess, I received hundreds of expensive bouquets of flowers a year and even more so since the competition began, but there was something about those daisies that meant a lot more. I kissed Luca's cheek and began to thread the daisies together to make a chain. When I'd finished, I pulled my diamond tiara from my head and gave myself a crown of daisies instead.

"I think I prefer you like that. You look more carefree. You've been so serious lately."

"I don't want to make a mistake," I answered honestly. "It's not just about me. It's about my kingdom too. It's a huge decision to make."

"I want to be honest with you now. I want to marry you. I came here because I wanted to help rule a country one day and that was all, but as the months have gone by, I've fallen in love with you. You really are beautiful although I see an ever-present sadness in you. At first, I put it down to the loss of your sister, and as time went by, I thought it might be the strain you are under. Now, I think it might be something else. I'd like to feel we can be honest with one another. Can you tell me what it is?"

I couldn't tell him. How could I? I was sad for so many different reasons, two of which he'd mentioned, but I was also sad about being away from Cynder. I was sad at how my life was turning out and the lack of control I had over my own future. I was sad how my own father was treating innocent people, and I couldn't think of a way to stop it.

"I'm sad because I'm overwhelmed by my own responsibilities." It was the closest thing to the truth I could tell him.

He squeezed my hand. "Then let me share those responsibilities with you. I may not be as good looking as Xavier, or as well loved in Silverwood as Leo, but I know how to be a prince, and I know how to look after a princess. I'd like to look after this princess if she'd let me." He pointed at my chest, right where my heart was.

"I..."

"You don't need to say anything. I can see in your eyes that you don't love me, and that's ok. Love is something that can grow. We barely know each other, but if you choose me, I'll work hard every day to make you feel safe enough that you could fall in love with me."

He kissed me then, and I let him. I let him because he was my only chance at a future. I didn't know if I'd ever see Cynder again, but Luca was right here beside me. He was the perfect man to take my side to one day rule the kingdom. I'd never love him like I loved Cynder, a love that eclipsed the way I felt about him couldn't exist. But Luca's kisses took my breath away which was more than I could wish for. We both ignored the tears streaming down my face. Maybe Luca didn't even notice, for however practiced his kisses were, they could never beat the innocent embraces I shared with Cynder on the shabby sofa of his apartment.

I gazed up to his window. The curtains hadn't moved. Something told me that Cynder was back on the run. In my heart of hearts, I knew I'd never see him again.

"I'm going to choose you."

I looked straight into Luca's eyes. The grin on his face was unmistakable which only made my heart break a little more. I had to pick someone, and between Xavier and Luca, there really was no choice. If I could ignore his playboy past, and he could ignore the fact I wasn't in love with him, maybe we'd make a good team.

"I didn't want to believe you'd choose me. Even though I was the only prince out of the four, I knew I had shortcomings and wasn't good enough for you. When you kissed me all those weeks ago, I'd hoped it was enough to convince you we should be together, but you still went on dates with the others. The time between our dates was so excruciatingly endless that I found myself wandering the palace in the hope I'd accidentally bump into you. I've always considered myself a romantic, but it is only with you that I realize I was nothing but a flirt and a cad. Right from the start, with you, I've felt different, like I've finally found someone I could make it with, be a partner to. When you spent that week with Daniel, I thought that was it. I was so torn up with jealousy that I couldn't eat or sleep, but the rules forbade me to interrupt you. I just had to wait it out. When you announced he was leaving, I was overjoyed. I thought maybe my letters had worked."

"Letters?"

"I wrote you every day. There was nothing in the rules about that. Didn't your father give them to you?"

I seethed on the inside. "No. My father didn't. I'm sorry, Luca, I didn't know."

"It doesn't matter now. All that matters is that I'm here with you and that you've chosen to stand by my side."

He cupped my face in his warm hand and kissed me again. My anger faded away as I melted into his kiss.

"I need to tell my father." I said much later "I don't know if he'll want to announce it now, or if I'll have to go through the elimination with Xavier as planned."

"And Leo."

"And Leo." I'd forgotten about having to have him officially eliminated too, mainly because he hadn't been an option for me for quite some time.

I stood up and brushed the grass from my gown. Xavi would die on the spot if she could see the mess I'd made of it. Luca picked up my tiara and handed it back to me.

"Where are you going? Our date has only just begun."

"I want to tell my father the news. No time like the present." I may as well get it over with as soon as possible.

"Good idea. I'll tell my parents too."

"No! I need to tell my father first. Could you please wait?"

"For you, anything." He kissed my hand and let me leave.

I walked slowly back to the palace, wondering if I'd made a terrible mistake. This was the second man I'd proposed to this summer. The second man I didn't love but was the best option available to me. The second man I'd asked to marry me in the hope I'd love him one day. It was a depressing thought. He wasn't the one for me, but he was the best choice for the kingdom. I remembered his stance on the Magi. One day, we'd make things right again, and on that day, Cynder would understand why I did what I had to do. He'd be free, like all of his kind. I only hoped he'd forgiven me by then because I wasn't sure I'd ever be able to forgive myself.

I found my father having a joke with Queen Sarina. I noticed he was standing as far away as possible from King Theron who was in discussion with Elise and my mother.

"Father, can I have a word in private?"

He excused himself from Queen Sarina and took me to his office. I wasn't sure exactly how he was going to take my news, but at the end of the day, he really didn't have any choice in the matter. Yes, he could tell me he wanted Xavier kept in the competition as long as possible, but the final decision had always been mine. Once it was announced to the public, he wouldn't be able to change it anyway. Part of me thought it might be better to tell the world before my father as I had planned to do with Daniel, but the next elimination was a couple of weeks away, and I was sick of playing the charade.

"I've picked Luca." I said it straight out before I lost the nerve.

"You are going to eliminate Luca? Wonderful. I've been waiting all day to stick it to that odious bore Theron. Xavier will make a great partner and leader I'm sure. You've made the right decision."

"No. You misunderstand. I've picked Prince Luca to marry. I want to marry him. I want Xavier and Leo eliminated as soon as possible. I'm sure if you called Sadie, she'd be all too happy to set up another broadcast at short notice."

My father frowned and didn't speak for a few minutes. When he did, his tone was gruff.

"I thought we had an understanding. Xavier cannot be eliminated."

I stood firm. "Yes, so you have said, but you also said that the final decision is down to me. I've made that decision, and it's to marry Luca. That can't happen without eliminating the other two men."

"This is not acceptable."

"It is acceptable, and it is what's going to happen. I didn't want to do this stupid competition in the first place, but I did because you asked me to. I chose four men out of a hundred, and I went on date after date in the public eye. I didn't want to do any of it, but I did because it is what you expected me to do. I've not complained at all, but now I've made my choice, and my choice is Luca."

My father nodded slowly. "Fine. I shall contact Sadie and ask her to come tomorrow. May as well get it over with. I'll expect you in your finest gown at midday for the formal announcement. I'll let Prince Luca know he is to be ready also. I assume you've already told him?"

"Of course, I have. Oh, thank you, Daddy." I ran to hug him, but he just huffed and barged past me.

It was only when I went to bed late that night that I remembered I was supposed to meet up with Leo. I'd left it too late, but I knew he'd understand after tomorrow's announcement.

Xavi fussed around me even more than usual the next day. She'd been told I was going to make a big announcement and had the perfect dress for me to make it in. It was an off the shoulder white number that could easily pass for a wedding dress had it been a little longer. Perhaps she had guessed what the announcement was to be.

I felt almost happy as I walked down to the stage area. There were so many people crammed into the palace grounds that I wondered how they could all breathe. They stretched as far as the eye could see, way past the gates of the palace. There were also many more cameras here today than usual. It seemed my father had invited all the networks, not just the one Sadie worked for. I was pleased to see it was still she that would be interviewing me though. I didn't like being interviewed, but I, at least, knew her.

I waited at the edge of the stage while she did her usual warm up of the crowd.

I'd hoped Luca would be around, but maybe he would join me after the announcement. It made sense. As my nerves increased, I found myself playing with the bracelet Cynder had given me. After today, I'd have to take it off. Only the

317

thought that I was doing this for him and the other Magi kept me going. I'd sacrifice my life with him if it meant his freedom. Once I was married, I'd have more say in the running of the kingdom and with Luca on my side along with his parents, I would work tirelessly to make the Magi free again.

Taking a deep breath, I waited for Sadie to finish her speech. She was working her way through a presentation showing pictures of the whole competition from the night of the ball to the official photos taken yesterday of the Thalian royal family.

I shed a tear when I saw Daniel among the photos and wondered what he was up to. I'd not seen him since the last elimination. I hoped he was doing well. We would soon be needing those chairs he was making for the palace, so I was confident I'd see him again sooner rather than later.

When the presentation finished, Sadie spoke directly to the crowd.

"There have been a number of highlights from the competition as you can see. We've watched Princess Charmaine blossom from a young girl into a woman these past few months, and now we are all gathered here for an important milestone in her young life. For tonight ladies and gentlemen, I'm extremely excited to announce that we are not eliminating one man, but two. Her Royal Highness, The Princess Charmaine has chosen the man she will marry in six weeks' time."

The crowd went ballistic. I had to stick my fingers in my ears for fear of going deaf as the thunderous sound of thousands of people cheering filled the air. I could just see some of the banners that they were holding up.

We love you Leo

And

Luca for Charmaine. I even saw one with Xavier's name and a girl's phone number on it.

"Without further ado," continued Sadie as the noise abated slightly, "Let me bring on stage Princess Charmaine."

I walked on stage to even more riotous applause. I could see more of the banners now. Many were supporting the three men left. A couple had Daniel's name on them.

I smiled as I approached Sadie, and waved out to the people. It took a full five minutes before the crowd had calmed down enough for me to be able to speak.

"What a welcome!" said Sadie.

"Thank you all. I'm very happy to be here, and I'm so grateful for your support through this competition. It's been a very difficult choice as you can imagine. All the men were wonderful, and any girl in my position would find it hard to choose. Eliminating Daniel last time was so much harder than I anticipated and the same goes for the two men I'm eliminating today. Having spent time with both of them, I can assure you, they will make fantastic husbands to two lucky ladies one day."

"Just not you, eh?" Sadie interrupted good-naturedly.

"I can only pick one man, Sadie, as you know."

The crowd laughed. I pulled so hard on my bracelet I could feel the tiny silver carriage digging into my skin. Cynder would be watching this. I wondered if his heart would break as much as mine had.

"A girl's heart is a complicated thing. For one man you may be his lucky charm, but sometimes, no matter what you do, you have to make a decision that is the best for everyone. Everyone should be free for that." I hoped that Cynder understood my cryptic message. I added the "everybody should be free" in the hopes he knew I was doing this so he could be free. I hoped he knew that I'd love him forever. "I've been free to make my decision; I just hope it's one you all agree with."

"Exactly, and if we don't, then there's always the two gorgeous hunks left for us, right ladies?"

There was another cheer, and the banners were thrust higher into the sky.

"Without further ado, let's put the kingdom out of its misery and invite the new soon-to-be prince of Silverwood to the stage."

I waited for Luca to join me. I could feel my charm bracelet cutting into my skin; I was pulling it so tightly.

There was a huge collective scream from the crowd as Xavier took to the stage. At the same time, the screen behind us showed his photo and the words "Prince Xavier."

The pain on my wrist stopped suddenly as the bracelet broke and flew across the stage.

The screen cut to me, and all I could see was my own expression of shock.

A Secret Uncovered

I raged at my father, but he fobbed me off with some story about finding Luca kissing one of the kitchen maids. I didn't want to believe him, not after everything he'd said in the garden, but I'd seen the way Luca flirted with a kitchen maid at the ball and at the back of my mind, I knew it might be true. I hated myself for thinking it. Luca had the reputation, but he'd treated me with such respect. I thought I knew him, or, at least, I thought I was beginning to. The full-on rush of love that hits you like a train had not happened with Luca the way it had with Cynder, but I can't deny that my heart had fluttered when we had kissed. And we had kissed. We'd kissed a lot, and somewhere between lunch with his parents and the meeting with my father, I'd fallen into a dream that maybe we would be something special one day.

That dream was now as broken as all my others. Now I had to marry a man I didn't even like. At least, I'd liked the other three.

Luca had been sent back to Thalia in disgrace alongside his parents. I wasn't even given the chance to say goodbye.

I left my father's office when he told me that his decision was final and if I didn't agree to it, he'd make Elise marry Xavier instead. That was not something I was about to let happen.

On the way back to my room, I reflected on how it was possible for my life to deteriorate so much in such a short space of time. Just a few months ago, I was looking forward to the summer ahead and to the ball in which Grace would choose a husband. Since then, not only had I lost the love of my life with Cynder, I had also lost the chance to save his life, or at least save him from a life in hiding. The police were still looking for him. Now they were going door to door searching every house for the pair to the glass slipper that had melted next to the bomb. They wouldn't find it, of course. It was still safely hidden in my room, but they would find him. There was no doubt in my mind. And unlike Luca with the influence of his parents, I doubted Xavier would help. He'd shown no interest in the Magi at all. In fact, he'd not really shown a lot of interest in anything. The thought of being married to him for the rest of my life filled me with bile. I ran to my room and threw myself down on the bed, but the tears wouldn't come. I wasn't just sad anymore. I was angry. I was absolutely livid with everything that had happened. I thumped my pillow, hoping to relieve myself of some of the frustration. It didn't work.

If only Grace were here. She would know what to do. I wondered how she would have felt in marrying Xavier. After all, if she were still alive, she would have been in my position. She would probably do it without fuss. She'd smile and do what was best for the kingdom, putting her own wants and needs last. Not that I could figure out why Xavier was the best choice. He had no royal connections. He didn't have the support of the people like Leo did. In fact, the only thing I could see that he brought to the table was a set of ripped abs. Nice in themselves, but hopeless in helping to run a kingdom. If only I knew why my father wanted him, then maybe I could understand, but my father had made it quite clear that he wasn't going to tell me his reasons. No, he was going to make me marry a man I didn't love, without knowing why.

It was so unfair. I needed Grace more than ever. I walked over to the door that separated our rooms. I'd only stepped through it on one occasion since her death, and then I'd run through it, not wanting to stay in the room for fear it might make me cry. I was already on the verge of tears, so what did it matter? I opened the door and stepped in.

It was musty. The cleaners had not been permitted in here since her death a few months previously. I opened her curtains and a window to let in some air.

Like before, the pain hit me in the stomach. Her room was exactly as she had left it. The doll she'd been given as a present on her birth was still on her bed. I picked it up and hugged it tightly. I could still smell her perfume slightly on it. Memories of her flooded back, filling me with grief as strong as it had been since the day she died.

"I need you," I whispered, but of course, she didn't answer. I placed the doll back on the bed and walked over to her shelving unit. Despite the extravagant gifts she'd received from well-wishers every day, the items she kept close to her were remarkably plain. A cheap teddy she'd won at a fairground the one time she'd been permitted to leave the palace, a postcard from a friend of hers, some old books that really should have been taken back to the schoolroom, and finally a photo of the three of us. Grace, Elise, and I. It was taken a couple of years ago, and yet, we all looked so young. Grace sat up straight with Elise gazing up at her, trying to copy her, and with me standing behind them, sticking my tongue out. I laughed. It represented the three of us so well; no wonder Grace kept it. I picked it up and held onto it. I'd find a frame and put it on my wall.

I picked up the teddy next, and something hard fell out, hitting me on my toe. When I looked down, I saw a small black leather-bound book. I picked it up, ready to put it back on the shelf, but then I saw it had fallen from the back of the teddy. The stitching had come away, and there was a hole just big enough to fit the book in. This book had been hidden on purpose. I opened it to the front page and realized it was a diary. Grace's diary.

I'd not known she kept one. Putting the teddy back on the shelf, I took both the photo and the diary back into my room. I'd just sat on the bed to read it when the door at the other side of the room opened. I quickly shoved the black book under my pillow.

"That was a surprise," said Elise, coming over and sitting next to me on the bed. She meant the announcement earlier.

"For you and me both!" I sighed.

"What do you mean?"

"I wasn't going to pick Xavier. I was going to pick Luca."

She opened her mouth in surprise. "I did wonder why you picked him. Whenever you talked about the four men, you rarely mentioned his name."

"That's because I had nothing to say about him. I still don't. Father chose him, but I don't know why."

"You aren't going to actually go ahead with it are you?" The big question.

"What choice do I have, Elise? I'm the heir to the throne now. I have to get married. If I don't marry Xavier, what will I do? Father got rid of Luca pretty swiftly. I've no reason to think he won't do the same to me if I don't cooperate, and then it will be you who has to marry Xavier."

"You are being paranoid. Listen to what you are saying. There's no way that father would banish you. You are his eldest daughter."

I wasn't so sure anymore.

"Wouldn't he? He's banished the Magi; he's banished Luca, all for his own reasons. Who's to say he won't do the same to me? He wants

Xavier as the prince, and that's that. Why are you here anyway?"

I knew I was being snappy, but it was ok for her. She still had Leo, and now she was free to go public with their relationship. What's more, our father didn't seem to mind.

"I came to tell you that Leo is in the library. He wants to see you."

What with everything that had happened over the last twenty-four hours, I'd completely forgotten about meeting Leo. Not that I really cared anymore. I'd already lost everything I cared about, but I'd let him down once, It would be rude to let him down again. Besides, I wanted to tell him what I'd found out about my grandfather.

"I'm sorry for snapping. Can you tell him I'll be down in five minutes? I can't stay another second in this dress."

I changed into my most comfortable outfit and met both Leo and Elise in the library. Leo stood and kissed me on the cheek. At the same time, he whispered in my ear.

"I have news. I can't tell you here."

"Let's go out into the garden," I said loudly in case anyone was listening.

But when we got to the front door, the weather had changed drastically. The beautiful weather of the morning had turned into a violent storm. The dark sky crashed with thunder and rain lashed down.

"That's it then!" said Leo. "We'll have to talk tomorrow."

"No!" I wanted to say that the weather wasn't so bad, but the trees were nearly being blown over with the gale that was blowing. To go outside would be madness.

"I know where we can go."

The only place I could think of that wouldn't be bugged was the servant's quarters. There was no doubt in my mind that the communal areas frequented by the staff would have listening devices, but even my father wouldn't stoop so low as to listen into the private lives of the staff in their own rooms. At first, I was going to take them to Jenny's room in the hope she'd understand, but as we walked down the staff corridor, I had a better idea. I opened the door to the room that had once belonged to Agatha. As she hadn't yet been replaced, I assumed it would still be empty. I was pleased to see I was right. There were no personal items anywhere, and the wardrobe was empty. It was the perfect place to have a secret conversation.

"Molly had a baby!" I blurted out as soon as I was sure we were not being listened to.

"I know, and in view of today's event's you are not going to like what I'm about to tell you."

It sounded ominous. What could my grandfather having a child possibly have to do with the dreadful day I was having?

"I'll start from the beginning. I met up with Zania Askham in a small town called Yorke, which is near the southern border. She was reluctant to speak to me at first as Yorke is one of the towns that the Magi are being driven from."

"I thought she wasn't a Mage?"

"She's not, but the story she told me was all about the Magi. A lot of her friends are, and the police are going after Magi supporters now." He walked around the room as he spoke and steepled his fingers together. I could see he was used to public speaking. "Eventually, I persuaded her to talk. A hefty sum for her granddaughter's college tuition did it. She told me that she did know Molly very well a long time ago. They were both very young and did the same job, except she got paid for it, and Molly didn't. Molly, like all the other Magi in the palace, were unpaid slaves. She said that even though they both were the queen's maids, in reality, it was Molly that did all the work, while she was in charge. As they became friends, Zania helped out Molly when the queen wasn't looking."

Elise interrupted. "But surely, it would have been easier for Molly anyway? She had a wand."

"No. Back then, just as it is today, wands were prohibited. Everything was done by hand. Despite their different backgrounds, the two girls became firm friends.

"After a few months, Molly caught the King's eye. She didn't tell Zania for a long time, but eventually, she let slip that she was having an affair with your grandfather, the king. Around that time, the king moved all the slaves into the staff quarters and built more in the same wing. He did it so Molly could come to his bed chambers without anyone seeing. Molly was placed right on the end by the servant's staircase. From then on, when she wasn't with the king or working, Molly and Zania spent all their time together. One day she told Zania that she was pregnant and the baby was the king's.

"The queen found out. How could she not, when the bump became apparent. She told your grandfather that she wanted to ban the Magi and especially Molly, but your grandfather wouldn't hear of it. He built Molly four bungalows on the grounds. One for her and the baby, and the others as decoys.

Officially, they were for guests, but it was Molly and her daughter that lived there. The others were hardly ever used."

"That's where you are staying now?" said Elise. "And Molly had a girl?"

"She did! When your grandfather died, your grandmother told your father the truth. He was a young man by then and had just succeeded to the throne. Immediately, he threw Molly and her daughter out onto the street. He paid Molly off so she wouldn't tell anyone the truth. She was true to her word and never spoke of it again. If anyone asked who her daughter's father was, she told them she didn't know. She ended up in Yorke, and when Zania retired, she joined her there. Molly died quite a few years ago, but her daughter is still alive."

"Who is she?"

"Her name is Ellen. She also lives a simple life in Yorke. Because she is only half Magi, she has so far been able to hide her true parentage from the authorities, but she has a son."

My mind whirled as I thought about the implications. I had an aunt and cousin out there somewhere.

Leo looked at me then as though he was about to drop a bombshell. When he spoke, he did just that.

"Her son's name is Xavier."

The Shock of the Truth

avier? Please tell me that you don't mean my Xavier?"

"If by your Xavier, you mean Xavier Gallo, then yes, I'm afraid so. Xavier is your cousin."

I stood up, feeling out of breath. The world seemed to close in around me as I fought to breathe. Blackness tinged the corners of my eyes.

"It's not that bad," Elise ran over and put her arms around me to soothe me.

"Not that bad?" I croaked. "I had a hundred men to choose from. Of the four I chose, one was gay, one was probably sleeping with a kitchen maid, one is our cousin, and the last one is dating you! I think on a scale of what's bad, this could very well be right at the top!"

I was hysterical, and the dizziness was beginning to close in. Elise guided me to a chair and put my head between my knees. Slowly, my vision began to clear, and my breathing returned to normal.

"I don't get it!" I said at last. "Why would my father want me to marry my cousin?"

"You don't think Father knows?" asked Elise, still fanning me with her hands.

I sat up straight. "Of course, he knows. There has been something going on this whole time. Xavier has been hiding something, and this is it. This is why father wanted him in, but I can't understand why. It makes no sense."

"I'm sorry to say this," began Leo, "and it's just a theory, but your father only had daughters. Maybe he wanted a male member of his family to rule the kingdom? He's of an older generation who may think it's for the best."

"Xavier doesn't even know how to put clothes on, let alone rule a country." I fumed at the thought of it. My father had never had a problem with having daughters, and we'd been brought up to one day rule. Nothing was ever denied us because we were girls. I didn't buy it. There was something else.

"I'm going to find Xavier...or Father. One of them is going to tell me the truth!" I slammed the door on the way out and marched through the palace. When I'd got as far as the entrance hall, my mother collared me.

"There you are. I've been looking all over for you. The dressmaker is here and wants to measure you for the wedding dress."

"I'm in no mood for wedding dresses," I replied abruptly. "Where is Father? I need to speak to him."

"He's out with Xavier. He thought it would be best to get to know his future son-in-law before the big day."

"He already knows him. When are they due back?" I could speak to them both at once. It would give me a chance to tell them what I thought of them.

"I don't know. I think your father mentioned taking him somewhere and that they'd be all day. It will give us plenty of time to sort out the dress. I want it to look perfect, and I'm sure you do too. Oh, and before I forget, Luca passed me a letter before he went home. He asked me to give it to you."

She fished around in her pocket before handing me a plain envelope. I took it and turned, planning to read it in my room.

"Where are you going? The dressmaker is waiting, and she's already been here for an hour. It would be rude to keep her any longer."

So I slipped the envelope into my own pocket and followed my mother to the dressing room. It seemed so empty without Xavi and her bevy of beauticians there, but there was a huge pile of white fabric and a tiny old lady with half-moon glasses and a tape measure in her hands.

I spent the afternoon being measured from head to toe before being swathed in every type of fabric imaginable. Swatches of every color of the rainbow and more were laid out for me to choose from, but all I could think about was the letter from Luca.

I found an opportunity to open it when my mother and the old woman were discussing the difference between baby pink and petal pink.

I ripped open the envelope and read. It was not the love letter I was expecting, just a hurriedly written note.

What did I do wrong?

L

What did he do wrong? Absolutely nothing, that's what. He must have been as blindsided by the announcement that I was going to marry Xavier as I was. What must he have thought as the photo of Xavier flashed up on screen? I wanted to write back to him, but I was sure he'd hate me now. Why wouldn't he? He must have thought I'd changed my mind. They say that you don't know what you've got until it's gone, and in this case, it was true. I missed him. Not in the same heart-wrenching way I missed Grace or Cynder, but I missed his presence. I missed the future he'd painted for us. I wasn't even sure what my future would be now.

After another few hours of bridal wear discussions, I was finally allowed to leave. I wandered through the palace aimlessly, not knowing which way to turn or what to do next. Cynder was gone, Daniel was gone, and Luca was gone. I felt like I had no one left to talk to.

I was just about to drag myself back to bed when Father and Xavier walked through the main palace doors. Both of them were soaked through to the skin after being out in the rain.

Good! It served them right!

I marched over to them. "I know! I know everything!" I shouted. They both looked at me. A curious expression came over Xavier's face. He actually smiled. My father, on the other hand, looked nervous as well he might.

"Let's talk about this in my office," he said, ushering me away from the members of staff, who had stopped what they were doing and were watching the spectacle I was making instead. Not that I cared.

As soon as the door closed behind us, I began to shout again, but my father cut me off.

"What exactly is it you know?"

"I know that my grandfather had another child. I know that Xavier is my cousin!"

My father sighed and massaged his temples. "How did you find out?"

"It doesn't matter how I found out. The question is why? Do you not think I'm good enough? Am I so bad that you'd have me marry a blood relative to help me rule?"

"There is nothing against the law about cousins marrying," Xavier cut in. The smirk on his face was beginning to annoy me. He was enjoying this. He wanted to be found out. Far from the gorgeous man I thought he was, the smirk made him look ugly. I wanted to smack it right off his face. "And we are only half-cousins remember?"

"Xavier, I think it best if you go and get dry so I can speak to my daughter alone."

Xavier looked put out by the request, but he headed for the door all the same. "Just make sure you tell her my plans for the future."

He opened the door and walked through it, giving me the opportunity to slam it behind his sneaky back.

"I only found out about Xavier when the positions opened for the ball. Of course, I'd known about his mother for many years, so I knew it was a possibility that she had children, but I hoped that she'd not tell them about their grandfather. I had gone to great lengths to keep the whole sordid story out of the press."

"Yes, you paid off Molly."

He seemed surprised. "So you know her name too? Not that it matters, not now. I was so angry with my father when I found out he'd cheated on my mother with a woman who was not only a maid but a mage too. It was a scandal and my mother never really got over it. I hated him, really hated him." He stood up and began to pace the room. "Of course, I only found out after he died, so I didn't get the chance to tell him what I thought of him. I paid Molly a huge amount of money to keep her daughter's parentage a secret, but it seems that I wasted that money after all."

"She didn't tell anyone. Her daughter already knew the truth. She didn't tell anyone either except for her only son."

"Well, her only son decided to blackmail me," he replied angrily. "He told me that if he didn't succeed to the throne, he'd tell the world the truth."

"You were being blackmailed?" It made sense now. Leo was wrong about not trusting a girl to rule. This wasn't about me. It never had been. This was about Xavier.

"Yes. What was I to do? I made sure he got an invite and kept him in the competition. Very soon, he'll get what he wants when he marries you."

"But why does he want to be king? He's shown no interest in it to me."

"He wants to keep Silverwood clean."

I was confused. "What does that even mean?"

"He wants it empty of immigrants. He wants the Magi out."

I thought about this for a second. Like everything else I was being told, it made no sense. "But he *is* a Mage!"

"His grandmother was. I think we can assume that by the time the magi blood got down to him, it was diluted enough to not work. He's no more a mage than you or I."

"But why does he want them all out of Silverwood?"

"I suspect for the same reason I do. He hates them. Maybe with him, it's jealousy, but what do I care? If he'll continue my work when I'm gone, then that's all I need to know."

Xavier might have been blackmailing my father, but they were on the same side. I could see that now. My father had spent years being angry at the woman that broke his mother's heart, and he'd blamed all Magi. That's why their rights had become less and less since my grandfather died. Xavier blackmailing him was just the excuse he needed to further his campaign of hatred over them.

"An entire group of people are being thrown out of the land because of an old man's indiscretion over forty years ago. You can't do this!"

"What choice do I have? He'll tell the press otherwise."

"So what if he does?" I countered angrily. "Maybe the people have a right to know the truth. Maybe then, when everything is out in the open, the Magi can come back, and we can start building bridges."

"I have no interest in building bridges with the Magi."

"I don't care where your interests lie anymore. I'd rather the royal reputation be ruined forever than marry that man."

My father sighed again and sat back in his chair.

"I'm afraid it's not that simple."

"Why not?" I demanded.

"Because it was Xavier that planted the bomb at the ball and there is currently another one hidden in the palace."

Daniel

The air flew out of my lungs in a whoosh, winding me with the impact of his words.

"Xavier planted the bomb?"

"Yes, but don't worry, I made sure that you, your mother, and sister were all out of the way of the blast zone when it detonated. You weren't in any danger."

"You...you...you knew about this?"

"Not at first. At first, I just thought he was blackmailing me. I'd hoped that when I invited him and helped you chose him as one of the five men, he'd back down. After dinner, he came to me, and we had a little chat. He told me then about the bomb. I was going to call the police on him, but when he put forward the idea that we could blame the protesters, it got me thinking. I'd been trying to get rid of the Magi for years. Sure they were ok to do the dirty work in the palace, but they were getting ideas above their station. To be honest, it didn't take me long to come around to Xavier's way of thinking. I waited until my three girls were out of harm's way and gave him the signal. When he saw some fellow from the kitchen walking through the corridor, he hit the timer. Ten seconds later our problems were solved."

"People died!" I cried out, unable to believe what I was hearing. "Innocent people! And an innocent man has been blamed for it!"

"I was kind of hoping he'd die in the blast, to be honest, but he managed to escape. He was only a kitchen hand."

"Only a kitchen hand?" I could feel myself start to hyperventilate again. All this time, he'd been on the run accused of murder when it was my own father and soon-to-be husband who'd done it.

"It had to be done. The Magi were getting too big, too powerful."

"They just want to go to university, to get jobs," I whispered.

"Yes, and where would that lead? To rebellion, that's where. I did what I had to do for the sake of this kingdom, and I expect you to do the same. You'll be marrying Xavier next week, and you'll keep quiet about everything I told you. If anything happens between now and then, such as the press hearing of this, we'll all be finished. You don't want to end up in jail do you?"

I left my father's office feeling faint. My whole life had turned on its head. I didn't know who I could trust anymore. If I couldn't trust my own father, who could I trust?

I wanted to go and shout and scream at Xavier, but I knew there was no point. Before he'd left my father's office, he'd smiled at me knowingly. His face, I'd once thought was beautiful was contorted into a thing of evil and just thinking of him made my blood curdle.

That night I lay on my bed in a daze, thinking back over everything that had happened in the past few months. Cynder had told me that he'd heard someone talking to my father right after the bomb had gone off. He'd thought it was a member of staff, but it had to be Xavier. They'd collaborated to use him as a scapegoat right from the start. He was just in the wrong place at the wrong time. At least, I knew the truth now. I'd always known that Cynder didn't plant that bomb, but it was a small relief to have it proven. Not that it helped him in any way. He was still out there somewhere and still wanted by the police. I was in no doubt that if he did get caught, they'd still sentence him to death.

Why wouldn't they? It didn't matter that he was innocent. They wanted the truth buried.

I was trapped in the palace by my duties, and if I didn't marry Xavier on the 26th of September as planned, he was going to blow us all up. If it was just me, I think I'd have let him, but it wasn't just me. It was Elise, and my mother, and Leo, and the staff. None of them deserved to die because one man...make that two men, hated the Magi over something that happened so long ago. Xavier wasn't even born when my grandfather died, but he'd learned to hate him as much as my father had. So many innocent people were already suffering because of an act of indiscretion. So much hate abounded and my future, far from being the one I had imagined of being the one to bring about peace between the Magi and non-magic's, had been torn away from me.

The next few weeks passed in a blur. Each day, more awful than the last. My mother made endless appointments to do with the wedding arrangements, and there was interview after interview, photo shoot after photo shoot with Sadie, all of which I had to hold Xavier's hand and smile through as though I was the happiest woman alive, all the while feeling like I was dying inside. The nation was in a frenzy of such excitement that not only did Xavier and I take up the front cover of every newspaper, but most of the inside columns as well. In fact, everyone in Silverwood was excited about the wedding except me.

I'd been forced to lie to Elise and Leo, telling them it was all a mistake and that I did love Xavier after all. Elise knew I was lying, but as time when on, she began to accept it. I mainly kept out of her way, just as I did with everyone. Xavier never let an opportunity go to remind me that I was under his control. If I did or said anything he didn't like, he'd casually let the hidden bomb into the conversation.

There was just one other person in Silverwood who I imagined would be as upset as I. Cynder would be out there seeing all the press coverage. There was no way he could avoid it. I wondered if he went to bed at night as tied up in knots as I felt.

Another man I'd managed to make unhappy was Luca. Every day I received a letter from him declaring how much he missed me. It got so difficult to read them that I eventually stopped, taking them to my room instead to read at a later date.

Wherever I was in the palace, I was aware that somewhere beneath my feet was a bomb, just waiting to go off. Xavier assured me that we were all safe as long as I turned up at the wedding and kept my mouth shut, but it hardly made me feel better. It didn't alter the fact that there were enough explosives nearby to kill everyone in the palace. Every slight movement or strange light I saw had me on edge. I couldn't sleep with my nerves stretched to the breaking from the fear and my dread of the wedding. Jenny was in favor of getting more sedatives from the doctor, putting my jitteriness down to nerves, but I talked her out of it. I needed to stay alert.

As summer passed into early autumn and the trees in the garden began to change color, I found myself out there more than ever. Except this time I was alone. There was no Luca to share kisses, nor Daniel to share jokes with. I'd even stopped glancing up to Cynder's apartment window to see if the curtains had moved. He was long gone, taking my heart with him.

Just a week before the wedding, on one of the last warm days of the year, I was out there again, preferring the fresh air to the stuffiness of the palace. I walked slowly, taking in the flowers that were still holding on. Soon the blanket of winter would come in and cover them,

and they would die until next spring. I envied them. I wished I could hide somewhere for the winter and wake up next spring when this nightmare was over.

I could still see no way out of it. I'd spoken to my father to see if a thorough sweep of the palace had been done by the guards to find the bomb and he insisted it had, but I wasn't so sure. He didn't seem to care anyway. Why would he? With Xavier as his son-in-law, it would continue the legacy of hate he'd propagated. I began to wonder if there was a bomb at all, but banking on there not being one was putting too many lives at stake.

A delivery truck drove down the driveway, breaking me away from my thoughts. So many delivery trucks had been coming into and out of the grounds, all delivering things for the wedding, but this one was different. It was different because from the front of the truck appeared a man with blond hair. It was a man I recognized. I ran to him and threw my arms around him, and like he had done in our last week together, Daniel spun me around.

"Finished the first batch of chairs. The next lot will be here next week. Come on, come look at them."

He looked so happy and exuberant, that for the first time in weeks, I smiled. Around the back of the van was a handsome man pulling chairs out and stacking them on the drive.

"This is Dean, my boyfriend."

Dean put down the chair he was holding and held his hand out to shake. I took his hand and grinned.

"It's nice to meet you, Dean. And, oh wow, these chairs!"

Dean picked up one of the stacks and began to take it to the palace doors.

I raised an eyebrow at Daniel. "Boyfriend?"

Happiness poured from him. "He's been helping me with the chairs," he admitted.

"I'm so happy for you," I said, hugging him again. "What does your father think?"

"My father has come around. I think the massive order of chairs for the wedding helped. Thanks for that by the way."

"It's no problem. I'm glad things worked out for you. I hope you and Dean can make it to the wedding. It wouldn't be the same without you."

"I must say I'm surprised you ended up with Xavier. I had money on the prince. You owe me fifty dollars!"

I pushed him playfully. "No can do. I'll be paying off chairs for the rest of my life."

"Seriously, though, Xavier?"

My facade dropped. "I don't want to marry him," I admitted, keeping my voice down.

"So why are you?"

I so wanted to tell him the truth, but if Xavier found out, who knew what would happen?

"It's complicated. I have to."

"You have to?" Now it was Daniel's turn to raise his eyebrow.

"I can't talk about it."

Daniel locked his arm in mine and began walking me down the driveway slowly. When he was sure that we were out of earshot, he turned to me.

"What's going on?" His voice was so full of love and concern that I broke down. He took me in his arms and held me while I wept.

"I'm being forced into it. Xavier is the one who planted the bomb, and there is another one in the palace. If I don't marry him, he's going to blow the palace up."

"What? Why hasn't your father gotten the police involved?"

"My father wants me to marry him. They both want the Magi run out of Silverwood."

Daniel just stared at me open-mouthed. "I don't know what to say, Charmaine. I'm so sorry. Can't you tell the press?"

"How can I? There are over a thousand staff members in the palace, not to mention Elise, mother, and Leo."

"Leo is still in there? I thought he was eliminated?"

"He's dating Elise. Father has let him stay on if he remains quiet."

Daniel's eyes widened, and he let out a low whistle. "Wow!" He mouthed the word, but no sound came out. "What about Luca? Is he still there too?"

"No. My father sent him home. Neither he nor Leo knows about the bomb. You are the first person I've told."

He hugged me again, probably to save him from having to say anything. What was there to say anyway?

"Is there anything I can do?" he asked, breaking away from me.

"No. Just come to the wedding. I'll need all the support I can get."

He wiped a tear from my eye. "I'll be there."

As we walked back up to the house, he bent down.

"Hey, what's this?" He picked up a silver chain that had fallen at the edge of the grass line. A small carriage and a small silver shoe charm glinted in the sun.

Before the Wedding

I awoke to my wedding day in much the same way I had done in the weeks previously—full of dread and feeling sick.

Elise bounded in and jumped on my bed.

"It's time."

"I know." I sighed. I'd spent the last week trying to come up with some way to get out of the mess I was in, but it was so much bigger than me. The whole kingdom was in a mess, but looking out of the window, my father was doing a good job of covering it up. White peacocks strolled around on the freshly mown grass, and millions of white petals were strewn over the back driveway. I knew that the front driveway would be even more spectacular, as it was in the garden there that the wedding was to take place. I'd watched as a huge marquee had been erected on the front lawn in case of inclement weather and this morning, as the sun was shining, they'd be setting out hundreds of Daniel's chairs in rows outside next to it.

"It won't be that bad, you'll see," said Elise, coming up behind me and wrapping her arms around my waist. "Look. The people are already out in force to get a glimpse of you. You can see them through the back gates. Jenny says that a lot of people have been camping out by the front gate for days to get the best spot to see you."

"Hmm."

"Does it matter that you are cousins? Not really. He's still utterly gorgeous, and really, we are only half-cousins. It's not like you are marrying a brother."

"I don't love him, Elise."

"I know. I knew when you told me you did that you were lying. I could see it in your eyes, but maybe you could learn to."

I knew she was trying to make me feel better, but she didn't know the truth, and I wasn't about to tell her. She'd be as devastated as I if she found out what our father had done.

"Where is Leo? Is he getting ready?" This was to be their first official date. Until now, they'd kept their relationship secret from the press, but with all eyes on me, they were now free to be together.

"He's been out for the last few days. He says he'd got something special planned for the wedding so expect a big present." She giggled, and I smiled at her. She was truly happy. I could see it in the way her eyes sparkled, which made me happy. At least one of us was.

"Come on then," I replied, linking my arm in hers. Let's go and get ready!"

As the chief (and only) bridesmaid, Elise was going to spend the morning in the dressing room with me.

When we got there, we found a huge table set out with fruits, baked goods, and champagne.

There were also so many people there that I could barely see Xavi, who stood in the middle looking flustered and trying to coordinate everyone.

"What's all this?" I asked.

Jenny appeared from the throng.

"This is your wedding breakfast. I know, traditionally, it's supposed to be with the bride and groom and all the guests, but many of them haven't arrived yet, so we are having a girls only breakfast in here while you get ready." She thrust a glass into my hand and poured champagne into it. "Your mother is already a little tipsy."

I searched for my mother in the crowd and found her talking animatedly to Alezis. I couldn't see that she was tipsy, but then my mother always knew how to be a lady.

I knocked back the champagne and grabbed a croissant. If these were my last hours of freedom, I might as well enjoy them.

The champagne numbed my brain, and after my second glass, I was beginning not to care what happened for the rest of the day.

I was just about to pour my third glass, when Xavi, pulled it from my hand and guided me towards Alezis.

"Nobody wants a drunk bride," she reprimanded. "I'll bring you some juice."

"I don't want juice," I called after her retreating form, but it fell on deaf ears. A minute later, she was back with a glass of orange juice. As usual, Alezis was gazing at my hair as if it might suddenly change color or do something exciting.

An hour later and the only hair he'd touched was the fuzz that had grown on his chin.

"Are you going to cut my hair? Because my ass is getting numb!"

"Perfection takes time," he murmured and went back to stroking his chin.

I was about to snap back again. I knew that it was hardly his fault that I didn't want to get married, but he was adding stress to an already stressful day.

Xavi came over and whispered something in his ear. Watching her expression in the mirror, I could see that something was wrong, but I was already past the point of caring. Maybe Xavier had dropped dead or run away, either of which would be a bonus as far as I was concerned.

No one thought to let me in on the secret, but as soon as Xavi left, Alezis got to work on my hair, cutting it and styling it in double quick time.

He'd put it in a half-up do and curled the bottom of it. It was beautiful as it was, but I knew that a veil would cover most of it once I was fully dressed.

As soon as I was finished, Elise took my place, ready to be made beautiful. How they could improve in the perfection she already was, I had no idea.

Makeup was next, and like Alezis, the three makeup artists who made me flawless rushed the job. Agneta was quickly brought over, and she powdered my face and applied mascara and a coat of pale lip gloss. I could see Xavi waiting impatiently by her side and tapping her foot. Something really must be up if Xavi was in a flap. I sneaked a peek at my watch, wondering if we were running late, but there were hours until the wedding started. We had plenty of time. If I stil had any doubt that something was wrong, a quick look in the mirror showed me the usually unflappable Jenny pacing up and down with a worried look about her. Even my mother seemed to be on her third or fourth drink.

"Xavi. What's going on?"

"Nothing." She answered a little too quickly. "I'm just excited is all."

Her expression showed anything but excitement.

"Less is more," she said, wrestling me away from Agnata's hands. Agneta sighed, but let her take me.

Unlike all the other times when I'd had to dress for an occasion in here, there was only one dress brought out. It was so far from the huge meringue style monstrosity I'd been expecting. There were no frills or layers or crystals or tulle. It was just a white dress. Long and elegant and as close to my style as it was possible to get without having holes in the knee and grass marks on the back. In short, it was stunning. The only bit of detail was a beige satin sash around the middle. I put it over my head and looked at myself in the mirror. I looked like me. Ok, me in a long white dress, but it was still me. Beneath the months of heartache and pretending to be someone I wasn't, it was almost a relief to see that I still existed in there. When my mother handed me a pair of white sneakers with pale beige laces, I almost cried. For the first time in months, someone had listened to me.

"Why?" I asked, slipping my feet into them.

She pulled me to one side, away from everyone else. "Because you stepped up at last minute to do a job that was never intended to be yours. In an extremely short time frame, you've had to grow up fast and in the public eye. You took on so much more than anyone could have expected of you and apart from a couple of hiccups along the way, you've done a marvelous job. The public adores you, and from a personal point of view, you are the bravest young lady I've ever met. I'm proud to have you as my daughter. That is why I listened to you when you said you didn't want a fancy dress. I thought on today of all days, you should have something you asked for."

Her eyes were moist which threatened to set me off crying. I hugged her tightly. She was right about one thing. Everything had changed, including my relationship with her. Once upon a time, she was like a fairy princess to me. Not only was she the queen, but she was also my hero. She must have noticed our relationship had changed over the last few months. Like a lot of other people in my life, I felt like I was losing her too.

"You look perfect!" She smiled as I did a little twirl for her. There was sadness in her eyes too. It should have been Grace standing here in the white dress. She handed me a diamond necklace, and I let her place it around my neck. Like the dress, it was understated.

"Are you ready? Your father has been waiting outside for half an hour."

"What for?" I asked, surprised. The wedding wasn't scheduled to start for hours.

"We've brought the wedding forward. As soon as Elise is dressed, your father will be escorting you to the gardens for the wedding."

"Why?" I asked perplexed. This whole charade had taken months of planning. The guests had invites for a certain time, the catering was ready to go for after the wedding, the media had been told five o'clock and the people had too. It made absolutely no sense at all to move it to the morning. "The guests won't even be here yet."

"Your father has had people calling the guests for the last hour to notify them of the new time.

I'm sure a few will be late, but it doesn't really matter, does it?"

"But why are we bringing the wedding forward?" Something was going on. I'd seen it with the way Xavi was panicking, and I could see it in the others. "What are you not telling me?"

"I don't want to worry you on your big day."

"Just tell me."

"Your father received intelligence that the Magi are going to stage another demonstration outside the palace walls. He's got police filling the streets, and all the palace guards are on maximum alert, but we thought it would be better to get the wedding done as soon as possible just in case there is a problem later."

It was funny how much this piece of information didn't bother me. My mother seemed more worried about it than I could ever be. The only thought in my mind was not one of a ruined wedding or for my own safety, but the fact that I might see Cynder again.

Xavi came over and with the aid of one of her helpers, fitted my veil. Elise, looking stunning as always in a form fitting beige satin dress with pink flowers in her hair, came over and handed me my bouquet.

We hugged and as I walked through the door to my future, I pulled the veil over my face. For the first time in months, I was hidden from the world.

"You look beautiful, my dear," my father said gruffly, kissing me on the cheek. I put my arm in his. What I really wanted to do was hit him with it, but at the back of my mind, I knew that as soon as I was married, I would be counted as a grown up, capable of making my own decisions. I might have been losing a lot of freedom, but I would also receive other freedoms. I'd be able to travel outside of the palace without permission, and I'd have some say in the way things were run. The police and other officials would have to obey me. I wouldn't be queen yet, but I'd be one step closer. And even though my father didn't know it, I was going to fight him on the laws of the Magi. No matter what happened later today, the Magi would have an ally on the inside. My father wasn't going to know what hit him!

The Wedding

I could already hear the music as I followed Elise out of the front door of the palace. The musicians had either managed to arrive hours early, or someone was playing a record on a player through a speaker. I couldn't see either way because at some point in the night a white fabric tunnel from the house to the wedding venue had been erected just so that no one could see me before I walked down the aisle.

I wanted to ask my father if there were Magi outside already, but I knew it would be fruitless. My heart thumped as we walked through the tunnel, and yet, all I could hear was the music and the sounds of thousands of people cheering. Unlike the televised events from my dates where the public had been invited into the grounds, the public was to be kept outside and the wedding broadcast on huge screens erected on the tops of the palace walls. Only a few people, who had been camping out for days, would actually see anything in real life through gaps in the palace gates.

Still, it hadn't stopped anyone, judging by the noise. I tried to make out whether any of the noise came from the Magi and if the screams and shouts I could hear were happy noises or ones of fighting. It all sounded happy, but it was so loud that screams of distress could quite easily have been hidden.

My mind was whirling with thoughts of Cynder. Was he on the other side of that wall right now, surrounded by other Magi who were protecting him? I fingered my bracelet, twisting the carriage charm around nervously in my fingers. Was I the first bride to walk down the aisle thinking of another man to the one I was marrying? Surely, I couldn't be the first, but unlike the others, I didn't have the luxury of calling the whole thing off at the last minute. I couldn't run away and leave it all behind. Where would I go? As we rounded the corner, a couple of guards opened the end curtains slightly. I got a peek at the rows of chairs, all decked out in beige ribbon with pretty pink flowers on the backs of each, matching both my dress and bouquet. Daniel had done an amazing job. They looked wonderful. They were surprisingly full of people. Amazing, as most of the guests had barely had any notice.

Elise turned and kissed me on the cheek before stepping out. If I thought it was noisy before, it was nothing compared to the rapturous applause and whistles that Elise's appearance illicited. The orchestra began to play the wedding march although it had trouble being heard over the crowd.

I stepped forward and breathed deeply. I was marrying a man whom I not only didn't like, but deep down despised. He stood for everything I hated and yet, the people needed this. They needed to see that the monarchy was still strong. Didn't they?

The curtains had been placed back after Elise had walked out so I couldn't see a thing. In just a moment, I was to become someone's wife. I began to panic and yet feeling the charm bracelet around my wrist was enough to keep me calm. Cynder was with me in spirit, if not in real life. And as the curtains opened to my future, I couldn't help but wonder if he was somewhere just over the other side of the wall.

The screams of the people elevated, and the orchestra increased their volume once again so I could keep step with the dum dum di dum of the wedding march. It turned out that it was an orchestra after all. I could see them now, to the side of the seated area, playing violins and cellos and all the other instruments that made up a full orchestra. Every seat was full. All the guests, the majority of whom I didn't know, had made it in time despite the early start. The sun was shining, and my mother had done a magnificent job of organizing everything. If it was anyone else's wedding, I would have called it perfect. Glancing up at the one screen I could see, I saw a petrified girl staring back. It took me a second to realize that it was me. I was not the brave woman my mother had talked about earlier, but I needed to be. I stood up straight and smiled my widest smile, transforming the scared looking girl on the screen into a happy woman on her wedding day. If I couldn't be her, I could at least pretend to be, the way I had done for the last few months.

I smiled at everyone, the guests, the cameras, and the priest who would be conducting the ceremony. The only person I didn't smile at was Xavier. He didn't deserve my smiles. At the front, I noticed that Luca, Daniel, and Leo were all there. They had been seated together in a prime spot for the cameras. All three beamed at me as I passed. If only things had been different. I would happily have traded Xavier for any of them, but right from the start, the whole thing had been rigged by my father. It didn't matter who sat in those chairs, I was always going to be walking towards Xavier.

At the front, my father took his seat, and my bouquet was handed to Elise who stood to the side. Xavier took my hand and gave me a sickly smile. As usual, his hand was cold and clammy, and I cringed as I held it. The thought of us producing an heir together someday was enough to make me sick. How had I ever thought him good-looking?

The crowd died down as the priest spoke.

"Dearly beloved, we are gathered here today..."

I zoned out as the reality of my situation finally hit me. Without realizing it, I'd been hoping that something would happen that would stop this moment. First, my proposing to Daniel, then to Luca. Just as late as an hour ago, I was hoping that Cynder would somehow leap over the wall and save me from it. But there was no one left to help me. Daniel was sitting next to Dean, their hands entwined. Leo and Elise were not seated together, but I could almost feel the love radiating between them. It seemed everyone had found their happy-ever-after except me. Actually, there was one person who looked as miserable as I felt. Luca was smiling, but like me, it masked pain. He was hurting. Maybe he really was in love with me. My heart broke a little more at the thought of it. Why had I listened to my father? If I'd have pushed a little harder with Luca, maybe it would have been him standing here instead of Xavier. I didn't love Luca, but I liked him a lot, and I liked his vision for the future of Silverwood. He was a good man, a man I would be proud to stand beside as his wife, a man I could see making a great leader.

"We are gathered here today to celebrate..."

I wondered what kind of leader Xavier would make. I was honestly surprised he'd managed to turn up in clothes to the wedding, so I wasn't holding out for much, and yet he'd managed to manipulate the king into marrying his eldest daughter, so I guess I wasn't giving him the credit he deserved. He was cleverer than he looked, and this terrified me more than the thought of marrying an airhead.

I barely knew the guy at all. Nothing he'd told me in our brief conversations was the truth. I didn't know who I was marrying at all.

"If anyone can show just cause why this couple cannot lawfully be joined together in matrimony, let them speak now or forever hold their peace."

I held my breath. This is the point where Cynder would jump over the wall or where Luca would stand up and declare his undying love for me. I found that I was hoping for literally anyone to stand up and give the priest a reason, but after a couple of seconds of silence, I realized that there was no one left to speak up. I was up here by myself. There was only one person I could count on to stop this wedding, and that was me.

"Xavier Simon Gallo, do you take Charmaine Elizabeth Mary Annesley to be your lawfully wedded wife?"

"Yes!" Xavier replied impatiently. He couldn't even be bothered to say I do.

The priest turned to me. I could feel my stomach tying itself in knots.

"And do you, Charmaine Elizabeth Mary Annesley, take Xavier Simon Gallo to be your lawfully wedded husband?"

I held my breath while the world came to a standstill. The once overly exuberant crowd outside had now hushed to complete silence as if the thousands of people were waiting to hear my reply.

"I..."

The seconds dragged out to a minute, and still, I was yet to give an answer. I could feel the eyes of hundreds of thousands of people boring into me and the weight of the decision.

"I..."

"She will," said Xavier, aware that I was causing a scene.

"She has to answer for herself," reminded the priest.

"Do you, Charmaine Elizab..."

There was a noise by the gate. One of the guards was shouting and running towards us.

"The Magi..." He toppled forward, and that's when we all saw the knife in his blood soaked back.

Somewhere, someone screamed. The image that had been on the screen of Xavier and I had panned around to show the toppled guard.

Outside, the rumbles of panic began, and the wedding guests dispersed, running in all directions. The gates that had once been our border to the outside world now had people climbing all over them into the grounds.

I watched in horror as the same could be said for the walls. The grounds were filling from all angles. I could hear the screams of terror from outside the walls, and scarier still, gunshots being fired.

Someone grabbed my hand and pulled me through the crowds of people. In the chaos, I was being buffeted around as people crashed into me. I couldn't tell if they were wedding guests or the Magi. The gunshots were more frequent now, filling the air with a staccato beat, to the chorus of wails and screams.

I was pulled, not towards the house, but to the back part of the garden, but I could see we weren't safe here either. The Magi had already pulled the back gates down and were swarming through. My savior swerved, pulling me back towards the house. I couldn't see who it was – I could only see their back, but it was either a wedding guest or someone else in a suit.

I wanted to stop him, to tell him that the Magi were our friends, but, of course, I couldn't. The Magi were not my friends. Just the handful that I had known knew I'd never hurt them, but how could I expect the rest of them to know that?

I was pulled towards the servant's entrance. I had thought we would be safe inside, but I could already see people fighting down the long corridor that ran the entire length of the palace. The person holding my hand tried pulling me right, but this time I finally did stop him.

"The safe room is through there," I said motioning to a door directly in front of us that would take us out to the main hall.

He turned around to see where I was pointing, and that's when I saw who had saved me

It was Luca.

Chaos

"Follow me."

It was my turn to guide him through the maze that was the palace. Screams filled the air, all way too close for comfort. People ran past us in a panic, not knowing which way to go. I didn't recognize any of them. Bodies littered the floor as the sounds of gunshots whistled past our ears. The way to the main entrance and the safe room below it was blocked, and so we had to run up the nearest flight of stairs to the next floor. From there it was easy enough to run through the empty corridors until we got to the main entrance hall. The doors were open, and people were pouring in. Men in uniform shot bullets almost aimlessly into the throng of people, and there was blood everywhere.

"The safe room entrance is down there." I pointed down to the doorway, now almost hidden by the sheer number of people in the hallway.

"Is there anywhere else we can hide?" asked Luca, looking along the empty first floor corridors.

"We can go up to the higher floors and hide in one of the rooms,"

"No, there are too many people coming in," I looked, and he was right. A steady stream of people were pushing their way through the huge front doors. People were already beginning to go up the stairs. Pretty soon, we would be deluged there too.

"What else can we do? The palace is massive. If we go high enough, we can get away," I said in a panic. Another minute and we were going to be trampled.

"Ok, let's go," Luca never let go of my hand as we both ran up the next set of stairs and kept running until we reached the top floor, my parents private quarters.

"This way," I shouted breathlessly, pointing at a door that would lead to the roof. I could already hear the stampeding feet of hundreds of people following right behind us and the sound of gunshots had not abated as we climbed higher. It felt like a full-scale war was chasing us.

Up one flight of stone stairs and we emerged onto the roof. I'd never been more glad to be wearing sneakers instead of heels. Luca pushed the door closed behind us. Without any way to lock it from the outside, we had to be content with sprinting across the roof and letting the others follow. We were almost to the other side when I looked back and saw a throng of people, also racing for their lives. I could see the panic on their faces. They were not up here to hurt us; they were fleeing just as we were. Gunshots cracked from the gardens below and when I hazarded a peek over the battlements, I could see the true extent of the mess. The whole wedding area including the marquee and the tunnel I'd walked down had been trampled, and thousands of people were still pushing their way into the swollen grounds. The sheer numbers of people astounded me. Not all of them could be Magi. I could see a couple of guards trying fruitlessly to stem the tide, but the people were still coming in.

"Why are they all pushing in?" I asked Luca.

He pointed to a plume of smoke outside the wall, then to another one. The Magi had set fires outside, and the people were coming in here for safety. The problem was, there weren't enough police in here to make up for the sheer number of people. As I watched, a policeman shot a couple of people trying to climb over the palace walls. The whole thing was a mess.

"Come on, we have to go." The roof was already beginning to fill with people.

Luca pulled me towards another door at the end of the roof. It led to a spiral staircase that would either take us up to the top of the highest tower or back down to the main part of the palace.

I pulled one way—upwards, as Luca tried pulling me in the opposite direction.

"There's no one up there," I cried in panic. The number of people on the roof was swelling, and already, I could hear gun cracks sounding out.

"But there will be soon. We'll either get crushed or pushed over the edge. We need to go down. The safe room is our only option."

I had no idea how we were going to manage it, but I followed him down the stairs. We were almost on the ground floor before we saw anyone else. Everyone, it seemed, had used the main stairs and not the servant's stairway at the back of the palace.

We ran past Jenny's room and then past Agatha's old room and down some more stairs until we were back at the main entrance. It was slightly quieter now although bodies littered the floor and the once white marble now shimmered with the blood of the fallen.

I had to step over a number of them until I reached the entrance to the safe room. The guard at the door had been shot, and his body blocked the entrance. Luca barged past me and pushed on the door. It didn't open.

"Try pulling it!" I cried desperately as a bullet whizzed right past my ear.

Luca had to pull the body of the guard out of the way, but the door still wouldn't budge.

"We need to put in a code. Do you know it?" he asked. I looked at the keypad. It displayed the numbers 0-9.

"I don't know. It could be anything."

"What date did your father ascend to the throne?" asked Luca, keeping much calmer than I felt. A shot rang out and a body hit me as it fell to the floor, smearing my wedding dress with blood and increasing the terror I already felt.

I gave him the date, but it didn't work. He then tried my mother's birthday and my father's. All in all, it took four attempts to get it right. It was Grace's birthday.

We ran through the door, slamming it shut behind us.

"Hello!" I called out; hoping to hear my mother's or Elise's voice, but only silence rang back.

"No one is here," I cried, trying not to hyperventilate. I could barely breathe from all the running and fear that was coursing through my veins. Somewhere out there were the people I loved, fighting a war I didn't understand.

"We have to stay by the door. Elise is still out there. The Magi might get her." I hated to say it. I'd been on their side this whole time, and now they were invading the palace, killing people. The thought made me feel sick.

"It's not the Magi."

"Of course, it is. They were demonstrating, and it turned into a riot."

"Shit!" Luca ran his hand through his hair. "The Magi aren't here at all. This is my fault. I never knew..."

"What's going on?" I'd never seen Luca so rattled. "How can it be your fault?"

"I'm so sorry, Charmaine. I never expected this. Really I didn't."

I stepped back from him, unsure of what to say.

"Daniel called me last week. He told me everything, how you were being forced to marry Xavier, how Xavier is blackmailing your father. I wondered why I'd been sent home so suddenly. I couldn't understand it, but when Daniel called, it all made sense. I met up with Daniel, and we got word to Leo too. Between us, we came up with a plan to halt the wedding. We dropped hints that there was going to be a demonstration by the Magi. That's all, I swear. The truth is, there aren't enough Magi left in the kingdom to really demonstrate, but we thought it might make them cancel the wedding, or at least postpone it until a later date while we thought of something else."

"There's no demonstration?" I asked weakly. "So what happened?"

"I don't know. I really don't know, but I know magic when I see it, and none was being used here today."

I was just getting my head around the whole thing when there was a fierce rapping on the door followed by Dean's voice.

"Open the door, quickly!"

Luca opened the door. Dean ran through it with an injured Daniel in his arms. His right thigh had a plume of red staining his gray suit.

Behind them, followed Elise and Leo. Thankfully, they both looked unhurt."

"Quick, get him over here," I said to Dean, pointing the way to the seating area. "Luca, can you stay here and listen out for my mother and father?"

"Sure!"

Dean carried Daniel to the sofa and ripped his trousers while I looked for a first aid kit. I found one quickly, but looking at his leg, it needed more than I could do.

"I'll clean it up, but you are going to need stitches," I said to Daniel who nodded.

I did what I could to clean it and wrapped the wound with a bandage. "I think the bullet went through. We'll get a doctor to see you as soon as we can."

"Thanks," said Daniel. "Listen. I have something to tell you."

"I already know. Luca just told me."

"We didn't expect this," said Leo, butting in.

"What happened?" I asked him "Do you know? I saw people climbing over the walls to attack. If it wasn't the Magi, who was it?"

Leo shook his head. "People have been lining up for days to be able to see you. By this morning, there were tens of thousands of people out there, all pushing to get closer. The four of us had to get a police escort in. It was madness. People were fainting from the crush. Now I can only speculate, but I think one of the police fired a shot. Maybe it was an accident, maybe he thought he'd seen one of the Magi, but for whatever reason, a shot went off causing panic and a stampede. The people you saw climbing the fences weren't Magi attacking, they were just normal people trying to get away from the crush. I saw the police firing into the crowd, obviously thinking that the Magi had something to do with this. To my knowledge, there were no Magi out there."

He put his head in his hands and wept. I'd never seen him look so vulnerable. "I'll never forgive myself for this."

Elise pulled him to her and let him weep on her shoulder.

"All you guys did was drop a hint that there might be a demonstration. You didn't organize one, and you didn't cause this mess. It would have happened anyway. The police have been in my father's pocket for years and have been trained to be brutal to the Magi without any thought. If there were too many people out there, it is because it wasn't planned properly and if someone fired a shot, it was because they were living in fear of what the Magi could do. This is why things need to change. I cannot live in a kingdom where there is so much senseless hate."

"What are you going to do?" asked Elise.

"I'm not going to marry Xavier for a start. I'll marry whomever I want, when I want, and I'll marry for the right reasons. I'll speak out instead of being the timid little girl I've always been. I'm not some kid in her elder sister's shadow anymore. I'm the future queen, and my parents will have to listen. I don't know how, but I'll fight until my last breath to get the Magi back into our kingdom."

"You won't be alone!" Leo stood and hugged me, quickly followed by Dean and Elise.

"No, you won't be alone." I turned to see Luca standing beside me. "I'll be with you. I'll stand beside you and fight for all time if you'll have me."

"Who's guarding the door?" asked Elise.

"There is a guard there now," replied Luca, not even looking in her direction "Charmaine, I wanted to ask you something..."

There was a shout from the other end of the cavernous room. We all turned our heads to see Mother being helped through the door by the guard. She looked almost delirious as the thick door closed behind her.

"Mother!" Elise and I ran to her. "Are you ok?"

She looked me straight in the eye, a hint of madness in her own.

"Your father is dead. You are now the queen of Silverwood."

After

In the days that followed, I didn't have the luxury of doing any of the things I said I would. My heart was too heavy, and so was that of the people. Leo had been right in his speculation. The Magi were not to blame. How could they be? There were barely any left, and those that were still in the country were in hiding. Reports indicated that it was actually the chief of police who had started the whole thing. He'd been so stressed about keeping the Magi out that he'd shot a small girl who was wearing a purple dress. She wasn't even a Mage, just a normal kid, but he'd shot her anyway in a panic. The terror had spread outwards like a disease, consuming everyone in a nearby radius. People began to flee, causing more hysteria. The police were overwhelmed and began to shoot other people such as those attempting to escape the crush by scaling the palace walls. From then on, it only got worse. Ten thousand plus people had all crammed into the surrounding streets of the palace, and there just wasn't enough room to accommodate them all. Many were trampled to death; too many were shot. It turned out a group of anti-magi had started the fires, proof, if I needed any, that I needed to stamp out the hate that my father and the local police had bred.

My father had been shot by one of his own policemen. It hurt, but in a way, I felt like justice had been done. Karma had reaped his soul. Xavier hadn't fared any better. His body was found days later in the clean-up. He'd been trampled to death like so many others. All in all, the final tally of dead was over three hundred although there were thousands injured. Jenny managed to escape by hiding in a broom cupboard for twelve hours, but she was one of the lucky ones. Many of the palace staff were either killed or injured. Sadie also lost her life although she didn't go down without a fight. Ever the professional, she carried on broadcasting, showing the people watching on their TV's the mess we had made of the kingdom. She even managed to get her own death on tape, carrying on presenting as she was trampled. The last I heard, she'd been posthumously awarded the broadcaster of the year. I thought she would have liked that.

The only good thing to come out of the whole mess was the fact that a thorough search of the palace had been done and no bomb had been found. It was just another of Xavier's lies—a way to manipulate me.

Once again, the Kingdom was in a state of official mourning, but this time I didn't object to the black dresses Xavi laid out on my bed every morning. She never asked for me to go down to the dressing room for which I was grateful, but one day I'd have to. Someday soon, I'd have to plan my coronation to officially take the title of queen from my mother. There would be no king and no prince regent or prince consort. I was going to do it alone. Well, not quite alone, Leo, Daniel, Luca, and Dean had moved into the palace and vowed to stay there as long as I needed them, and need them I did. I don't know how I would have gotten through those dark days without them. They took charge of everything from the cleanup to opening up the grounds to care for those injured.

About three weeks after the wedding when the dead had been buried, including my father, I found myself alone in the garden with Luca.

October had arrived, and winter was closing in fast. I was wearing black trousers, and no one seemed to mind.

We walked the pathways silently holding hands. He'd not left my side in the past three weeks and had helped me keep my head above water at a time I felt like I was drowning. He'd become as good a friend as I could hope for.

He was there for me, even when I stumbled upon Grace's diary that I'd hastily hidden when Elise entered my room. It had fallen down the side of my bed, and I'd forgotten about it. When I read it, I found out that my father had told Grace she had to marry Xavier. Grace had refused, and there had been a huge argument. The date she'd written about it was the day before she died. I had no proof, but it seemed extremely convenient that it happened that day. I ordered the police – or what was left of them to exhume her body, but before they got the chance, Pascal, the head chef came forward and admitted adding poison to her cocoa on the orders of the king. My own father had murdered his eldest daughter to get his own way. I was pretty sure Xavier had something to do with it too, but I'd never know for sure.

Throughout it all, Luca stayed with me, holding my hand all the way.

He took over on days when I couldn't even find a way to get out of bed, and came to me every evening to keep me company. It was he that organized a criminal trial with regards to my father, and it was he that kept the whole sordid thing out of the papers. The monarchy was as unpopular as they had ever been. We didn't need to add murderer to the list of crimes my father had committed. One day, I'd tell the people the truth and beg for their forgiveness, and I knew that Luca would be holding my hand as I did so.

We carried on with walking our path through what was left of the gardens. The flowers had all been trampled, and as it was coming up to winter, I'd not asked the gardeners to plant more. I'd never seen the gardens look so sorry. The palace had been cleared of debris, but there was months of renovation work to be done. Daniel and Dean had taken on that particular project although Dean had to do most of the work while Daniel's leg healed.

I felt Luca stop and squeeze my hand.

"I wanted to ask you something that day when we were in the safe room, but we got cut off. I've not found a good time to ask again, and truth be told, I'm not sure there will ever be a right time, but I have to ask you, or I'll hate myself."

"Ask me."

"When I came here, I wanted to rule a country. For the longest time, it was all I ever thought of, but then I met you. I've watched as you have been dealt a world of problems and heartache and I've watched you deal with it all like a queen. You know I love you. I'm honored to say that I know you and I'm excited by your presence. Whatever your answer is, I promise I'll stay here and help you through the next few months while you find your feet and I'll speak to my parents about becoming an ally with Silverwood. Even if you say no, I'll understand, but with my deepest part of my soul, I hope you don't. Charmaine Elizabeth Mary Annesley, will you marry me?"

There was no ring and no getting down on one knee, but I saw love and truth in his eyes. My mind flashed to Cynder, the boy who had stolen my heart all those months ago, but it had been so long since I'd last seen him. I felt the charms he'd given me, resting upon my wrist and I wondered if it was time to take them off, to shed my childish crush and finally grow up. I had a kingdom to run and who better to run it with than a man who was already a prince? With Luca by my side, one day, we'd make sure that Cynder was a free man. All of the Magi would have equal rights and live freely among the rest of us. No more would they be slaves or second-class citizens. They would be free. This was the only way I knew how to save him.

I looked into Luca's eyes. I liked him a great deal, and he'd proven his loyalty and love to me in so many ways. One day I'd learn to love him too. I kissed him slowly and felt myself melt into him as I always did when we kissed. One day soon, I was going to be the queen, and I needed my own king by my side.

"Yes," I murmured, "Yes, I will."

The End

Lucky Charm

Chapter 1

I felt the weight of the royal crown bearing down as the bishop placed it firmly on my head to a rapturous applause and the bright lights of the media. Six months since my father had died and I was now the official Queen of Silverwood.

The national anthem played as cameras flashed, blinding me with their brightness. My only job was to stay still and look regal as the massive congregation sang.

When the music had stopped and the cheering had died down, Luca came bounding over and gave me a kiss on the cheek. He held my hand as I stood, trying not to fall over with the weight of the bejewelled monstrosity on my head. He looked resplendent with his immaculate royal attire decked in golden trim and epaulettes. I, on the other hand looked like a royal golden meringue with the biggest dress Xavi had ever dared to dress me in. It was white with a golden lace overlay that nipped in at the waist before billowing out at the skirts. Over the top I wore a golden velvet cape edged in ermine that trailed along the floor behind me.

I walked down the aisle of the huge cathedral arm in arm with Luca who was doing his best to keep me upright. I tried not to think about the next time we'd be making this particular journey. In five months time we'd be doing the same walk only then it would be on our wedding day as husband and wife.

Despite the all time low ratings of popularity for the monarchy, a surprisingly large number of people had turned out for the coronation. The cathedral was packed with the kingdom's elite, not to mention various celebrities and royals from other lands, and the roads outside of the cathedral were crowded with people. I gave Elise a quick smile as I passed and she smiled back. She looked more radiant than ever, probably due to her honeymoon glow. Leo had proposed to her at Christmas and with mother's blessing, they'd had a discreet family wedding in the palace on New Year's Day. The only people they'd invited were family and Daniel and Dean. I envied them for the intimacy of it. My wedding plans were shaping up to be a complete nightmare of epic proportions thanks to my mother and Xavi collaborating. In my mother's mind, I needed a wedding even more spectacular than the last one to make people forget what had happened at it. As many people had died including the groom and the king, I thought having a bigger wedding cake and better dressed bridesmaids probably wasn't going to cut it, but I kept my mouth shut and let her plan it her way.

I tried to get my wedding out of my mind and concentrate on putting one foot in front of the other without losing my crown or tripping over the long skirt I was wearing. As everything was being televised and shown to tens of thousands of people throughout the kingdom, I knew any misstep would result in more damaging press for our family.

Security was at an all time high to prevent the same disaster as the one at the palace six months ago, and as I left the cathedral, I was flanked by ten guards specially brought in from the Silverwood Army. They led me through the snow to the awaiting golden carriage, but it was Luca that helped me through the door with my large skirt.

Thousands of people screamed and cheered as we were taken through the crowd lined streets back to the palace. I waved and smiled as I was expected to do and tried not to look as uncomfortable as I felt.

"How are you feeling your majesty?" whispered Luca in my ear.

I turned away from the crowds for a second to look into his handsome face. "Exhausted," I replied honestly. "You?"

"I'm feeling like the luckiest man in the world right now. I cannot believe I'm going to be marrying you in a few months. You look every inch the queen and if it wasn't for the eyes of every person of Silverwood currently watching us, I'd be kissing you right now."

I smiled. I wanted to kiss him too, but I couldn't be seen to be kissing him in public before our wedding day. Instead, I reached out for his hand and squeezed it.

We lapsed into an easy silence. I felt comfortable in his presence and couldn't think of anyone who I'd prefer to be with on the day of my coronation.

There is one other

The voice in my head piped up. I couldn't think of Cynder. Not now. I ignored the little voice and instead concentrated on my new role as monarch.

"My father made it look so easy," I said, sighing.

"Your father was a tyrant and a murderer," Luca reminded me.

"Yes, but the people loved him. They hate me."

"They hate all royalty because of what happened. You've told the people the full story. You can't make them believe it."

It was the truth. As soon as I found out that my father had died, I'd gone to the press to tell them the truth about the riots. I'd also gotten Cynder cleared of all charges. What I hadn't expected was for the people not to believe me. No one wanted to hear the truth that it was the fault of my father and Xavier when it was convenient to carry on blaming the Magi.

"Why does no one believe it?" I asked Luca for the thousandth time.

"Because for a long time, people treated the Magi like dirt, fuelled by the belief that they were to blame for all of Silverwood's problems. No one wants to be the bad guy and so it's easier to believe a lie than to face up to what they have done."

I knew he was right, but it was of little consolation. I'd naively thought that I could tell the truth and invite the Magi back and everyone in Silverwood would be happy. I soon found out that anti-magi feelings ran much deeper than I had expected. My father's legacy of hate had lived on even if he hadn't.

I turned back to the window and plastered on my fake smile again. There were so many people out there and yet nothing about it seemed real.

I looked at the crowds as the six white horses pulled the carriage through the heavily guarded gates of the palace. Even now, six months after the riot, I could still see a number of people demonstrating against the Magi. Today was not a special occasion for them. It was just another excuse to bring their plaquards and spew their vitriolic bile. They had been there all winter. Not even the harsh weather conditions we'd experienced had put them off. When the Magi themselves had demonstrated last year about their appalling treatment, the police had used brute force to move them. These guys were left alone.

When my father had died, I'd tried to hire back all the Magi staff that had lost their jobs at the hands of my father. Most of them had just disappeared and the few I did find were too scared to come back because of the anti-magi demonstrators. I'd even resorted to hiring a private investigator to track down Cynder and

Agatha, but he'd not been able to find either of them. Agatha's aunt and uncle's house had been ransacked and no one knew or would tell where they had all gone. Cynder had just vanished without a trace.

It was believed that the majority of Silverwood's Magi had fled to The Kingdom of Thalia, so I could only hope that Cynder and Agatha had found safety there.

The carriage came to a halt at the palace doors and two footmen opened the door and helped me out. The palace itself looked better than ever after all the restorations that had been done on it and the only reminder of the disaster that had happened all those months back was the lingering smell of wet paint. Paint that had been used to cover up the blood stains and new plaster filling the bullet holes in the walls.

"I'm going to get changed," I said as Luca and I entered the main hall. The dress was weighing me down and I couldn't wait to get out of it.

"Do you need any help?" Luca replied, eyeing up the multitude of buttons.

"They are just for decoration," I smiled. "I think I'll be ok. Why don't you get changed too?"

Luca nodded but I could see he was put out. Royal protocol demanded that we weren't too intimate until our wedding night, so apart from the occasional stolen kiss, we'd not had much in the way of intimacy. I'd not asked how many women Luca had been with. I didn't want to know. He was far more experienced than I and used to getting what he wanted. The long wait until we were married was difficult for him, but apart from kissing him when no one was looking, there wasn't much I could do about it. He was living full time in one of the guest houses in the grounds. Of the four, his was the only one occupied now that Leo had moved into the main palace.

I watched him leave before running upstairs to my room. Xavi had laid out a simple but elegant dress for me to wear for the rest of the day. I heaved a sigh of relief as I took the heavy crown from my head and eased myself out of the hefty gown. I laid myself down on the bed in my underwear, reluctant to get changed and go out to face the next part of the day – Meetings with the press followed by a huge banquet of celebration.

My room felt emptier than ever now that Elise wasn't in the adjoining room. I'd grown up in the middle room between my sisters and now both of their rooms stood empty. Elise had been given her own suite of rooms after marrying Leo. I'd get my own suite when I married Luca. The rooms were ready for me but I hadn't once been to look. I had too many memories in my old room.

I stood up and made my way over to the window as I had many times. Peeking through a crack in the curtains, I looked out over the snowy white grounds to the apartment that had once been occupied by Cynder. I'd spent so many fruitless hours gazing at the window, hoping that I'd see the light on or any other sign of life in there.

Not that I needed any reminders of Cynder. He pervaded my every thought, and at night he filled my dreams. I'd been naive when I thought agreeing to marry Luca would help me forget. Nothing helped me forget but in truth, I wasn't sure I wanted to. He was still out there somewhere. Still on the run, despite no longer being a wanted criminal.

I went back to my bed and picked up the chain from the bedside table. The small silver carriage glinted in the sun. I'd not worn it in months but I couldn't bring myself to put it away in a drawer. No matter how many times my head told me that marrying Luca was the right thing to do, my heart wasn't buying it. I slipped the bracelet on my wrist and pulled my dress over my head.

Taking a deep breath, I stepped out of my room, ready to take up my duty as the new queen of Silverwood.

End of Chapter one

Princess Charmaine is getting married. She should be happy right?

The kingdom is in turmoil after the death of the king, and it's up to Princess Charmaine to set things right. With her coronation looming and an upcoming wedding to sort out, she barely has time to worry about the people of magic that so desperately need her.

Still on the run from the police and no longer wanted in the kingdom he once loved, Cynder is forced to find another way to live, but when a chance encounter puts him back in touch with the love he lost, he knows he must do everything in her power to save her.

Lucky Charm is the second book in the Charm series, a reverse fairytale based on Cinderella by USA Today bestselling author J.A.Armitage. Take everything you think you know about fairytales and turn it on its head.

Acknowledgements

There are many people I'd like to thank for help in the making of Charm. The biggest thank you goes to my Reading Army. So many of you helped to make this fairytale a reality. Whether you beta read, came up with names for the characters or just offered moral support – I can't thank you enough! Special thanks to Amanda Williams, Jennifer Delgado, Stephanie Pittser, Trina Clausen-Adams, Judith Cohen, Lenka Trnkova, Seraphia Bunny Sparks, Tara Campbell, Kalli Bunch and to all the others in my Reading Army. I really couldn't have written this book without you.

And to RP, my biggest supporter and bacon sandwich maker.